Bridging the gaps between poets

P|O|L

P|O|L ■ 2023 ■ 1

Poetry Out Loud

Short Stories | Prose Poems | Reviews

P|O|L

Issue : 05 | Year : 05 | June 2023

Advisory Board
David Lee Morgan
Ashoke Kar

Editorial Director
Gauranga Mohanta

Editor in Chief
Uday Shankar Durjay

Associate Editor
Louise Whyburd

Section Editor
Sudip Chakroborthy

Managing Editor
Joseph Inhong Cho

Administrative Assistant
Sudip Bishwas
Anindita Mitra

Special Correspondent
Dayal Dutta

Jacket Design
Ashraf-ul Alam Shikder

Publisher
S Pen Union London
E: poetryoutlouduk@gmail.com
Available at Amazon - Paper Back and Kindle
Price: £10 | $10 | €15 | Tk. 500 | Rs. 350

Contents

Part One

Author Profiles (12-35)

Part Two

Article (34-47)
Subrata Kumar Das

Part Three

Short Stories (48-175)
Finn Hall | Sarah Leavesley | Daniela Andonovska Trajkovska | Bipradas Barua |Saleha Chowdhury | Nasrin Jahan | Mojaffor Hossain | Moom Rahman |Nahar Alam | Kazi Rafi | Tareq Samin | AKM Abdullah

Part Four

Prose Poems (176-200)
David Lee Morgan | Gauranga Mohanta | Maria Starosta Sumana Ray | Sudip Biswas | Lipi Nasrin | Louise Whyburd

Part Five

Short Stories (201-307)
Premendra Mitra | Syed Shamsul Haq
Ashraf-ul Alam Shikder | Taghrid Bou Merhi
Shakil Kalam | Moynur Rahman Babul | Ahmad Raju
Anindita Mitra | Anukul Biswas | Aliza Khatun | Mridha
Aladuddin | Uday Shankar Durjay

Part Six

Prose Poems (308-329)
Louise Goodfield | Rajashree Mohapatra | Ataur Rahman
Milad | Laura Whelton | Shamim Hossain | Sujit Manna
Mirela Leka Xhava | Roksana Lais

Part Seven

Book Reviews (330-345)
Dr. Nitai Saha | Pina Piccolo | Piyali Basu | Louise
Whyburd

Editorial

Nowadays, everything is changing so fast. We crave to read unknown stories from unfamiliar worlds. As the Danish physicist Niels Bohr probably said, "Predictions are hard, especially about the future." Therefore, the author's job is to write speculative fiction about future life. Though not entirely accurate, it entertains us and allows us to discover something new, whether it be new fears, dreams, or ambitions for humanity's advancement.
We always clarify with poets that POL is unsuitable for traditional poetry; it is a platform for prose poetry. However, poets remain confused about prose poetry, believing anything other than rhyming poetry falls into that category. 'A prose composition that, while not broken into verse lines, demonstrates other traits such as symbols, metaphors, and other figures of speech common to poetry.' If we look back at the beginnings of prose poetry, such as Amy Lowell's 'Bath,' Russel Edson's 'Metals Metals,' David Ignatow's 'Information,' and many more, we can gain a better understanding. Editing is the most crucial part of publishing a magazine. We need to focus on various aspects of the content while ensuring a quality read.

In this issue, we place more emphasis on short stories rather than prose poetry. Before we began, we invited a few selected poets, even though we received numerous short stories and prose poems. We always strive to include all the content, but the quality of writing and suitable translations often fall short of the standard expected by our readers. Each year, we receive requests to translate many authors' writings into English, and we try our best to assist them.

In doing so, we have discovered a few translators with a strong command of translation. Ashraf-ul Alam Shikder is not new to us, but Shuvra Bhowmik and Haimanty Chowdhury have started doing an excellent job. In this issue, we decided to publish some classic Bengali literature. 'Telenapota Abishkar' (originally written in Bengali by Premendra Mitra) is a modern classic short story translated by Haimanty Chowdhury. When I discussed POL with Shuvra Bhowmik, he expressed great excitement about utilizing his knowledge and translation skills, which makes us proud. Ashraf-ul Alam Shikder, a big-hearted person, is unforgettable in his dedication to POL. We were thrilled when he designed a new logo driven by his passion and interest. Furthermore, he has done a few translations for us. The POL team is grateful for his dedication, despite his physical health condition. Ashoke Kar always helps with every aspect of POL. He has translated many Bengali poems into English since the beginning of POL. POL is always grateful for Dr. Gauranga Mohanta's ideas, contributions, translations, proofreading, editing, and more. Without his dedication, POL would not be possible. Louise Whyburd is a vital part of the POL team. Despite her busy schedule, she deserves recognition for her passion for POL. Diligently, she works hard with a keen eye, extending beyond POL to make it a professional platform. For the first time, Subrata Kumar Das from Canada has written about Canadian literature in POL. In his article, he mentions

Margaret Atwood's 'Alias Grace,' Alice Munro's 'Runaway,' Michael Ondaatjee's 'The Skin of a Lion,' Rohinton Mistry's 'A Fine Balance,' M. G. Vassanji's 'The Assassin's Son,' and many more. I must mention poet David Lee Morgan; I am impressed by his friendliness and sincerity whenever I meet him. The POL team is proud to have him.

We always aim to deliver outstanding work to our valuable readers. POL is not just a magazine; it is an open platform for unveiling literary ideas and sharing them with others. We are committed to continuing our journey and making each step memorable.

Part One

Author Bios

Fin Hall, the New Pitsligo-based poet and artistic organiser extraordinaire. Fin is the host of Like a blot From The Blue, a poetry and spoken-word event transcending the boundaries of the physical and digital welcoming in hundreds of creatives from across the globe as well as a regular open mic night at The Blue Lamp Fin is a profoundly experienced poet with a career spanning decades. On-stage, Fin performs with a beautiful sensitivity. He isn't afraid to broach upon themes of old age, hope, love, and loss but reserves a potent and fiery attitude against injustice. Fin is also a filmmaker, collaborative writer, performance poet and this year, as well as adding a second regular venue for his Blot shows, will be producing the New PitsLigo Spoken Word Festival

He has two solo collections, Once Upon A Time There Was, Now There Isn't, & Solidarity (A short collection of rant political poems) , 2 Collaborative, Joined Up Writing 1 and 2, where over a 200 writers from around the globe are part of it (book 3 is almost done) and has well over 20 pieces published both online and in books from Australia, China, India USA, Canada and U.K. At the moment he is also getting ready to publish a book by 70 different writers aged over 70, and next year he will have another collection out, but this time his daughter will be part of it.

Premendra Mitra (4 September 1904 – 3 May 1988), a renowned figure of the Kallol era, was a versatile Bengali poet, novelist, short story writer, and film director. He is well-known for creating beloved characters in Bengali literature such as Ghanada, Parashar Varma, Mezhkarta, and Mamababu.

Throughout his career, Premendra Mitra received several prestigious awards, including the Rabindra Award, Academy Award Padma Shri, and Desikottam.

In 1932, Premendra Mitra published his first poetry collection titled 'Prathama'. His poetry is characterised by humanism intertwined with a revolutionary spirit. During his early years, he released three collections of short stories: 'Panchashar', 'Benami Bandar', and 'Putul O Pratima'. Through his writings, Premendra Mitra skillfully depicted the complexities of human relationships, the intricacies of the human mind, and the struggles faced by the middle and lower classes.

In addition to his poetic and prose works, Premendra Mitra authored numerous detective stories and novels featuring the detective character Parashar Varma, who was a detective by profession but a poet at heart. He also introduced the character Mamababu, who appeared in several adventure novels and short stories that captivated teenage readers.

In the Bengali literary world, **Syed Shamsul Haque** is known in one word as a 'satisfying writer'. Throughout his long literary career, he has left the indelible mark of his talent in various art and literature domains, including poetry, stories, novels, and plays. His writings beautifully capture the emotions and feelings of Bengali middle-class society, using simple words and rhythms. Born on December 27th, 1935, in the northern district of Kurigram, Bangladesh, Syed Haque was the eldest among eight brothers and sisters. His first published piece was a story in a magazine called 'Agatya' in 1951. Since then, he has showcased his talent in various literary fields, ultimately receiving the Bangla Academy Award in 1966.

Bipradash Barua was born on September 20, 1940, in Chittagong (renamed now as Chottogram). He wrote extensively on different genres of literature: stories, novels, essays and research works, juvenile stories, and children's novels. Also, he has written Biographies on Environment.

Stories include Sada Coffin (1984), Juddhajoyer Galla (1985), Biranganar Prem (1987), and Alaukik Chumban (1995) are notable, while novels like Acena (1975), Muktijoddahara (1991), Bhitara Ekjon Kande (1996) and Ami Tomar Kache Samudrer Enti Dheu Jama

Rekhechi (1997) and *Fire Takate-i Dekhi Bangabandhu (1997)* have received wide acclaim.

His essays and research works have covered an array of interesting areas: *Kabitay Bakprotima (1976), Gautam Buddha: Deshkal O Jiban (1986),* and *Gachpala Tarulata (1995).*

His writings on Environment have been successful in arousing curiosity among the reading public. His books include *Kacher Pakhi Durer Pakhi (1979), Sat Samudra Tero Nadi (1994), and Nadi Mekhla Bangladesh (1994),* which are worthy of attention.

Besides offering a cornucopia of pleasurable reading materials, Barua has been primarily a short-story writer. A unique blend of human life and nature has been the focal point of his stories. Also, he has dealt, in a classical style, with the working people and the natural phenomena of Bengal. The Liberation War of Bangladesh has been depicted in his stories in many ways. He got the coveted Bangla Academy Award in 1991.

Nasreen Jahan (born March 5, 1964) is a Bangladeshi author, novelist, and literary editor. She began writing in the early eighties and gained fame through her novel *'Urukku'*. She received the Phillips Literary Award for this novel, as well as the Bangla Academy Award for her overall contribution to Bengali literature. Her first novel, *'Urukku,'* was translated into English by Kaiser Huq, and she won the Phillips Literary Award for it in 1994. Her second novel, *'Chandra's Prothom Kola,'* was published in 1994 but received a less enthusiastic response compared to her first novel. In 1995, at the *Ekushey* Book Fair, she published a novel titled *'Chandralekha Jadubistar'* and *'Chaar Pasher Batigulo Nive Asche'* based on freedom fighting. The following year, her long observational novel *'Sonali Mukhosh'* was also published at the *Ekushey* Book Fair. Her later novels include 'Lee', *'Krush Kather Konna'*, *'Shankhonartoki'*, and *'Eshwarer Baam Haat'*.

Saleha Chowdhury is an author who has written over 80 Bengali novels, short stories, essays, poems, columns, and two collections of English poetry. Born in Rajshahi, Bangladesh, in 1943, she served as a lecturer at Dhaka University from 1967 to 1972. Later, she relocated to London with her family and worked as a schoolteacher until her retirement.

Chowdhury's works predominantly focus on portraying human beings with their virtues and flaws. Additionally, she has translated 25 English books into Bengali, including works by Peter Carry, Michael Ondatje, Roald Dahl, Pearl S. Buck, Nelson Mandela, Hemingway, John Steinbeck, Marquez, and Irving Stone, among others.

Her literary contributions have earned her numerous accolades, including the *Annaya* Award, Bangla Academy *Probasi Lekhok Puruskar*, *Asraf Siddiqi Gold Medal*, *Lekhika Sanggha Puruskar*, and *Ayesha Foyez* Literary Award. She has also received a Merit award from Washington DC for her English poems and was a runners-up in a prize competition.

Subrata Kumar Das is a writer, curator and organizer based in Toronto. He has twenty-nine books to his credit. His Bengali book on Canadian literature, published in 2019, received huge applause.

Born in Bangladesh in 1964, Subrata completed his Bachelor's with honours and Master's in English from Rajshahi University, Bangladesh. Since January 1990, he had taught English language and literature at tertiary and college levels for more than twenty years.

A winner of Gayatri GaMarsh Memorial Award for Literary Excellence in 2018, Subrata was short-listed for the Top 25 Immigrants Awards in Canada in 2021.

Subrata participated in the Toronto International Festival of Authors (TIFA) in 2020 and 2022 and led teams of Bengali writers. His recent autobiographical book was released in Toronto on March 04 last, on his 59th birth anniversary.

Mojaffor Hossain is a fiction writer of contemporary Bangla literature. Starting his career as a journalist and now working as a translator in the Bangla Academy, Dhaka, he has published six books packed with awe-inspiring short stories, which, in recent years, have attracted much acclaim from both general readers and literary critics. His signature style is using native realities as his settings and giving them magic-realistic or surrealistic colours. He has received Exim Bank-*Anyadin Humayun Ahmed* Award for his short story collection 'Atit Akta Bhindesh', Abul Hasan Sahitya Award for *'Paradheen Desher Swadheen Manushera'* and *Kali O Kalam* Sahitya Award for *Timiryatra*, a novel. He has also been awarded *Arani Sahitya Puraskar* and *Boishakhi* Television Award for his stories. He is also known as a translator and literary critic and published 15 books so far. His other notable works are South Asian Diaspora literature, *Pathe Bisleshane Bishwagalpo* and *Bishwasahityer Katha*.

Louise Whyburd is a creative writer who lives in the South-west of England. Louise has always been creative, she studied a BTEC national diploma in Performing Arts during her college years and has also worked on a stained-glass window art project which is still displayed in the Steam Railway Museum in Swindon. She continued with her creativity into adulthood through her passion for cooking and art and rekindled her love of writing during lockdown. Louise has had poetry published in a selection of collective poetry books which have been sold across the world in several different languages. She has also written an article for a London published Hindu cultural magazine. Louise's writing is very much inspired by her life experiences and unique perspective on a vast array of subjects from nature to politics.

David Lee Morgan has travelled the world with his saxophone, as a performance poet and street musician. He has won many poetry slams, including the London, the UK, and the BBC Poetry Slam Championships. He has featured at St Anza, the international poetry festival in St. Andrews, Scotland, LINGO, Dublin's poetry and spoken word festival, and at the Isle of Wight festival.

He is a longstanding member of the Writers Guild and holds a Ph.D. in Creative Writing from Newcastle University. He lives in London, grew up in the USA, was born in Berlin, and considers himself a citizen of the planet. He has been published in numerous magazines and anthologies and has two volumes of poetry published.

Gauranga Mohanta, a well-known writer with a PhD in English Literature, has authored twelve books. His notable works include "Robert Frost: A Critical Study in Major Images and Symbols" (2009) and "A Green Dove in Silence: Forty Prose Poems in Translation" (2018), which have the ability to captivate readers. Alongside his literary pursuits, he held positions in the civil service and served as a lecturer at various universities. Presently, he imparts knowledge on Modern and Romantic Poetry at the Bangladesh University of Business and Technology. Furthermore, Gauranga actively contributes articles, poems, and translated works to magazines. Residing in Dhaka, he endeavours to organising the annual Dhaka Translation Festival, guided by the motto of "Unite through Translation".

Sarah James is a prize-winning poet, fiction writer, journalist, and photographer, also published as Sarah Leavesley. Her poetry has featured in the *Guardian*, *Financial Times* and Forward Prize anthologies, as well as in a café mural, on the BBC, on buses, city pavements and in the Blackpool Illuminations. Author of eight poetry titles, an Arts Council England funded multimedia hypertext poetry narrative > Room, two novellas and a touring poetry-play, her latest poetry collection is *Blood Sugar, Sex, Magic* (Verve Poetry Press, 2022), winner of the CP Aware Award Prize for Poetry 2021. She also runs V. Press, publishing award-winning poetry and flash fiction.

Laura Whelton is a 45-year-old woman living in Cork city. She studied Fine Art and trained to be a chef in Fine Dining. She also studied Sociology, English and History of Art. She has some level 5 Fetac courses behind her also, she enjoys concerts, wine, music and literature. Laura has been published widely in Books, zines and blogs.

Moom Rahman was born in 1971. He is a prolific writer from Bangladesh. He is a full-time writer. He writes short stories, dramas, poems, translations, screenplays and essays; he is comfortable in writing in all genre. He is very passionate about everything starting from cooking recipes to advertisement copy to thoughtful essays, he considers everything to be part of his writing. He dedicates his whole life to writing.

Lipi Nasrin, born on 3 April 1971 in Bangladesh, completed her master's degree at the University of Rajshahi and obtained a Ph.D. from the Institute of Biological Sciences within the same university. Currently, she holds the position of Associate Professor of Botany at Satkhira Government College in Bangladesh. She has authored four poetry books in Bangla: 'Noisobder Nissongo Prohor' (Lonely period of silence), 'Godhuli Ronger Chhaya' (The shadow of twilight), 'Nilombon Madokota' (Suspended obsession), and 'Nistol Melancholy' (Fathomless Melancholy), as well as a collection of short stories titled 'Rater Brishti' (The Rain of Night). Her short stories and essays are regularly published in various literary magazines in Bangladesh and abroad. Some of her poems have been translated into German and featured in an anthology called 'Ein Weg Zum Träumen-Teil-1' (A way to dream part-1) from Austria. Translated versions of her poems have also been published in the UNBANGLA ANTHOLOGY, titled 'Under The Blue Roof: Poems of Bengali poets from New York.'

Dayal Datta is a Bangladeshi poet, born and raised there. In his poems, various inconsistencies of society, socialism, patriotism and international affairs are observed. Though he is a banker, he wrote numerous poems with a deep love for literature. In addition to writing in regular magazines, his writings in various international magazines and journals are popular. He is deeply engaged in various literary, social, and cultural endeavors, actively organizing events for the Bangladesh Udichi Shilpi Group and serving as a member of the Executive Committee of Khelaghar Mahanagar North. Despite his busy schedule, he has also established himself as a respected income tax lawyer.

Tareq Samin is a Bangladeshi secular-humanist author. He is the editor of the bilingual literary journal Sahitto. He has authored eight books. He edited two books of Anthology of International poetry which included 22 poets from 20 countries. His poems have been translated into more than 20 languages of which English, Spanish, Chinese, German, French, Italian are just a few to mention. His poems, short stories and articles have also been published in more than 25 countries. He received the 'International Best Poets Award-2020' from The International Poetry Translation and Research Centre (IPTRC), China and the Greek Academy of Arts and Writing. He has been awarded 'Honorable Mention' in Foreign Language Authors category for his poem 'Another Try' in 'The prize il Meleto di Guido Gozzano Agliè' poetry competition held on 12 September 2020 in Turin, Italy. In July 2021 he won Naji Naaman Literary Prize 2021. Tareq Samin is a Martin-Roth-Initiative Scholarship Alumnus. As a Martin-Roth-Initiative Scholarship holder, he was a guest writer in Goethe-Institute, Kolkata, India and Kathmandu, Nepal. In 2021, he was also an International guest writer in Château de Lavigny International writers-in-residence, Switzerland.

Kazi Rafi is a fiction writer in Bangladesh (B-1975). Kazi Rafi has eleven novels and six volumes of stories to his credit. He is a postgraduate in English literature. His first novel Blurred Dream of Sassandra compassionately depicted the simplicity of West African life. The gruesome description of the cannibal area and culture of the tribes enriches the reader's horizon of experiences. The art of story- telling, the similes, metaphor and Irony of life, characterization, subtlety of diction, thematic grandeur impressed the readers. For this novel the author was awarded with HSBC-Kali O Kolom Award-2010 which is one of the most prestigious award in

Bangladesh and Bangla literature. He has fifteen more books published from Bangladesh and he received three more awards including '*Nirnay* Gold Medal-2013' in his possession for the outstanding performance in the era of Novel and Short Stories.

Ashraf-ul Alam Shikder, (28 February 1964) was born in Bangladesh, is a full-time writer but even though designs pre-press, web, adverts; writes film scripts and poetry. He is the author of The Art of Writing a Script. He has been working for a few advertising agencies since 1990 as Creative Director. He also worked for Ad-film, Tele-Drama, Music Videos, TV-programmes and TV-films as a freelancer.

Dr. Nitai Saha is an Associate Professor of English at Munshi Premchand College, Siliguri. A Post-Graduate in English Literature from North Bengal University, he obtained his M. Phil degree in 2001. Dr. Saha earned his Ph. D. on W. B. Yeats in 2007. He has in his credit several books, say, Books Way Edition of Eugene O'Neill's The Emperor Jones, Studies in R.K. Narayan's The English Teacher (joint editor), and Daniel Defoe's Robinson Crusoe: Context, Text and Criticism (joint editor). His book 'Unquiet Dreams: On Rereading W.B. Yeats's Poetry' is a much acclaimed publication. A number of his articles have been included in various anthologies of critical writings on different authors. Besides, he has published some illuminating papers in several journals of repute.

AKM Abdullah is a poet, story writer, editor (dashwebmag -Bengali and English) and the author of 8 books (6 poetry, 1 novel and 1 storybook; all are Bangla version). He was born in Bangladesh, currently living in the United Kingdom. More than a hundred English poems have been published in many anthologies and literary magazines. In A World of Despair (English Poetry Collection) to be published soon.

Roksana Lais is a bohemian person who loves to travel and to know different cultures and people. Humanity and nature attract more than anything. Writing and painting is her passion. She loves to write fiction from the experience of life. She enjoys living a simple life with the love of nature and dislikes human cruelty, lies and dishonesty. Roksana Lais: Author, Poet, Story writer, and Novelist Born in Bangladesh now lives in Canada. Her published books: Looking for the Dream City, Bluewater in The Moonlight, At the Unknown Stream, In the middle, The Journey of light, Golden Light in Sraabon Moment, Lattar to Sky.

Daniela Andonovska Trajkovska (February 3, 1979, Bitola, North Macedonia) is a poetess, a scientist, an editor in chief of two literary journals ('Rast'/ 'Growth' by Bitola Literary Circle and 'Contemporary Dialogues' by Macedonian Science Society), and editor of literary magazine 'Stozher' issued by Macedonian Writers' Association, a literary critic, a doctor of pedagogy, university professor. She is co-founder of the Center for

Literature, Art, Culture, Rhetoric and Language at the Faculty of Education-Bitola, a member of the Macedonian Writers' Association, Macedonian Science Society – Bitola - was president of the Editorial Council for 2 mandates and now she is the Head of the Department for Linguistic and Literature, a member of the Slavic Academy for Literature and Art in Varna, and Bitola Literary Circle. She has published 3 university books, 2 books of short stories, one poetry book for children, 9 poetry books in Macedonian language and 5 poetry books in English, Italian, and Arabic language. Her poetry is translated into 40 languages. She has won several literary awards and the most important are: 'Krste Chachanski' for prose (2019), National 'Karamanov' Poetry Prize for the poetry book 'Electronic Blood' (2019), Macedonian Literary Avantgarde for 'House of Contrasts' (2020), 'Abduvali Qutbiddin' (2020, Uzbekistan), 'Tulliola-Renato Filippelli' for the poetry book 'Electronic Blood' (Italy, 2021), 'City of Galateo-Antonio De Ferraris' (Italy, 2021), Literary Criticism Award in 2022, 'Dritero Agolli' Award (Albania, 2023) and 'Aco Shopov' for her poetry book 'Math Poetry' (by Macedonian Writers' Association in 2021).

Sumana Ray hails from Tripura but currently resides and works in Mumbai. She has been a productive writer since her college days. Born and raised in Tripura, she now works and lives in Mumbai. Her poems and stories get regularly published in magazines and journals. She has also written four books titled *Uran, Jolorob, Rangiye Diye Jao, and Imon Rater Kuasha.* All of these have been very well received by the readers. She has been invited and honoured at International literary festivals, wherein she has presented her works to an audience of distinguished personalities from the world of Bangla literature. She studied Mathematics and loves to play outdoor and indoor games. She is fond of music, travelling and she enjoys long rides on her bicycle. Sumana's determination is admired by many as she works very hard to maintain the work-life balance. She has come a long way but remains passionate about writing and continues to pursue excellence.

Mariia Starosta lives in Ukraine in the city of Lviv. Author of two poetry books "Two Worlds" and "A Woman With The Smell of Smoke". Plans to publish the third bilingual collection "Reflections of A Woman". She teaches Ukrainian language and literature at the Lviv Linguistic Gymnasium. Married, raising a son and a daughter.

Anindita Mitra was born on 17 May 1982 and is influenced by the philosophy of Rabindranath Tagore. She believes in humanism and detests fundamentalism. Mitra writes poetry, stories and articles. *Ebong Aparajita* (Bangla) is a collection of short stories, published in 2018. She lives in Kolkata, India now.

Aliza Khatun was born on February 2nd 1981, in the village of *Arunbari* in the *Chapainawabganj* district of Bangladesh. She studied M.Sc in Mathematics at Jagannath University, Dhaka, Bangladesh. Aliza Khatun is the eldest of four siblings. She is the mother of one son. Living in *Satkhira* district headquarters, she works at a humanitarian international organisation & quot; *Rishilpi* handicrafts limited & quot; as an executive HR. She published poetry: *Noishabdo Chhona Jal, Modhyarater Khame, Bhangonkal, Srabon Janala, Rodmakha Chitthi, Gahine Daho, Aradhya Pother Dike, Mumurshu Mokame;* and published proses: *Borgamati, Vatir Tane, Agun Gonja Mati, Roktosamudra O Ekush Akkhyan.*

Mridha Alauddin was born in February 1978 in Kangshi, Wazirpur, Barisal. His writings are regularly published in the country's national daily newspaper and literary magazines. Mridha is a poet who is conscious of rhythm. Here are some of Mridha's published works: 'The Mind Goes to The Sun' (poems). Published by Rel Gachh, Moghbazar, Dhaka-1217, in 2005. 'Next Winter Men Will Become Sunlight' (poems). Publisher: Barnes and Noble, New York. 'Butterflies Have Become Some Fishes' (poems), and 'A Few Poisons Needed' (Doha's poems) published by Mohammad Liaquatullh of Student Ways, 9 Banglabazar, Dhaka-1000. Mridha has received several awards and honors, including the Atish Dipankar Gold Medal, Bangabhumi Literary Honor from Bangabhumi Sahitya Parishad, Pinnacle Literary Medal from Pinnacle Littlemag, and the Crest of the Bengali Muslim Literature Association along with a gold medal. Currently, Mridha is working at the Kalbela newspaper.

Piyali Basu was born into a critically acclaimed family in South Kolkata on November 11th. Her father, the late

Sri Prasoon Basu, was an eminent writer, renowned political personality, and a popular book publisher. Piyali completed her master's degree in Bengali literature from Jadavpur University and later obtained her PhD from Dublin, Ireland. She is known for her Bengali poetry, particularly her experiments with various poetry forms. She has published a total of eight books. After residing in Ireland for 23 years, she moved to the United Kingdom two years ago and currently resides there.

Shamita Das Dasgupta (b. 1949) is a cofounder of Manavi, the first organisation to focus on violence against South Asian women in the US. She has taught psychology, gender studies, and law at the Rutgers University and NYU, authored five books, written a bunch of academic papers and monographs, and is still conducting training for DV and SV practitioners in the US and India. In her retirement, she is enjoying writing mystery stories in Bengali.

Rajashree Mohapatra, born in Odisha, India, holds a master's degree in History and Journalism and Mass Communication from Utkal University, Odisha. As a teacher, she is dedicated to her profession. Additionally, she is a postgraduate in Environmental Education and Industrial Waste Management from Sambalpur University, Odisha. Rajashree has committed herself to being a Social Activist, working with non-governmental organisations to advocate for social justice, environmental issues, and human rights in remote areas. Poetry, painting, and journalism are her passions.

Shamim Hossain was born on August 7, 1983 in Rajshahi, Bangladesh. Although poetry is his only worship in life and death, he is equally proficient in fiction. He is the author of poetry books: *Varendra Prantare Vasanta Name* (2007), *Pakhi Pakhi Bhoy* (2011), *Upamanser Sobha* (2012), *Shital Sandhya Geetal Ratri* (2013), *Dhaner Dhatri* (2015), *Dumurer Ayu* (2017), *Him Yantrangsha* (2021), *Ek Turhi Chhoy Burhi* (2008), and *Gachbhai Nachbhai* (2017). Besides he edits the art and literature magazine 'Nadi'. He has received several awards such as the *Kali O Kalam Tarun* Poet and Writer *Puraskar* (2015), *Rupantar Sahitya Puraskar* (2013), *Rajshahi Sahitya Parishad Puraskar* (2011), *Adhayan Shishu Foundation Puraskar* (2006), Vishal Bangla Sahitya Puraskar (2017), Poet-Editor Anwar Ahmad Smritipadak (2017).

Sujit Manna is a bilingual poet, writer, and translator. He was born on September 23rd of 1997 in a village named *Khasbarh, Paschim Medinipur* of West Bengal (India). Graduated in English literature, and he started writing regularly in 2015. He is already a published author of five books. His poetry showcases the yin-yang of society. His writings exhibit love in its purest form. He has some interesting notions about today's writings in English which belongs to India mainly in Bengal. An avid reader and collector of great literary gems, he considers himself a labourer of phonetics. He wants to represent himself via his work.

Borche Panov was born on September 27, 1961 in Radovish, The Republic of North Macedonia. He graduated from the 'Sts. Cyril and Methodius'; University of Skopje in Macedonian and South Slavic Languages (1986). He has been a member of the 'Macedonian Writers Association' since 1998. He has published: a) poetry: 'What did Charlie Ch. See from the Back Side of the Screen' (1991), 'Cyclone Eye' (1995), 'Stop, Charlie' (2002), 'Tact" (2006), 'The Riddle of Glass' (2008), 'Basilica of Writing' (2010), 'Mystical Supper' (2012), 'Vdah' (The Breathe of Life) (2014), 'Human Silences' (2016), 'Uhania' (2017), "Shell" (2018), 'A Room of my Time Zones' (2021); and several essays and plays: 'The Fifth Season of the Year' (2000). He has also published poetry books in other languages: 'Particles of Hematite' (2016 - in Macedonian and Bulgarian language, published in Bulgaria), 'Vdah' (2017 – in Slovenian, published in Slovenia), 'Balloon Shaving' (2018 – Serbian, published in Serbia), 'Fotostiheza' (Photopoesis, 2019 – Bulgarian, published in Bulgaria), 'Blood that Juggles with 80000 Thoughts' (2021 in Croatian, published in Croatia), 'Underground Apple' in Arabic language published in United Arab Emirates in 2021 by Rawashen Publishing House, and 'Underground Apple' in English language (translated by Daniela Andonovska-Trajkovska) and published in Netherlands by Demer Press in 2021. His poetry was published in a number of anthologies, literary magazines and journals both at home and abroad, and his works are translated into 38 languages. He has won several literary awards such as: Premio Mondiale 'Tulliola- Renato Filippelli'; in Italy for his book "Balloon Shaving" (2021), International Award of Excellence 'City of Galateo-Antonio De Ferrariis&quot' (Italy, Rome, 2021), Premio 'Le Occasioni'; in Italy (among 662 participants), and Sahitto Literary Award 2021.

Ahmad Raju is not only a storyteller but also a poet, novelist, and painter. He has been writing since childhood and regularly publishes his works in various literary magazines, including prominent national dailies in his country Bangladesh and abroad. One of his notable achievements is winning the Best Story Award in the *Arani* Story Competition-2013 for his story *'Mukut'*. In 2015, he received the Best Story Writer Award from the Australian newspaper Suprabhat Sydney. Raju is the author of several works, including '*Swapnachur*' (a collection of poetry), *'Meghbalika'*, '*Chhayabati*' (collections of short stories), and *'Nihshobder Adhare-Alo'* (a novel). Additionally, he serves as the editor of the literary magazine Gangchil.

Mirela Leka Xhava, born in the city of Elbasan, Albania, is a poet and writer. She graduated in Albanian Language and Literature and worked as a Librarian at the University of the City. She also served as a correspondent for the newspaper "Elbasani". In 1999, her first book titled "I do not love winter in the eye" was published. Mirela has since published her poetry in various national and international literary magazines. She has actively participated in contests and anthologies, receiving positive evaluations. Additionally, she engages in translation work from French for several literary magazines in Albania. Her latest book of poems, titled "Flowers of the Montesquieu Street," was published in September of this year. Mirela currently resides in Bordeaux, France, with her family, where she continues to write and pursue her literary endeavors.

Uday Shankar Durjay is a versatile writer, excelling as a poet, essayist, and translator. His works have been widely published in newspapers and magazines. Originally from Bangladesh, Durjay currently resides in the UK. His writing journey began in 1996 with the publication of his work in the 'Doinik Jessore.' Durjay pursued his education in Business Information Systems at the University of East London and obtained an MSc in Management from BPP University in the UK. He has authored several notable works, including *'Likhe Rakhi Bishuddho Atmar Ratridin'* (Keep writing the day-night of the innocent souls), *'Joma Rakhi Nirjatito Nakkhatrer Abidhan'* (I Preserve The Dictionary of Exiled Stars) a collection of Bengali poetry, and *'Western Avenuer Aronnodin'* (The Woodendays of Western Avenue), a Bengali translation of selected English poems. He has also compiled a collection of Bengali articles titled *'Probanddho Sangroho'*. In addition to his writing endeavors, Durjay serves as the editor of POL, and he also holds the editorship of *Spandan*, a creative magazine focused on Bengali literature. His contributions to literature have garnered recognition, and he was honored with the Shahitto International Award for Literature in 2021.

Part Two

Article

Subrata Kumar Das

An Immigrant's Quest for CanLit

To an immigrant Canadian, it is a very tough question 'Which are the best novels in Canadian Literature' or 'Who are the most celebrated poets of the country?' or 'Who are the most loved Canadian memoirists?' or 'Which playwrights overwhelmed the nation?' Is it easy to reply for an immigrant to ask, 'Who are the frequently uttered poetic lines written on Canadian soil?' 'Which New Brunswick writer has conquered the readership to the farthest west of Vancouver? 'Who are the First Nation major authors of Canada?' All these are unbelievably tough because an immigrant does have his or her own literature, and it is not that easy to cope with new literature in a very short time. More than that, Canadian literature, though written in English, is possibly not on any curriculum outside Canada. So, when Canada becomes one's land, it becomes challenging to merge with it, to grab from its culture, and to dive into its literature. And to speak the truth, nothing happened differently to me, an enthusiast of Bengali literature, who migrated from Dhaka, a far-away South Asian city, frequently focused in Canadian media for primarily negative reasons.

Before leaving for the North American city in 2013, we only knew some names of Canadian fictionists. The names of the Canadian fiction writers that we crossed back home included Michael Ondaatje, Rohinton Mistry, and Yann Martel, and who else? The South Asian connections between the earlier two and 'Life of Pi,' set in a sub-continent context, were possibly the components that caused some sort of interest in me and in many like us. The international reputation of Carol Shields or Margaret Atwood might climb the reading table of a Bengali reader also. But how frequent was that? Or before the 2013 Nobel, how many Bengali readers and writers were truly acquainted with the works of Alice Munro? When the bigwigs of world literature fall upon our own way, it does not sound easy to discover their recent powerful works. Nothing different happens when writers emerging within the borders of my own vast land named 'Canada' get included among those dignitaries.

Let me confess first. I was a man of literature and, more than that, a man of novels. My enthusiasm was so sky-high that in 2003 I initiated a website on the novels of Bangladesh. But what a sorry saga that I do not know even a little about the novel genre of my new land! I cannot even try to know even, because whenever I do make any effort to know, the question hovers over me how much can I know at this post-fifty age? And it seemed very impractical to start with zero at this stage of life. And with almost knowing nothing more in this regard, I had spent the first two years in my Toronto life. By this time, the names like Alice Munro for her getting the Nobel and Margaret Atwood for her coverage in the international media came up repeatedly. I dared to look at their books, but I dared not dive into their works. Hundreds of thousands of books by Canadian writers are shelved in the one hundred branches of Toronto Public Library (TPL), but I could not reach them. For the previously inconceivable services of TPL, I can now hold any of the titles online or can do, for up to fifty, pick those from my nearby branch, but I could not utilize them. Thousands of books are kept in the bookstores, but I could not touch them. It was not that they were expensive because used books at low prices are available at Toronto stores, but I could not love them. I, Subrata Kumar Das, who did have a personal library of more than five thousand books in my Dhaka home, and wrote enormously on Bangla literature, especially on Bengali novels, could not leaf through the Toronto books because they seemed to me very unfathomable. Because I always believe a book is actually not an individual book in itself. A book is a part of the whole work of the author. A book is a part of the entire genre. A book's significance is indebted to creating the complete literature written in that language.

In such a dissatisfactory and unhealthy status of mind, one day, I did a tremendous job. I did not know beforehand that it was going to be enormous. The tremendousness erupted through a stoutness of mind. What was that?

But before that, let me tell you about the preparation for that moment. After two years of my stay in the new land, I started working on Canadian Literature. I started because I had no other alternative but to start. I started because, as a man of literature, I could bear my ignorance no more. My plan grew in me in such a way that I had to do something which would eradicate the obstacles on my way to penetrating Canadian literature.
More than that, I envisioned writing on Canadian Literature, popularly known as CanLit. As there was almost nothing in Bengali on Canadian Literature, this world full of assets started waving to me from afar. I knew CanLit was unknown to me and millions like me. A desire to do something which would help those millions to easily access the literature of Canada began to spring in me. I knew well my Bengali fellows were aware of the literature of England and America and even that of Russia, America, French, or even Germany; even the language of that literature, not English, but Canadian literature, remained to them unknown though the lion share of it is composed in the language that is known to the literati of Bangladesh.

With this view in mind, for about six months, I have been browsing Canadian literature, especially novels, as I am more comfortable with this genre through the internet. I started leafing through some books, borrowing from the library. Like a collegiate student, I began to take notes down on them. Alongside many other social and literary activities, I was secretly enjoying the discoveries of a mere boy in a newer world. But I could realise that development could not be achieved as per expectation. From the hundreds of unknown writers from the hundreds of never-heard-of great books, it was not very easy for me to keep pace. And at last, that sweetest morning came in my life when I, having no significant income at all, decided to buy a bunch of books. I decided so because I knew if the books lay before me all the time, it would be easier to befriend them.

On a weekend morning, I decided to visit a nearby Value Village on Danforth, where many used things, along with books, are sold. I had no hurry. Standing before the shelves of fiction, I began to look at the back flaps. Among the many, I began to select the ones by Canadians. After someone hours, I found my basket full of Canadian books, mostly novels. Now was the time to be selective. I picked the award-winning ones and found that the number was almost twenty. With a satiated soul, I discovered myself as a saint, with nothing around me, having nothing else in me. Only books and books written by Canadian writers. I paid at the counter and took a TTC bus. Taking a seat in a quiet corner at the back, I brought out all the books one after another. I returned home, and my wife found me with special brightness. My journey with Canadian novels started.

For the next few days, my only job was to google the books, and their writers, take notes, and do cross references. It was a pleasant journey I had made after a couple of years.

Unlike the general assumption, the looks and conditions of the books I had bought were not any oldish. Most of them were in better condition than the books of the public library. Returning home, I put them with much care on my bedside table. The whole table, though small in size, appeared to me something like a big flower bouquet. Whenever I stayed near that, I bowed down over them or took a flower out of the bunch and got its fragrance.

Margaret Atwood's 'Alias Grace,' Alice Munro's 'Runaway,' Michael Ondaatjee's 'The Skin of a Lion,' Rohinton Mistry's 'A Fine Balance,' M. G. Vassanji's 'The Assassin's Son' began to dazzle on my table. Gabrielle Roy, Anne Michaels, and George Elliott Clarke accompanied them. Mostly fiction, mostly novels, as this genre draws me more all the time.

But gradually, now I had got smarter. Now I dared to borrow books of CanLit from Toronto Public Library. The previous inconvenience had been conquered by now. Reading CanLit, or at least swimming into them, had been a pleasure by then. All these positive nods allowed me to welcome the other creations by the authors who had already visited my home.

So, Margaret Atwood's 'Survival' walked to my home from the Dawes Road branch, my home branch. I browsed; I made several attempts; I tried to get into what

Atwood actually wanted to say in her 1972 book, considered a milestone in shaping CanLit in the real sense. And after some days, I understood that I had understood nothing. But I got elated to get some flicks on the timelines that had made the CanLit as we see now.

So, Atwood's 'Hag-Seed' (2016) also walked my poor abode. All my searches encouraged me to read that as it was a modern retelling of William Shakespeare's 'Tempest.' The novelization of the four-hundred-year-old play had made the news in the media. Hag-Seed was one among the other four in The Winter's Tale, The Taming of the Shrew, Othello, and Macbeth. Some more were expected to come out later. But sorrowfully, I was little able to get a taste of the new creation of Canada's legendary literary star though I was happy to know that in the fictionalized recreation of Shakespearean plays, one wordsmith was from Canada, my present land, the land I possibly love most.

Neither Alice Munro could draw my attention. I tried to understand my failure. The points that came up before me included: i) I don't know the landscape of many of her stories; ii) the characters of her stories don't seem to be very familiar; iii) the psychologies of the characters are different from the Bengali minds; etcetera. But by then, I had learned a huge amount of things about Munro. I knew her 'Lives of Girls and Women' is not a compilation of stories; rather, that is a novel. Many have defined the book as the only novel of the only Nobel-for-literature-winning from Canada. It is autobiographical, but many said that it is not a truly biographical one. The protagonist of the book is Del Jordan, an adolescent girl who was brought up in the Ontario area. And thus, the 'Bildungsroman' or 'the portrayal of the artist as a young woman' provided me with much enlightenment as this feature of any novel attracts me more. All the major 'Bildungsroman' novels that I have loved to read time and again got a new member in the list.

By then, I had learned that in Canada, there are a good number of writers who represent the whole nation or a city and work for national or community arts. I had already known George Elliott Clarke as the parliamentary Poet Laureate of Canada. I also knew that Clarke had been the Poet Laureate of Toronto City since 2012 and got the new appointment only in January 2016. I attempted my copy of his novel 'George and Rue,' published in 2005. I got wondered if George represented the black community. I felt happy that George's stories and poems hovered over the arrival of black people in Nova Scotia hundreds of years before.

By then, I had learned that Anne Michales had been the Toronto Poet Laureate since January 2016. And so when I saw her 'Fugitive Pieces' in the bookstore, I didn't hesitate to spare a second lest any second customer might bag that. I leafed through it, but I failed to get impassioned to go through it. I felt sad that I could not love the novel, which had received at least twelve awards. I felt desolate that I was not worthy to enjoy a Trillium Book Award-winning, City of Toronto Book Award-winning novel. But I also had many reasons for not liking them. So I did not get completely frustrated, nor did I give up my whole project.

Days passed by, but those days were not like the days previously passed when I had no knowledge of CanLit. Many new insights began to embellish me with many-faced knowledge regarding the literature of my new country. I began to realisee that I would also be able to make a 'can.'

The collection that I have brought helped me a lot to start a journey. It was not more than twenty, but it gave me enormous support to go forth. I read one or two books by an individual writer, but I studied huge stuff online on him or her. Taking notes on them helped me develop my insight. I began to discover the thin invisible threads among them, began to connect the threads between the writers, and began to understand their status in the whole bulk of Canadian Literature.

My thirst began to rise up, as is the general feature to put new steps. To speed up that journey, Nilima, my wife, accompanied me after some days. It was also a Value Village shop around Eglington Square.

On my first visit to buy CanLit books, I was an unknown in a new land – almost no writers on the big shelves appeared known to me, and almost no book seemed that known to me. But today, things have changed. Among the many writers shelved across, I got some very much acquainted with me; many of the books sounded familiar.

On the previous day, only two hands were to carry, but this time four hands were ready to carry the goldmines. We carried them home, fondled them with much love, and caressed them with great care.

Now the big volumes of Don Gillmor's 'Kanata,' Laurence Hill's 'The Illegal,' Gabrielle Roy's 'the tin flute,' David Adams Richards 'mercy among the Children,' Anne Hebert's 'Kamouraska,' Noah Richler's 'This is My Country, What's Yours?' began to glitter on my table. The glows overpowered me, my bedroom, and my whole living place. The glow accompanied me all the time, all my hours and minutes, all my thoughts and moments.

Now I know the great Canadian authors named Ann-Marie MacDonalds, Vincent Lam, Catherine Govier, Joseph Boyden, Timothy Findley, Margaret Laurence, Susanna Moddie, Thomas King, and Sara Jennette Duncan, just to name a few at random.

The fat volumes began to give a happy feeling. But I started worrying as well. How to go through novels comprising more than three to four to five hundred pages? How to go through the eight hundred-odd pages of 'The Luminaries' by Eleanor Catton? But I felt the impulse to touch the book – the Governor General Literary Award Winner book of 2013. This novel by Catton, the Canada-born New Zealand author, got the Man Booker Prize also. How come I won't read the books of this creative figure of only thirty, whose debut novel 'The Rehearsal' came out only in 2008? How come

I won't read the historical novel 'The Brothers Sisters' by Patrick de Witt, the Vancouver writer? In the year when this magnum opus was published, he was hailed by two national awards in Canada. This book brought him the Governor General Literary Award, Rogers Writers Trust Fiction Prize, and many more. And I should not be afraid to go through the three hundred-odd pages of this noted fiction writer! I knew I had to start. But how?

To make my way through CanLit, I began searching which books on the history of Canadian literature were available in the Toronto Public Library. Immediately I got 'Canadian Literature in English: Texts and Contexts' and William Herbert New's book 'A History of Canadian Literature .'I got some more like John Moss' 'A Reader's Guide to the Canadian Novel' and 'Canadian Writers at Work.' All those provided many more inputs to enrich me, extend my horizon, and help me move forward. By now, I have become more aware of the early Canadian literary pieces, the individual development of Canadian English and Canadian French literature, and the ages through which Canadian literature had run through the centuries.

But I felt that my attachment to the library books on the history of Canadian Literature would not impact me as much as they should have. I browsed those, underlined horrendously, and returned them to the library with all my observations. If that was so, then certainly reading them for my own study would not contribute when I would need those. And so, I began new searching.

One day, while researching the 'used books shops in Toronto,' I got one 'Re: Reading.' They do have many branches across the city. Google gave the address of the nearest one, which is not very far from my home.

It was a day that multiplied my happiness in Toronto hundred times. As per my Google search, I reached there in 30 minutes. Not a very spacious shop it was. But there had been a huge number of tall shelves jam-packed mostly with books. Saying a 'hello' at the front desk, I confessed that I was a new one in the city and country also, and for the first time I was there in that shop, and I was trying to search for books on and of Canadian Literature. The lady took me with her, showed me the signs on the shelves, and at last brought me to a place where I found a sign like 'Canadian Literature.'

'Re: Read' gave me many, among which a critique on Lucy Maud Montgomery touched me much. The unbelievably popular writer of Canada of the early twentieth century, by then, was not unfamiliar to me. Browsing on her life and works also added value to my reading. But the online study could not give me the strength to encapsulate a long article on her – a full view encompassing her writing career. But the new book would surely be a referential resource at my writing desk. I always believed literary criticism helps a reader to understand a text better, and books on literary criticism open many untrodden avenues for a reader. And all these possibilities shrouded my mind with many unseen possibilities.

This book made me happy, but this was not the book that made my day. Rather I like to say; it actually made my year. It actually made a project idea in me – it boosted me to write a Bengali-language book on Canadian Literature, the literature which is globally known as CanLit.

The book was voluminous, one of twelve-hundred pages. It was 'The Oxford Companion to Canadian Literature.' I did not know such a book I would ever own on CanLit. I did not know such an extensively informative book would always be my companion. And the truth is, I, a poor man in Toronto, could 'afford' such invaluable work in reality at only 12 dollars.

A new illumination began to encircle me around the clock. It did not let me sleep for the first few days. Entries like 'Novels in English,' 'Novels in French,' 'Poetry in English,' 'Poetry in French,' 'Biography and Memoirs in English,' 'Children's Literature in English,' 'Drama in English,' and 'Essays in English' made me sleepless.

'Novels in English' is an essay of 38 pages, contributed by many. The long essay has many separate parts which are written by scholarly persons. The parts have been like: 'Beginning to 1900', '1900 to 1920', '1920 to 1940', '1940 to 1960', '1960 to 1982', 'Other talents, other works: 1960 to 1982', '1983 to 1996', 'Other novels: 1983 to 1996'. Now I can use a marker as much as I wish, underline the significant lines whenever I need, and write my notes around the pages and thus use my study as and when I need.

A copy of 'The Oxford Companion to Canadian Literature' at my home has empowered me to work more precisely, more devotedly, and more meticulously. Now, similar books from the Toronto Public Library will pose more contribute to my research. Now Richard Lane's 'The Routledge Concise History of Canadian Literature,' 'Canadian Graphic: Picturing Life Narratives,' 'A Reader's Guide to the Canadian Novel,' 'Novels and the Nation: essays in Canadian Literature,' 'French-Canadian & Quebecois Novels,' 'Measures of Astonishment: poets on poetry,' 'ECW's biographical guide to Canadian poets' became supportive of continuing my work.

Now I gradually got aware of how the literature in Canada started and, how the different provinces came up with their own literature and thus contributed to the bulk of Canadian Literature, how the French-language literature enriched the CanLit.

And consequently, in 2018, I felt empowered to write a Bengali-language manuscript on Canadian literature, and now I feel blessed that my Murdhonno, Dhaka, came forward to publish that one into a book in the following year.

Subrata Kumar Das is an immigrant Bangladeshi writer now living in Toronto.

Part Three

Short Stories

Finn Hall

The Witch of the Dark Water

Near the village of Pitsligae there is a wide open, but very dark loch. In fact, there is one large loch and three smaller ones. On an island in the middle of the big body of water, known as the Blake Loch of Turclossie, legend has it that there lived a witch. Now witches aren't always bad and scary, in fact most are not. But, as it is with people in general, you do get the odd one who is very, very nasty.
This witch falls into that category.
The loch sits in a peat bog, and as in most peat bogs, faeries also lived there. They played among the cotton grass, and hid in the heather. Deer was known to come down to the waterside, as well as hares and occasionally a family of cranes. But over the years sightings of smaller birds became less.
The faeries couldn't understand why this was.

They started finding skeletons of small creatures, including ducks and moorhens littering the banks and surrounding foliage. Strange little holes in the ground started to appear.
Now faeries don't like puzzles and mysteries, so they set about trying to find out the cause of this calamity. Around the body of water they built several wooden hides, not like bird watching hides, more like little fences. Over the days they took turns in sitting behind these barricades, keeping an eye out for whatever was creating this carnage.
One grey evening, as autumn was turning into winter, two of the lookouts heard a sort of whooshing noise. At first they weren't sure what it was, due to the light, but soon saw it was a flock of migrant birds. They smiled to themselves. They heard another sound, very similar to the first. And thought nothing of it.
Not until the birds suddenly started making all sorts of noises and were flapping about as most of them, in a frightened manor, took off into the air.
Being very alert now, the watchers peered through the gloaming to see the witch had left her island and was snatching and grabbing the poor creatures and eating them, feathers and all. Leaving nothing but bones lying on the dark ground.
She then, using her long and bloody fingers, started digging in the damp peat and soil and pulled out long wriggling worms, which she swallowed whole.
The faeries were sickened at such a sight.
"How could she do this? They said, "We all live in harmony here. Nature abounds."
The witch, heard them, but not knowing who or what

said these words, jumped on her broomstick and flew back to her island.

The following morning the faeries called a meeting. All that could gathered in the circle midway between the water's edge and the trees. Discussions took place and a decision was made. They decided that in one week they would all gather at twilight, when they knew, as happened every year, a colony of Brent Geese were known to stop off and rest here for a few days.

So on the given day, the faeries strategically placed themselves around the area. Some on the banks of the water, others amongst the reeds and grass. Sure enough very little time had passed when the flock of geese descended, tired and weary, to their temporary abode.

A good time passed, and nothing happened. The birds continued to rest, feed and chat to each other. The guardians were just about to call it a night, planning to return the following evening, when they just about heard the strange sound caused by the broom flying witch. She had only time to grab but one or two of the poor birds before the faeries put their plan into action.

They immediately cast a spell making the air so heavy that the surprised witch could not take off, then the chief fairy, Cavoch, jumped up in front of the malevolent being, and cast an extremely powerful spell.

She turned the witch into a tree. A tree that could never grow, and never die. The tree sat far enough back from the edge of the dark water, that the little birds could sit on its branches and peck and sharpen their beaks, without fear of falling into the water.

And there to this day it remains.

Some say that if the sunlight and conditions are just

right, you can see a shimmer as the captive witch tries to escape her tree shape.

But the spell is so strong, that after enduring the pain, she lets out a shrill scream and ceases the futile attempt to escape.

Sarah Leavesley

Beyond the Lake

Everything starts when the lake freezes. Leaning over the snow-laden edge, Becky flinches as a girl stares up at her from the ice.

What the…! Becky's chest tightens, her heart thumping. She tries to slow her breathing and think. The face isn't a strange warping of her own reflection, though something about the girl seems strangely familiar. The same blue tinged with green eye colour, maybe Becky's nose when she was little. But this face is a stranger's, a child that Becky doesn't recognise, with blonde hair and a ferociously intense gaze.

A ferociously intense and alive gaze. The girl's outstretched fingers twitch slightly beneath the glassy surface. Becky's about to reach out when she hears her brother calling.

"I'm here, Tim, by the willow." She turns towards his voice. "You're not going to believe this!"

But when Becky looks back, the girl has gone, leaving only a crazy-glazed expanse splattered with broken twigs and trapped leaves. No fresh-water clarity. No creepy mystery either. Still, she shivers, and the soles of her red shoes slip. As she tips forwards, she sees the girl's pale face rising up to meet her, then nothing; Becky's head hits the ice and she blacks out.

By the time Becky has come round, she's cradled in her brother's arms; he's muttering about the treacherous ground, not going out without him, and the foolishness of her red shoes.

"Anything could have happened!" Tim sniffs. "If the lake hadn't been frozen, you'd have been at the bottom, drowned."

Becky shivers again, but not at the thought of drowning. Her brother's suffocating anxieties are full of controlling contradictions: the perils of winter, yet the winter ice that saved her.

"Tell me you weren't trying to get across!" Tim clamps his arm around Becky's waist and hoists her into a position that makes it impossible for her to walk without holding onto him for support. "It's too slippery, too thin. The ice could break."

She nods and lets her brother lead her towards the house. She puts her fingers to the bump on her head to cover a backwards glance at the little cottage, lights shining, on the other side of the glistening lake.

The next morning the lump on Becky's head is a purple-blue bruise – almost the colour of the lake in summer, not that she's ever been in or on it. No swimming, no sailing, no crossing to the other side by any means, Tim is emphatic about this. Not even a smile when she joked once about walking on water instead, just her brother's habitual frown, which only gets deeper.

"I was thinking I might head out," she ventures after breakfast. "An invigorating walk, to help the swelling heal."

"No, Becky!" Tim scowls. "I'm too busy to go with you. And if you faint again…it's cold and slippery."

"But I don't feel weak at all now, not even the hint of a headache."

"No!" He grabs her wrist.

"Ow!" she exclaims.

"I'm sorry." Tim loosens his grip. "I didn't mean to hold so tight. But it isn't safe for you to go alone; I'd barely trust my own feet in these conditions."

"I won't be out of shouting distance," she promises. "Just a five-minute stretch, around the house."

"Absolutely not. Be sensible." Her brother's voice has taken on its over-loud, pleading tone. "You'll only want to push on further. Remember what happened last year."

"I know." She nods. "You were right about not training."

"A stupid idea struggling on your own, dancing, when you've got me to take care of you!" He folds his arms across his chest.

"It was a daydream," she agrees. "But, you know, you don't really need me here."

"Of course, I don't need you." He glares. "What I need is to protect you from yourself. Have you taken your…"

"Yes, yes," she interrupts. "I've taken my pills – Dr Glover!"

"Is that meant to be funny?" He frowns.

"I'm sorry, Tim. I don't mean to cause you hassle. You do take care of me well. I wouldn't even go beyond the garden."

"Not in this weather, Becky. Open the window if you want fresh air!"

Tim stomps out of the lounge, closing the door loudly and firmly behind him. Becky hears the scrape of a chair across the kitchen tiles and guesses that he's positioned himself in precisely the right spot to make it impossible for her to get to the outside door without pushing past.

Becky sighs. Her brain is prone to tormenting her with strange ideas, but what does Tim expect when she's little else to stave off unrelenting boredom.

Dancing does exhaust her, but it also excites her. Music is in her bones, as much if not more than the occasional psychosis which haunts her mind. The ice-girl isn't a hallucination or stir-craziness though, Becky's sure of it! She leans the unbruised side of her forehead against the big window. The glass is bracingly chilly but the lake and distant hills so beautiful, white and unscuffed. Bar for the cottage at the other side of the lake, the nearest houses are doll's house small, a far glitter of lights at night.

As she stares out, Becky catches a ripple of movement in the glass. The girl's face! Her small eyes are distraught now, lips moving as if saying something, weed tangled in her straw hair… Shocked, Becky pulls away, burning her hand on the hot radiator. When she turns back to the window, there is nothing there but a small patch of damp near to where she'd rested her face: the mist of warm breath held too long against a cold surface.

A week later, the lake is still frozen; Tim is still refusing to allow Becky or himself leave the house.

Becky hasn't spoken to her brother about the girl – why give him something else to fuss over, he'd only think her delusional. But the child's increasingly anguished face has eased into every reflective surface: the bathroom mirror, the black TV screen, even the steel sink. Although never more than a filmic sheen that disappears as soon as Becky blinks, Becky feels, no, knows, that the girl is real.

As Becky shifts her weight between the stairs on her way up to the attic, the floorboards creak. She'd assumed they might and the sound doesn't scare her.

When she reaches the top, the attic is exactly as it always has been: quiet, relatively dust-free, winter sun shining directly through the skylights. All their parents' things are there, neatly boxed and stacked, as untouched as if time itself has frozen.

Feeling her stomach muscles clench, Becky hesitates. Sorting through their stuff might be too much. Tim would probably have a fit if he knew. Defying her brother without him knowing though is a small, if childish, triumph against being stuck inside.

Becky lifts down two boxes and sits cross-legged beside them. Picking up the family albums, she goes through holiday pictures, birthday shots, memories that she has forgotten and places which she doesn't recognise, though she can see her younger self in the photos. She lingers over the candid-camera moments caught by a guest at her parents' ruby anniversary party.

As Becky moves the album to look more closely at one of the photos, a picture slips from behind the cover – it's the girl! Becky's fingers tremble, as she examines the battered snapshot, marked *Isabelle Glover, Shrewsbury, 1996.* Glover, so the girl is family. 1996, six years before Becky was born, when Tim was four...

Is that it? Becky continues looking through. No more pictures of the girl. Just Tim, her parents and Aunt

Beth at various sea-sides. Becky flicks onwards faster – still nothing of Isabelle. Taking the album in one hand, Becky shakes it firmly.

A discoloured fragment of newspaper flutters like a giant moth to the floor. *Family's Tragic Drowning* – a heavy sickness churns Becky's stomach, but she can't stop. She reads on: *seven-year-old girl…Isabelle Glover…drowned…distraught parents said…her brother, Tim…submerged rocks…the only one to see her go under…* Becky struggles at first to link the words to their meaning. As what happened sinks in, the scrap of newsprint shudders from her grasp, falling to rest in the dark gap between her parents' broken chest of drawers and Tim's old briefcase.

By the time Becky has reached the cottage at the other side of the lake later that day, it no longer seems strange to her that the door should be opened by a ghost. Nor that the ghost should be her sister. It's reassuring though to see Isabelle smile as she had in the photo, rather than the trapped expression reflected in every shiny surface at the house. Not a trace of weed either in her sister's shiny brushed hair. On her feet, a pair of red shoes – an almost perfect match for Becky's except many sizes smaller.

All the questions that had blizzarded Becky's thoughts give way to a silent numbness, as Isabelle moves to one side to let her in. Snow has flicked up over the top of Becky's wellies and melted to a squelching slush around her feet. Isabelle holds out her hands.

Without a word, Becky levers her boots free. She pulls off her wet socks and passes them to her sister, who hands her some white satin slippers. Through the window, Becky can now see Tim, zig-zagging a path across the lake towards the cottage, the scuffed ice behind him as jagged as a saw blade.

Placing Becky's socks and wellies by the stove, Isabelle takes a chair and climbs on it to reach for something from the kitchen shelf. As Tim unlatches the cottage gate, Isabelle pushes a music box towards her sister. It's the kind that Becky dreamed of having as a child: a mirror lake surrounded by sparkling snow with two skating figures balanced on the water's frozen edge.

"Wind it, but only when you're ready," Isabelle says. Then, she opens the door and steps out, coatless, towards their brother.

Tim pushes the gate open, and Becky realises that he's smiling for once. He's carrying her red shoes, and sets them down on a tree-stump, before taking Isabelle's hand.

Becky watches them walk together towards the lake, her brother shortening his grown-up stride to match the seven year old's butterfly steps. As they reach the edge, Becky twists the music box's clockwork handle. Driven by hidden magnets, the tiny skaters begin to dance in looping circles across the mirror. Outside, Tim and Isabelle trace their own elegant figures of eight across the frozen lake, across the thin ice that Tim had warned Becky might break.

When the tune starts to fade, Becky forces herself to turn away from Tim and Isabelle. On the music-box mirror, the tiny skaters falter then stop. Becky puts the music box back on the shelf, then glances at the lake outside. No sign of her brother or sister, no marks from their dancing, or footsteps away from the bank – the surface is smooth and entirely un-scraped, as if they'd never been there. Or as if they've sunk through the thinness without a trace, the ice healing over behind them. On the tree-stump by the gate, Becky's bright red shoes are white with snow, their buried shape blending peacefully with the garden landscape.

Becky opens the door and glides, coatless, down the path. Her skirt flutters with sudden gusts of wind, but she isn't cold. Stopping at the tree-stump, she touches the red shoes. She no longer feels pulled to put them on; these white slippers fit better, and with them her movements are freer, less forced and more fluid. Gracefully adagio at first, then faster with pas brisés, Becky dances towards the glittering lake.

Daniela Andonovska Trajkovska

The Last Drops of Coffee and Time

Janko's days were all the same. He would open the Faculty's café at 8:00 am. On Monday mornings, he always opened the café half an hour earlier so that he could clean the Espresso and Macchiato machine. If someone asked for Espresso or Macchiato, he would briskly say, "Sorry! It's Monday! You can get one later." Then he would smile and start coughing. Thus, everybody knew that on early Monday mornings, they could only have Turkish coffee, Nescafe, Cocoa, and Hot Chocolate, but no Espresso or Macchiato. Tea, however, was available at any time.

'They', in fact, were just a handful of professors who used to drink their morning coffee at the Faculty before starting their lectures. Some of the students would also sit in Janko's café, eating pretzels, cheese buns, and salty rolls on the photocopied materials placed on their table, pensively turning the pages filled with dry bread crumbs.

From 8:30 am to 10:00 am, while everybody had classes, Janko would sit alone behind the counter, taking small sips from his small bottle of rakija that he used to hide among the mineral water crates and the big pine cones he collected in the Faculty's yard.

At 10:00 am, there was a long 30-minute break, and the students, along with the professors, would go out to the yard to have a cigarette and a cup of coffee. Janko's café was actually located in the Faculty's basement, and one of the windows overlooking the northern side of the Faculty's yard was the spot where he received his customers' orders. The customers would have to bend down and knock on the window several times; Janko would open the window, take their order, and then close it again. He had one ground rule: he never hurried. There was time for everything, and he never opened the window if he was not quite ready. Once he was done with the order, he would climb the ladder leaning on the inner side of the wall, open the window, and shout, "Professors!" or "Coffee is ready!" Then everybody rushed towards the window, the same window frame through which Janko saw the world. They would stretch their arms to pick up their cups of coffee, in which Janko's thoughts were floating—thoughts that he never uttered out loud, thoughts that refused to go home, as there was no one there waiting for the 49-year-old Janko. The worth of Janko's life was 20 denars per Turkish coffee, Espresso or Macchiato, or tea, and 30 denars per Nescafe. Very often, the professors would try to reason with him, claiming that he could not survive on the sum he was charging as he would have to spend it on his next supplies, but he would only raise his hand to stop them without saying a single word.

From 10:45 am to 12:30 pm, everybody would leave for their next lectures, and Janko would be alone again behind the counter, drinking the last drops of rakija without which his hands would shake, and his tongue would be tied. At 12:45, he would go out to collect the tables in the yard where a short while ago coffee was served to the future professors, presidents, managers, or perhaps the future shop assistants working in boutiques, marketplaces, and waiters—all of them holding a university degree in a society with the largest number of university graduates and the smallest number of decent job openings. Janko would then clean the ashtrays in which the academic citizens were burning down their critical thoughts and wash the cups in which the squandered time was the only residue.

At 1:00 pm, he would lock the café and go home, but nobody waited for him there. Very often, the professors would ask Janko to fetch them coffee in their office, and he would place the cup on the tray with two bags of sugar on the left-hand side and a little plastic spoon on the right-hand side, along with a glass of water, and start climbing the stairs. His hands were shaking, and many times he would spill the coffee, so he would go back to make a new one. Having placed it neatly on the tray, he would start his climb again. Sometimes it would take him half an hour to deliver the coffee, but the professors knew that he needed time to go up and down the stairs several times before he could make it to their office. He thought nobody noticed that. The hardest blow for him was when he would spill the coffee upon entering a professor's office. Then he would apologize and swiftly turn back to replace it with a new one. He would never give in when the professors insisted that he should leave the spilled coffee. He was even offended by it, though the biggest offense ever was when the professors would venture to get their coffee from the tray themselves instead of allowing him to do that. The professors have come to realise that, and nobody interfered with Janko's job.

Janko had the same time schedule both when there were students and professors at the Faculty and when there were none. There were days when he would sell only 11 coffees, sometimes 5 coffees and a tea, for instance, and there were days when he was the only person to drink a cup of coffee in his café. On these days, it was as if time had plotted against him, attempting to kick him out of the only place where he wanted to be: in the window frame, behind the counter, or on the table next to the counter. But he never changed. He would always open at 8:00 am and close at 1:00 pm. He never changed the price list either.

Today, I found out why the café had been closed lately. "A stroke," they said. He lost his memory and does not recognize anybody. He cannot even recognize his own brother. He cannot speak or get out of bed. He doesn't like visitors either. He doesn't even look at people's faces; he only looks at the red sky framed in the window. At 8:00 am, he opens his eyes, and at 1:00 pm, he closes them and keeps them closed until the next morning.

Translated from Macedonian into English by Prof. d-r Silvana Kolevska Neshkovska

Bipradas Barua

A Father's Dream And A Princess

A *Doyel* is twittering at dawn. The bird's tender tweet sounds more like a whistle. While working in the kitchen, the mother calls her son: "O my boy, listen!" Meanwhile, Bokul, with his skates on, is already out on the road. The mother keeps talking under her own breath: "Repeatedly, I told you to have something before going out; hardly do you have any strength in your body; I wonder how you will go running!"

He is all skin and bones and is in poor health. Even though he is skeletal, he is lanky. He is a freshman in college. With the *Poush* setting in, it is shivering cold, and the sky is overcast with mist. He looks even taller, having worn the sports trousers-suit, which includes a hooded jacket. He bought this sportswear at a lower price from Bongobazar, a popular makeshift market of ready-made garments which are meant for export but rejected by foreign buyers for non-compliance with specifications. The blue-white-black warm trousers suit is trendy, but his awkward-looking, longish hollow-cheeked face, pointed nose, and cheekbones stand out like a drought-stricken person.

The waist-lace of the trousers is loosened up to his knees; the hoody's string tied around his neck is swinging as well. Although his roller skates have caused wear and tear from their two-year usage, the made-in-

England skates still look grand. Their tips are sharp-edged. He goes roller-skating faster on the road, churning out loud sounds. However, he brings the speed down while negotiating bends on the rugged road, littered with potholes and road humps. Thinking that he might hit a flat road for a smoother ride, he goes in a north-south direction from Nawabpur road to Bongshal through Aloobazar, and therefore, he veers onto Bongshal. The north-south road is comparatively better. With the mist becoming compacted, visibility turns poorer. It would be good if he could go up to Ramna Park. Five-six people are likely to join him there. Meanwhile, two dreams 'princesses' come out of their Shiddeswari apartment. While speed-skating, he feels like snatching away their headscarves. Over a period of time, he has mastered the art of scooping up the hat from a person's head in a flash while running on skates. At the Shishupark skating ring, he has aced his skating skills to knock off the hats of the other skaters while retaining his own cap intact on his head. Shishupark opens in the afternoon, not in the morning. If he gets a move on now, he will be able to catch up with the beautiful Shiddeswari princesses. Meanwhile, they have caught sight of each other and struck some sort of a compromise; after all, there should be a limit to teasing remarks. Having said that, the girls also don't fall much behind in good-humored bantering. They have let Bokul know where they live; he has given his address as well.

He starts to go slowly as the road is full of cracks and craters. To fend off the chill, he pulls the cap onto his forehead. Thereafter, he gives his ears to the dream princesses, bursting out laughing. Meanwhile, a rickshaw passes by, almost kissing his legs; the man-driven three-wheeler rattles away, shattering his dreams. He can no longer see the caps of the princesses who are wearing blue sweaters and Jeans pants. He thinks they must have reached either *Minto* or *Bailey* Road by that time. Right at that time, he sees a fleshy and bushy-bearded man, clothed in a long dirty coat, at the end of the road. Even though he is the only person on foot on the road, Bokul gives an evasive look. Who can come out on the road so early on a cold morning? Finally, the rotund man comes into Bokul's view. The man is walking unsteadily. Is he drunk? This is what strikes his mind first. He doesn't have any empathy for a drunkard. Just because of the man's appearance and his body shape, he has managed to draw Bokul's attention. He is enviably tall; the frame of his glasses appears to be quite thick. Although he is not markedly on view due to fog, his heavy legs are pounding against the road, with intermittent stopping. As he himself is on roller skates, he is getting closer. His speed is like that of a pedestrian. Pulling his skates to the side of the road, the man stretches his hands out toward the closed door of a shop to stop himself from a tumbling fall. Bokul takes no time to realise the fact that he is not a drunkard. Maybe the man is sick. As Bokul reaches the spot, they are in close proximity to each other. Hanging on to the shutters of the shop, the man, the thickset skater, comes to a grinding halt. Bokul pulls up at the same spot. The man is trying to unbutton the collar-tight shirt under his coat with one hand while putting in his efforts to support his body weight with the other one.

Reaching closer, Bokul thinks he must do something for the man. Simultaneously, the laughing faces of the princesses come alive in his mind.

Meanwhile, through his thick-frame glasses, the man hauls up his turbid eyes and sees Bokul standing near him. The man is breathing heavily; as he cringes in pain, it becomes manifest in his face. Somehow, the man manages to unfasten the shirt's neck-tight button, and then placing his left hand on the right side of his chest; he tremulously said: "O my boy...!"

Bokul is shaken to the core of his heart by that particular phrase.

This is what Bokul's mother calls him: this is her special way of expressing her concern for her son. Quickly Bokul sits down, opens his skates in a jiffy, holds them under his armpit, and rushes to the man.

Somehow, the man musters some energy and says: "My boy, could you help me reach my home? Just a stone's throw..." Silently, Bokul stands very close to the man and stretches out his shoulders toward the person. Clasping Bokul's shoulders with his right hand, the man trudges alongside him. The man's weighty hands and huge body are leaning against the boy, who is as thin as a rake: what a polarity! With the man's body weight gradually becoming heavier, he appears to be contorting with wincing chest pain. In his imagination, Bokul visualizes that the Shiddeswari girl skaters, with their tresses flowing in the air, are gaining momentum. He thinks he is getting late. Also, they are listening to music to be in sync with the skating tempo. The cloud-coloured princess croons some lines of a Tagore song:

Amar Noyon Tobo Noyner Nibir Chayay

Moner Kothar Kushumokorok Khoje

(My eyes seek in the depth of your eyes' shades

What will stir my thoughts and blossom them)

While listening to the song, Bokul speeds up.

Even though the man is finding it difficult to catch up with Bokul, he doesn't want to fall behind. Bokul is quite keyed up while the man is getting hurt to keep pace with him. Intermittently, the man is gasping for breath. Looking at the man's face, Bokul becomes aware of this fact. Maybe, they want to go separate ways, and that is why they go speed-walking on the skates to the best of their abilities. Surprisingly, they aren't talking to each other. The street is completely naked: no people or vehicles! A street dog passes by, looking casually at them. Crows utter a caw, and the girl's song melts into thin air.

At a slow pace, they reach in front of the gate of an old house. The plaster of the brick pillars on both sides of the gate has been stripped away; however, the gate of the door is made of tin. With a slight push, the gate goes off the latch. After a few paces, they meet a set of wooden steps leading up to the second floor of the old house. A stockpile of rubbish has been dumped on the ground; a door that has gone to rack and ruin comes into Bokul's view. The stairs start to creak as they climb up. Reaching the door, the man somehow brings out the door key from his pocket and gives it to Bokul. The ramshackle door opens with a dying squeak. It is pitch dark inside the room. He gropes for the switch to turn it on, and then he leaves Bokul to walk one or two paces, all by himself, to hit his sofa like a thud. Even the old spring-supported settee refuses to keep quiet: it releases a squeal to welcome its master. The hefty man keeps his eyes closed, reclining his weighty body against the sofa. He feels himself recoil at the rising pain in his chest. Not knowing what to do at this point, at first, Bokul looks at the man, pans his head to see the run-down furniture soon after, and finally, he pays serious attention to the man. It is at that time the man opens his eyes and mouth to talk.

Anxiously, he says, "There is a moving slice in my heart."

His sudden dramatic disclosure renders Bokul clueless about what the piece is all about and why it is on the move. Realizing what the boy has been thinking about, the man says: "The war ended a long time back, but still, there is a particle in my chest. Of the four, three were taken out; one is still there."

He is talking about *Muktijuddho;* Bokul understands. Then the man must be a *Muktijoddah* - it is the boy's avowal. Immediately, Bokul goes two steps forward toward the man. Still, then, the boy doesn't know what his name and identity are - which sector he has fought in and what type of fighter he has been. The boy becomes interested in him when he gets to know that he is a *Muktijoddah*. Bokul's father was a *Muktijoddah*, too. Barely can he remember his father. Listening to a lot about his father from his mother, Bokul has formed an image of him. In his imagination, Bokul sees his father as a combatant - once, his father was about to be buried under chunks of the earth in a trench; his fellow fighters dug him out, and he was saved from the jaws of death. Finally, he returned as a victor.

The man says: "It was a face-to-face encounter; right away, they started raining down."

To let the man spurt over his outbursts of emotion, Bokul asks: "What did they do?"

The man replies in the form of another question: "Do you know what 'jittering' is?"

Giving him a nodding disapproval, Bokul says: "No."

The man says: "It is the language of war. It is a sort of patrolling. It is about a group which advances through the defence line of the warring sides very carefully to know about the exact enemy position and their weaponry."

The man adds detail to make it clear to the boy: "While we started jittering with a group of ten people, we fell into the hands of the enemy, and the enemy began to shell our position from a distance. Four splinters from the bombs hit my chest and hands." While elaborating on the incident, he becomes ashen-faced; his eyes turn depressingly dreary, and his face shows signs of acute pain. He writhes in agony., Bokul quickly asks: "Should I call a doctor?"

The man replies: "I think I'll be okay if I can take some rest. Maybe, the night duty is taking a toll on my health. I couldn't take rest for a single moment."

The boy comes up with an advice: "Then go to bed..."

The man asks: "Are you in a hurry? Do you have time on your hand?"

Bokul reminisced about his skating - Park Road, Mintoo Road - he skated alongside the Shiddeswari princesses, with their long loose hair wafting in the air, and he hummed the rest of the lines of the Tagore song, of which the dusky princess sang only two lines before.

Atur dithite shudhay shey niroberey

Nivrito Banir sondhan nai je re

Ojanar majhe obujher moto fere

Oushrudharay moje

(Anxiously, my eyes seek a message in the silence

But I can find nothing anywhere there

And so in the unknown, inconsolable,

They drown in a vale of tears!)

Bokul draws himself back to reality: now he is in the men's room. Without much thought, he says: "No-no, I am not in a hurry. I am done with skating." Then he keeps the skates on the floor.

"Could you find me the medicine? Maybe, it's somewhere in the room. They are tablets. It may be in a tray in the drawer." While requesting the boy to do the favor for him, the man tries to get up from bed, but he falls down, hitting the floor with a clonk.

Bokul rushes to the spot. Sitting beside the man, the boy says: "Let me hold you. Could you get up?"

With his half-shut eyes, the man looks at Bokul, but actually, he gazes into space, far beyond the boy's face. Trying to sound compassionate, Bokul says: "Don't you have anybody else?"

Coming out of his reverie, the downcast man gives voice to his frustration: "My wife is on a long break to Cumilla." This is a downright lie; his wife has left him forever!

"Shall I send a telegram to her?"

"No-no, it's not necessary. She just went yesterday." While saying these, he slumps into the settee, being downhearted.

Meanwhile, the boy wends his way into the next room. The small room contains a reading table and a bedstead. 'Happy Birthday, Naila' is written on the wall. Bokul clenches his fist at the name 'Naila.' In pent-up annoyance, he speaks under his breath: "Is it right to go on a holiday, leaving your sick husband?" A cup and two books are on the table. What a mess everywhere! With a look of disgust on his face, he then steps into the next room, pulling the curtain of the partition door. Even though this room is a small one, it has a big bedstead. On the wall, there is a photo illustrating the scene of Muktijoddah: the man in a beard, hiding in a trench, is aiming his LMG at the enemy. The caption under the photo is titled: Reza Ali During Thakurgaon Operation. Now the boy knows the man's name: Reza Ali. To look for the medicines, the boy pulls the drawer of the tumbledown half-secretary table open. Next to it is a helmet of a soldier on a stool. This helmet appears to be the same as the helmet in the photo. Bokul couldn't help but touch the protective gear of the soldier. He remembers his mother instantly. His mother said that his father had a helmet, too. She has given it to the Muktijoddah Museum. He doesn't reminisce about his father. When Bokul was only four, his father died in 1980. A bullet remained embedded in his chest, and it was made known

the day before his death in a hospital. Reza Ali has a bullet splinter in his chest, too. Will there be a mishap as well?

He exerts force to open the drawer, the one on the lower side of the row. On a small tray, three bullets, a fat pipe, and an old pocket watch are there. Besides these things, there is a brass bayonet. As the boy starts rummaging through the drawer, he finds two tablets on the tray - Brufen, the painkiller. What will happen after the pain subsides? No-no, a physician should see him. The man's treatment shouldn't be only tablet-dependent! He is such a burly man, yet he is so fatigued! Impulsively, the boy picks up the pipe Reza puffs on. As soon as Bokul catches a whiff of it, it starts to spew out an odorous admixture of burnt tobacco and an old stench from the pipe itself for not being used. Putting it in his mouth, the boy takes a drag on it. What a foul smell! Given the fact that he has had a sniff at it, he begins to think of himself as a grown-up man. Subsequently, he puts the helmet on his head and stands erect. In reverential gratitude, Bokul genuflects on the man who is close to the age of his martyred father. By showing his respect to Reza, he also pays a rich tribute to his own dead father. After that, the boy quickly but affectionately keeps the items in their places. He has had an interest in knowing what is there in the second and third drawers. Involuntarily, his hands make a move toward the second drawer, but he keeps his intent in check. It's not good to sneak a glance at someone else's things! Meanwhile, he scampers off to the kitchen, thinking about Reza. The boy needs to have some water to help the man have the tablets, but some people take tablets without water, too! Who knows what Reza will do? The kitchen, the plaster of which has come off in layers exposing the bricks, is just next to the room he is in at the moment. Things are all untidy here, too. A glass and a jar filled with water are there.

Returning to the room with tablets and water, he finds Reza Ali overtired and somnolent. His eyes are closed. Bokul thinks the man is fast asleep. The boy is confused about whether or not he should call the man. It seems Reza Ali is sleeping like a log. If it is so, then it is well and good. Is he in a deep sleep or in his last sleep? The boy is nonplussed by the whole affair. Putting the glass on a small tripod, Bokul advances toward the man and taps on his shoulder to know how his stimuli react to the boy's voluntary twitch. With no riposte coming from Reza Ali, Bokul is in two minds: is he slumbering or comatose? The situation gives the boy palpitations in his heart. Once again, Bokul calls to mind his father. His mother told him that his father went blacked out after he had returned from the bazaar. No sooner had he fallen grievously ill than an ambulance was called to take him to the hospital. He was diagnosed as having a hemorrhage from his chest injury. Surgeons sweated over to save his life; they even carried out a surgery on him to get the bullet out, but it was of no avail: he died.

Bokul darts across the lane to the main thoroughfare, looking for a place to make a phone call. Won't he get it? If the marts were open, there could be a possibility. Unfortunately, the area is surrounded by tea stalls, makeshift betel-leaf shops, and lodging houses. Big retail stores are closed. The boy scampers off to Nawabpur Road. Blaring the siren, an ambulance is coming from the northern direction at a great speed.

Raising both his hands, Bokul stands in the middle of the road and shouts at the top of his voice: "Stop, stop, stop." The ambulance screeches to a grinding halt near him. Two-three rickshaws and a few pedestrians are around the spot. Assuming that an accident has happened, the bystanders hurry to the spot and form a ring around the vehicle. One of them calls out: "Does it sound credible that accidents are caused by ambulances? Is the world going in a reverse direction?" Being wildly enthusiastic, another one says: "Lay hold on the driver! Take him captive."

Bokul replies: "It's not an accident. A man is seriously ill. He has to be taken to the hospital."

The ambulance is almost empty; it is going back to its destination with a doctor in there. Having the approval of the doctor, the driver allows Bokul to get into the vehicle.

Reaching the man's house, two people scurry to fetch Reza Ali. The man has stayed unconscious, and checking his pulse; the doctor places his stethoscope on his chest to examine how he is doing. Immediately, the doctor gives him an injection and asks the people to put him on the stretcher. The two helpers find the man quite heavy to be carried to put the man on a stretcher. While Reza Ali is being moved, the wooden house and stairs start to make a horrible squeaking noise. Bokul and the doctor lend their hands to the stretcher-bearers so that they can carry the sick man through the stairs with ease. As the situation demands the boy to become the temporary owner of the house, the boy keeps the house key in his pocket. The boy is full of malignant hatred when he doesn't find any clue to the answer: why is Reza Ali's wife away at this critical time? Conjuring up an evil image of the woman, Bokul once again feels like landing a blow on her. Giving a thumbnail sketch to the doctor of what has happened to the man, the boy says: "Five bombshell- splinters entered into his chest in a face-to-face encounter with the enemy during *Muktijoddah*. Of them, one is lodged in there. Now he is having severe pain from it." Right at that moment, Reza Ali opens his eyes and takes a good look at the boy who was in his house before he lost his sentience. This is the boy who has brought the man home from the road. Without saying a single word, he closes his eyes once again. The doctor says: "I am taking him to the hospital. It is not the kind of disease that can be treated by keeping the patient at home."

Minutes later, he opens his eyes once more and says: "O, my boy, could you do me a favor? I have a sister at Bramhanbaria. Please send her a telegram."

To relieve him of anxiety, Bokul says: "That's fine; you don't have to worry at all. I'll do everything."

While giving the boy her address and money, Reza Ali's eyes look aggrieved. "Don't lose time; just rush. Thank you," the man sounds a little keyed up while saying that.

Now the stretcher is on the ambulance, and the ambulance speeds its way through to the hospital, blaring the siren. When the boy recollects that he has left his skates in Reza Ali's house, he returns to that house and enters the house by opening the lock of the door. The boy thinks every house has a distinctive smell associated with it. This time the boy gets the classic aroma of this house. Immediately, the boy envisions his mother's activities: his mother went to the balcony from the kitchen; she was watering the rose plants on the tubs. Lots of roses - red, yellow, blackish, and rosy - bloomed on the plants in the containers; the blackish one was non-native. From there, she went to the Bokul, a locally-grown flower, counter where the orchid, which was stuck to the mango tree, was placed; she sprinkled some water on them with her hand; Cautiously, she was dusting off dirt from some leaves; the frame of a large-size photo of his father was hanging from the wall; in the photo, his father was wearing a soldier's helmet; crows were cawing outside, while Doyel, a local bird, was whistling; the sun was about to peep through, and the mist was yet to clear away.

Bokul goes skating all the way to the Telegram office. Negotiating a bend at the north-south road, he proceeds toward the telegraph office, and no sooner does he take a turn than he listens to the song which floats across the place. At times, he sings the song; sometimes, it is the unidentifiable voice of his father, and occasionally, it is the girl whose breezy rendition catches his attention, too.

Duare Ekesi Rokto Rekhai Padma-Ashon

Se Tomare Kisu Bole?

Tobo Kunjero Potho Diye Jete Jete

Batashe Batashe Betha Dei Mor Pete-

Bashi Ki Ashay Vasha Deye Akashete

Se Ki Keho Nani Bojhe?

(Before it's a door, I drew a blood-red lotus message

But did it say anything to you?

As I pass through your arbor

To every passing gale, I bared my heart

Doesn't anyone understand what makes a flute play

Until its notes pervade the sky?

Bokul has never sent any telegram to anybody. A lady is at work in the office. Maybe, her duty is not over yet. Going to her, he says: "I'd like to send an urgent telegram." The lady keenly observes the boy who is with his skates. Then she says: "Will you be able to write, or shall I write it for you?"

Her words hurt his feelings. "Certainly, I can. Please, give me a paper," he says.

The lady gives him a form. As Bokul doesn't have a pen, he asks for it. He reads up the form, written in English. While writing the address, he finds himself in a problem. Reza Ali's handwriting is smudgy. The paper the man has written his address on is ripped. In the sender's column, will Bokul write his name? Won't she know

Bokul? Will she be convinced that it is from Reza Ali? How about sending the telegram in Reza Ali's name - will he write the phrases like 'seriously ill; come sharp; medical hospital'? As he crosses out the first word, spoiling the form, he requests the lady for another form. Instead of giving him a new one, the lady at the counter asks him to return the one he is holding in his hand. Nervously, Bokul keeps looking at her. Without telling him anything, she does the job for him. What a relief! Bokul gives TK 20, the telegram charge, to her while giving Reza Ali's address to the lady to fill out the form appropriately. Bokul is simply clueless as to why Reza Ali is not asking his wife to come here at this critical time of his life! What sort of a man is he?

Thereafter, he rushes to the hospital. Taking the necessary information from the Emergency Department, he goes to the surgical ward number seven straightaway. Finding an attending physician there, Bokul asks him: "A patient named Reza Ali came by ambulance a little while ago. How's he now?

The doctor asks: "Is he the man who has a shell splinter in his chest?"

Bokul seems to be ready with his answer: "Yes. He didn't have any problems for a long time. All of a sudden, it has started to move."

The doctor enquires: "Is the X-ray done? It is tough to understand why it has happened, a difficult case. Please wait outside. I'll update you after I come to know about it. What I know is that he will undergo an operation. The operation theatre is just beside it. Just wait."

The doctor goes inside. The smell, patients, nurses, and support staff in the hospital encourage Bokul to retrieve his forgotten memories. He is overpowered by a mixed feeling - a miasma of medicine and people's breath creates a different world in the hospital. Simultaneously, he goes through a spell of an emotional rollercoaster in his mind: his father was a Muktijoddah, but he didn't see the war happening before his eyes. Reza Ali, a true Muktijoddah, works day and night in shifts in the factory. Not only can Bokul listen to the repeated striking sound in the aluminum plant, but they also can see the smoke rising from the chimney of the facility. Bokul's memory provides him with a series of more powerful yet clear images: he can see Reza Ali's room in the two-story wooden-floor house, enveloped in darkness. Bokul just can't accede to the apathy of Reza Ali's wife toward her husband. Perhaps, she has completely lost her interest in her husband! Coming out of his hypnotic state, Bokul faces reality: hospital affairs. When is the surgery going to happen? Is it already over? Or is it underway? Why isn't the doctor here yet? Does it mean that Reza Ali is being operated on? Once Bokul came to the aid of a person who was run over by a speeding bus, smashing his legs. Hardly he could understand the psychology of the city-dwellers! The nearby people crowded around the spot of occurrence, but they didn't come to his rescue. They didn't think it was the call of the hour; instead, they resorted to vandalism: they started shattering the windshields of the bus, although it was necessary for them to get hold of the bus driver first. It was as if smashing the bus into smithereens would set the victim's legs right. Bokul finds his father in Reza Ali. The picture of the operation theatre flashes through his mind. Right then, he calls his mother to his mind. Certainly, his mother is thinking about him! Even though it is a holiday, he is supposed to go back home by now. Bokul thinks his mother will be convinced once he explains the whole situation to her. Moreover, she will be happy to know that he has helped a Muktijoddah. Under the veneer of her manifest happiness, she tries to hold back her tears inconspicuously. On again and off again, she bawls, remembering his father and thinking about the looming uncertainty about what will happen to her son in the future. Once Bokul saw his mother crying: waking up in the middle of the night, he saw her whining. When asked, she opened up and told him a lot of things about what he had said to her while he was dying. Again, the scene of his father firing bullets from his stun gun came alive in his mind again. It happened during a face-to-face encounter to keep control over the Shuvopur bridge. Bokul superimposes Reza Ali's face on his father's.

He loses his balance when his feet hit the pair of skates. His entire body, particularly his hands, and legs, are shaking. Does surgery take that much time? In a flash, Bokul conjures up images of war scenes: Muktijoddahas and Pakistani military were locked into a face-to-face battle; between the Muktijoddahas and the Pakistani occupation army, there was the no man's land, and he went on a 'jittering' mission out there. While crawling, he didn't know when he had entered into the enemy-fortified positions. There was an uneasy calm; the moon looked dead; it was chilling cold at night, with heavy mist blanketing the entire area. Even the cry of an owl was a remote possibility. Perhaps jackals and dogs also knew how to stay away from the battlefield. The sounds of the fog falling in drops, the moon's speechless communication, the susurration of the night in the combat zone, and the heavy breathing of the enemies were the only happening ones. He had learned about daredevil attacks from the book titled *Guerrilla Theke Shomukhjuddhe* (From Guerrilla War to Face to Face War). Also, he had come to know what was meant by 'the sound of silence.' He thought he was going on a 'jittering' mission, piercing the pitiless silence; he was trying hard to remove the layer of the dense fog with his hands, and he was putting in his best efforts to do away with the shadow cast over moonlight by the bamboo cluster to find out a pathway. The air clung to the toxic smell of the burning gunpowder of the previous day's battle. Even the smoke rising from the ground bore that sort of noxious smoldering stench. Bokul would get the same kind of foul smell when Reza Ali would puff on his pipe.

Bokul's chest stomps in staccato fear. Instead of the man, Bokul thinks he is lying etherized on the operation table, and the powerful light above the bench is getting dimmer. He has an uncanny feeling that an armored tank is rumbling through his chest! It is as if he is lying near a live mine to take the detonator out of it. Consumed by the thought, he seems to be running short of breath. His heart starts beating faster. Due to restlessness and excitement, he begins sweating heavily: one splinter has been taken out; another one is just near that one, and again he feels edgy, dreading the situation. Then images of the huge figure of Reza Ali and the six-foot-tall physique of his father come to his mind one after another.

Slowly but surely, Bokul becomes weary; maybe, his thoughts get tired as well. His sneaking feelings appear to be dull and dreary, but actually, they are not totally gone. Maybe, they have fallen quiet for a while. He is conscious of the fact that Reza Ali is being operated on: doctors are busy cutting up Ali's affected body parts and then sewing them up. A beaming smile is forcing its way through the cloth, covering Ali's face; it means the operation is successful; a saline solution is being given in his hand; he is now shifted to the stretcher from the operation table; a nurse and a doctor are pushing his trolley hospital bed out of the door slowly. Bokul's all thoughts come to a dead halt at that moment.

Coming out into the earmarked waiting area, a middle-aged nurse cries out: "Who has come for Reza Ali?"

The unspecified sudden shout makes Bokul jump up in unnerving anxiety. It is as if he has woken up from sleep. In response, he instinctively answers: "It's me."

In a sweet but deep voice, the nurse replies, denoting utter disbelief: "You? You are just a very young boy! Isn't there anyone elderly in the family? Anyway, he will regain his consciousness after some time. Now, there is nothing to be afraid of. Finally, everything ended quite well. It was a difficult surgery, though. Yes, the danger is over, and your *bap (*father) will be okay. He is a very strong man, indeed! Otherwise, how could he join the Muktijoddah? Really, he is a solid man!" Surprisingly, Bokul doesn't react to the word *bap* uttered by the nurse. Instead, he asks her quickly: "How long will he take to recover fully?"

The nurse replies: "Until the rose-bud flowers into a full-blown rose, he might have to be on bed rest. It's not a very long time, is it? You won't realise even how quickly time goes by. No worries!"

Bokul asks: "What will be his bed number?"

The nurse says: "Bed number 71 under ward number seven. Just go and tell your mother not to worry. And take this. Keep this piece of iron as a token of remembrance. This is the one that moved. Even the last evidence of the enemy shouldn't be kept in the body, but it has to remain before our eyes in order to reminisce about what had happened. That is why so many things have been preserved in the Muktijoddah Museum."

Bokul stretches out his hand to take the piece of iron that has been rusted away. He loves the nurse's motivational words and takes a good look at the thing in his hand.

The nurse keeps on saying: "This splinter was lodged near his heart. Even the doctor couldn't identify the reasons why it started to move after such a long time! It might have happened due to some mental traumas. Even if it is a sleeping enemy, it is always good to have it eliminated once and for all. It's gone; the danger is over. My boy, you just go and give the message to your mother. However, if you have something to say to your *bap*, you can say."

Bokul is in a fix - what should he say? His father was a Muktijoddah, but he is no more in this world. Reza Ali is still alive. Bokul doesn't remember when and what he had said to his father. Although he is searching for the appropriate words or expressions to tell this *bap*, he is not getting them. In a hurry, Bokul says: "Kisses and hugs for him. Joy Bangla!"

Smiling endearingly, the nurse says: "I'll let him know."

Firmly holding the iron piece in his fist, he again says: "I wish him a speedy recovery, and I'll be back here in the afternoon. Let him know that, too."

Holding the skates under his armpit, Bokul begins his journey back home. He needs to tell the whole thing to his mother, who, he thinks, must be worrying a lot. As so many things have happened over a very short period of time, Bokul feels he has to share the entire incident with his mother to release his pent-up emotions. Anything other than this - whether going skating again or having a good meal - is of no significance to him at the moment. Only, he reminisces about the princess who not only had given him an iniquitous and inquisitive look but also exchanged one or two words with him. Whenever he gets a glimpse of her, he muses on the Tagore song that she had hummed. He keeps cogitating on the tune until it turns out to be one of his favorite songs. While walking back to his house, Bokul is warbling the song with a soprano voice:

Amar Noyono Tobo Noyoner Nibiro Chayay

Moner Kothar Kusumokorok Khoje

(My eyes seek in the depth of your eyes' shades

What will stir my thoughts and blossom them)

But instead, the face and the deep-set eyes of Muktijoddah Reza Ali come alive in his mind. Simultaneously, Bokul remembers his father, too.

It seems now he is missing his father way more than before. His mother's powers of recalling events of the Liberation War have helped him form an indelible image of his Muktijoddah father in him: he was a well-built six-feet tall man with a soldier's helmet on his head. The picture, hanging from the wall in the room, stirs his imagination. All of a sudden, Bokul has a strange feeling that he has outgrown his age. Still, he thinks it would be better had his father had been there; not only could he tell him so many things, but also he could listen to a lot of war stories; also, he could hear the history of how the country was liberated. A living history. It would be an invaluable experience listening to the history of Muktijoddah either from his father or from someone who had seen it happening instead of knowing it from history books. Indeed, it would be a thrilling adventure to have learned what the face-to-face fight was like!

Bokul jumps on a rickshaw to hurry back home. While the man-driven three-wheeler is negotiating its way to the destination, the face of the new Bangla teacher at his college comes alive in his mind. He is a writer and a Muktijoddah. Bokul remembers the first day of the teacher's class: some students in that class expressed widespread dissatisfaction when he mentioned Bangabandhu as the 'the best Bangali of the century.' Immediately, The voice of Bokul's mother hits his ears: "O, my boy." In coexistence with his mother's voice, the voice of Reza Ali reverberates with emotional intensity in Bokul's ears as well. He thinks it is worth waiting for a person like Reza Ali at the hospital, keeping all the other duties in abeyance.

Bokul's mother opens as soon as he knocks at the door. In a manner revealing her angst, she asks: "My son, where have you been? Come on in and see who is waiting for you!"

Even though he hears what his mother has said, he doesn't pay much attention to them. Firstly, he needs to talk to his mother about Muktijoddah Reza Ali. Affectionately, he puts his arms around her neck and says: "Listen, I have taken Reza Ali, an injured Muktijoddah, to his house first. This iron piece was in his chest. He has had to be operated on to remove this splinter. I am coming from the hospital now; you will go, too. Let's go..."

Before he is through with his utterance, he sees the very dusky-complexioned Shiddeswari princess standing behind his mother. Behind her is her other companion. Bokul is unable to believe his eyes: all his words dried up.

Pleadingly, his mother says: "Firstly, listen to them why they are here for. Then I'll listen to yours as well."

The cloud-coloured princess says: "There is a competition at Gulshan. We need to practice at the ring. Would you like to form a pair with me?

The couplet of the same Tagore song keeps ringing in his ears: *Amar Noyono Tobo Noyoner Nibir Chayay*

Moner Kothar Kushomkorok Khoje

(My eyes seek in the depth of your eyes' shades

What will stir my eyes and blossom them)

Translated from Bangla by Haroonuzzaman

Saleha Chowdhgury

I Lost Your Address

Ayon first saw Lily at Vincent Boulevard in Paris. Lily was buying flowers at a flower shop. Ayon was then studying in Paris. His exam was over. Ayon would return to the country in two days. One day by chance, he saw a nice French girl speaking in broken English. Dark long hair, a cute face, and a sunshine smile like Audrey Hepburn. The smile hypnotized Ayon, and he tried to get closer. Ayon's full name was Farid Hossain Ayon. And that Monalisa girl was Lily. After a little formal talk, Ayon asked -'Where do you live?'

She showed him the house where she lived. A tall ten storied white building. She said without hesitation, 'Would you like to come in, please? Let's have a cup of tea.'

This sudden invitation surprised Ayon. No one in the west invites anyone like this. They just talk, standing on the doorsteps for hours.

Ayon entered. A small flat. At the top of a ten-storied building called Al Carta. Lily had started a new job at a cake shop. Recently she broke up with her mother, and now she was living alone. 'Mom and Dad live separately .'She said. Mother is French. Father is Indian. Lily was the daughter of a broken family. A stunning beauty with an olive complexion. Olive complexion with dark eyes covered with thick eyelashes. Her hair is also dark. She looked like a classic painting of an old master.

They were gossiping while they were drinking tea and eating pastries. Then after a little while, Ayon said, 'Lily, I like you. And your smile! Dear God, it looks a bit like Monalisa. You invited me in, and you know I did not expect it so soon ?" 'My smile!' She blushed and covered her face with her palm. 'Yes, Lily, it's divine! And the dimple! my God, it's so cute!" Ayon was staring and couldn't take his eyes off. 'Sorry, Lily, forgive my staring!' Lily removed her palm, and it was obvious she liked him too. 'I like your face, Ayon. It's kind of cute too, And you are also olive green.'

Then both of them laughed. They were sitting on leisurely wicker chairs. There were two cups of tea and pastries on the round table and some flowers in a vase.

The whole city of Paris was visible from the small tenth-floor balcony. The city of Paris, with its wings, was spreading out. There were some flower plants on the patio. It seemed Lily loved flower plants. This balcony did not have lots of space to make it the hanging garden of Babylon, so some scattered plants and pots instead.

Lily said, ' Creating a flower garden is my hobby. But how can I make a garden here? So I have a miniature garden. I go for a walk in the garden when I have time. Do you know how many extensive gardens there are in this city?'

'Not quite, Lily. I lived here for a year. Busy with my study, and in two days' time, I would go back home. If you like a big garden, then I suppose you must marry a rich man with a big house.'

'You think so!' Lily smiled, 'No, Ayon, I would not marry. I mean, not just yet.' Lily was a little playful and said, 'I haven't met any rich man yet, and moreover, it's not on my immediate list to do so.'

Ayon said with a naughty smile, 'I wish I had a big house. But I can always rent a big one if you wait a little. But in the meantime, I have to go back home. Would you wait for me?'

Lily did not say yes or no. But Ayon was kind of desperate to get an answer.

'I would come back from the country and look for you.'

'All right. Then we will talk again. When are you going back to your country?'

'The day after tomorrow. Ish! It's really breaking my heart to think it even.

'I met you a few hours ago, and now we are friends. And we are talking about breaking hearts, marriage, and waiting. Sometimes things happen quickly.' Lily replied, 'So sad you are leaving the day after tomorrow. How I wish you could stay a little longer. Can you delay your going back a little?

'I am afraid not.'

'Not to worry. Let's make our time together a bit memorable then.' Lily's conversation was charming, and she had no hesitation in expressing her true feelings.

They were walking around Paris. The tour of Paris is an incredible experience. Ayon, as well as Lily, fell in love with Paris when they saw Lily's favorite places. He might have seen these places before, and Lily too, but not in each other's company. The incident took place before the day Ayon left for the country.

Lily bought a Vincent blue tie and gifted it to Ayon. Ayon was astonished. Sort of dumbfounded.

Lily said with her sunshine smile, 'I liked this tie very much. You will wear it with a suit. The shop was there. We just walked past it. It sells the best Vincent blue tie. Then she expressed, 'I like everything about Vincent van Gogh. What a pity! He died so young .' Tears come to my eyes when I see his drawings. He was mad about being loved. But he never found true love during his life.' Saying this, Lily sang a few lines of Starry Starry Night.

How do you try to say to me
How you suffered for your sanity.

'Yes! Just fighting to prove that 'I'm not crazy. It was not easy. Don't you think so, Ayon?' Lily continued.

'What amazing pictures he painted just to maintain his sanity. How many pictures! If Vincent were alive now, I would love him to death. A lot of love!' Saying this, Lily drifted off to another world. It was the day they met. A few hours and, Ayon promised he would come tomorrow early in the morning and spend the whole day till midnight with Lily.

Holding her hands, Ayon said, 'You know something, Lily, Vincent is no more. Maybe someone is looking for love, just like Vincent. A drop of love from heaven pouring down to quench someone's thirst.'

Lily smiled. With no words, she just came closer.

On the first day, for supper, Lily cooked something in the eight feet by ten feet kitchen and entertained Ayon. French omelets filled with crushed mushrooms and cheese. It was so tasty.

She said, 'I often eat out. Today I cooked for you. Tomorrow I will take a day's leave. You and I will go around every nook and corner of Paris.' Truly Ayon was feeling sad. An unexpected meeting made Ayon think twice before leaving this fabulous place. Paris! A word of wonder. But some urgent work back home stopped him from staying a little longer. He was upset about it.

'Sweet memories! Go back home, Ayon, with a bottle of memories, just like a bottle of perfume.'

'I am going back to my country not only with memories but with your essence too. You are my Lily of the Valley.' Every moment was a joyful, heart-touching conversation, and holding each other's hand was terrific too. As if dear God granted a day and a half for Ayon to know for the first time how a true loving companionship could change everything. But Lily's expression was not telling her feeling. As if something was hidden. Something was unspoken.

The two sat at a small dining table facing each other. He looked at her face many times. Sometimes forgetting their manners, he was staring at her endlessly. Dark hair, dark eyes, olive complexion, cute dimples and classic beauty. Lily was one in a million. Or maybe just one in the whole universe. One bottle of sparkling wine and two plates of French omelets. What a wonderful time! Then tea and fruity cake before departure.

But Lily said, 'Not wine for me. I'm drinking spring water. Have some wine if you like. Today's memories are unforgettable. I feel overjoyed.'

'Don't you drink wine?'

'I do. But not now.' She did not wish to make this subject longer.

She planned the next day's tour. 'We will have a boating trip. We will see Paris on the boat. We will get on the boat after seeing some spectacular places first. Come with me. I know the city of Paris like the back of my hand. Its lanes and by lanes, roads and highways, avenues and boulevards, landmarks and gardens. I mean, I know everything.'

What was the name of the park? Ayon forgot the name. Whatever it may be, it was a botanical garden. They sat under a tree and ate cookies. The park is pretty as a picture. The trees are fabulous. The flowers were enchanting. The cool breeze is soothing. Then nothing seemed more beautiful than the trees. The day was pleasant. They were blessed with lovely weather. Not so cold and not so hot. At first, she was wearing a sweet purple cardigan. After a while, Lily took it off and tied it around her waist. Her hair was flying around her face. Off and on, Lily pushed her hair back and then tied a band around her hair. Her cute face lit up with a heavenly smile. Her forehead was smooth and bright. Ayon was thinking someone with a beautiful forehead had a name. But she forgot that word.

Standing next to the Eiffel Tower, she said, 'We have to see Eiffel Tower climbing up to the top. I promise you it would be the best memory to keep it in your heart. The Eiffel Tower by night is a wonderful sight.'

'If necessary, I will roam around all night, walking with you wherever you take me.'

'We will see some pictures in Louvre.'

She knew the metro route well, as if the map of the metro rail was in her brain. She showed him all the exciting places without looking at any maps.

Sometimes looking at those stunning places, fabulous pictures at Louvre, Lily's eyes were full of tears. Was it the beauty or Ayon's company? It was hard to tell. At Louvre, she just said, 'Beauty does that to me. Makes me tearful.' And at Louvre, she was kneeling before some enchanting pictures to praise it with all her heart. It was not the age of mobile phones or selfies then. And they did not have a camera.

They both had tutti-frutti ice cream at Arch the Triumph. And whatnot. As if two teenagers were having the time of their lives.

'I ate a lot today,' said Lily, 'because you are with me.'

They saw Mark Sagal's paintings on the roof of 'Opera Garnier .'Though he had come here before, he never had seen any of Mark Sagal's artwork here. Ayon realised that Lily loved art, and her knowledge of art was astonishing. She approached a big building and said, 'Here live the helpless people. And the wounded soldiers.'

A sudden tour at Pompidou Center too.

She said, 'One can come here and spend the whole day. We don't have that much time. We'll stay an hour. The house of the Church called Pantheon is charming.' Ayon had lived for nearly a year in Paris. But he did not know about all these as if Lily lent her eyes. And he saw as much as people could see in a day.

Looking up at the sky, Ayon was thinking of a little drop of pure water to quench his thirst, but he did not realise that he was spending a whole day near the lake of Periyar and a crystal fountain named Lily. Only the feeling of love was blossoming, and Ayon understood he would come back again and spend the rest of his life with Lily. Ayon could not figure out what was so attractive. Was it the Indian touch in Lily and her wayward style? Or her talk or gossip. Or her infectious giggles. Now and again, a few lines of songs or a few lines of poems. And an abundance of joyful gestures. The sun shines on the beautiful forehead under her dark hair, then in a bun. While looking at it, the similes he could think of - the foamy cup of coffee was her joyful gesture and the touch of black coffee in Lily's deep, dreamy eyes. Lily was looking at a basilica. 'Look, Ayon, all the great creations of the world are due to religion. Large temples, mosques, churches, and basilicas are created for this reason.' Ayon nodded his head. People always tried to please God.

Lily said to Ayon, 'Listen, Ayon, I think sometimes people are really weak. That's why big buildings, pictures, and gardens are made for gods and goddesses.'

'That's right,' said Ayon, 'In fact, we are weak. Do you know something? I'm going to visit Notre Dame and say a special prayer. Let's see if the God of Notre Dame grants it.'

' Probably you will wish, after reaching your country, you get married to a beautiful woman,' Lily said jokingly.

'No. My prayer would not be that. You got a big zero for guessing such'. Said Ayon.

'Then a good job?'

'Ummm. No.'

'All right. Something else.'

'Let's have lunch at one of the restaurants next to Notre Dame and get on the boat and see Paris by boat on the Seine again. All right?'

'Why not. You have a special prayer, and me too. Let's do it.'

'Have you ever loved anyone?' Ayon asked suddenly. Lily smiled mysteriously. 'I will tell another day.' Lily looked away and avoided that topic.

'Not today?'

'No.'

Then Lily changed the subject. 'Hey, you don't take turtle sauce to eat fish. You do not like turtle sauce?'

She put some turtle sauce on Ayon's plate. The topic of love ended here. The conversation stopped for a little while.

She spoke again and recited some short poems on the river Seine. 'Boating in Seine/ A city majestic and clean.'

At one point, Ayon bought a bottle of Nina Richie. The perfume was Lily's favorite. He said, 'It's for you, lovely.'

Then afternoon became evening on the river. The professional cameramen took pictures of them as they boarded the boat. They said, 'It's a lovely couple.'

Ayon was a little upset that there was no picture of the flower garden with them two sitting under a lush green tree. No picture of holding tutti frutti ice cream with joy.

But the picture on the Seine was quite good. The professional photographer did his best. Ayon and Lily took two copies of the photos, and she said she would keep this in her collection. The two of them sat and realised how wonderful everything becomes when two souls sit side by side with a bit of love between them— for a little while in silence, just watching the river in the dusky evening. 'In silence, things grow/ And we know He lives in silence .'Lily uttered again.

Ayon did understand that this girl named Lily was a miracle. He whispered, 'Strange thing about the miracle; a miracle sometimes happens.'

Lily sighed, and her smiling face whispered -'It's Dylan Thomas.' Another line I like is- 'Do not go gentle into that good night.' Ayon said, 'No, Lily, no rage. I got more than my fair share.' Ayon thanked God for knowing this poem which he could share with Lily.

How long does a day last? The considerable sun will one day become a black hole and erase the name of the sun. Who knows what shape this world will get and what its name will be?

The day is over. On his way home from the Eiffel Tower at night, Ayon said, 'Will I ever see you again?'

Taking a 100 franc note from her bag, she wrote her home address and phone number. She said, 'Any time, Ayon.'

Ayon wanted to hold her for a long time before he said goodbye. He wished he won't let her go that night. But the fulfillment of this special wish seemed difficult then. Ayon will have to return to his country tomorrow. He needed to pack. Timidly Ayon put a little kiss on her lips. He was afraid to do more Lily would be cross. He was not sure crossing his limit may annoy Lily. So just a sweet kiss.

Lily said, 'When you come here again, we will go straight to the Palace of Versailles for a whole day.' Ayon could not understand why Lily was wiping tears with a tissue. She said, 'Keep in touch, Ayon. I won't forget you. Because? You do not need to hear all the reasons.'

Holding her hands, Ayon said, 'I will keep in touch.'

He carefully kept the one hundred franc note in his moneybag. He said in French, 'Je la Adore.' He heard this sentence somewhere. Lily laughed, hearing French from Ayon's mouth. She just said, ' Cherry! On se reverra.'

Ayon knew the meaning of this sentence. He understood Lily was telling him, 'I love you. I love you. I will see you again.'

Then a cloud came down from the sky, and Lily said, wiping her stupid drop of sadness, 'Adieu, my friend.'

The pain of that separation was in Ayon's heart for a long time. It was like a sharp needle was piercing somewhere in his heart. Yes, pain sometimes feels like that.

Then when he wanted to call her before boarding the plane, he realised that the moneybag was lost, where the one hundred franc note was carefully kept. He did not keep any money there, lest it should be spent by mistake. But everything is lost. Someone grabbed the moneybag from his hip pocket. Sadly, in pain, he, like a crazy one, was just trying to remember the phone number, but in vain. It was coming in the wrong numbers. And the plane flew away.

He uttered himself, 'Vincent Boulevard. Vincent, Vincent,' Then 'Starry, Starry Night.' Then Nina Richie, but not the right number and the address.

Ayon knew that he would never forget a name and the one-and-a-half day they spent together. This name could never be erased from his mind; he wrote it in many pages of his diary. Al Carta is ten storied houses. 'Dis' means 'ten'; he also knew it. Some feelings, too, were shattering.

He thought he would return next year and go straight to her house. The top apartment is on the tenth floor. From the balcony, you could see the whole city of Paris. Below that building is a flower shop. The first time where he saw Lily buying some flowers. A girl of fantastic beauty, East and West, the twine did mix. Lily Roy. Father was Indian, mother French.

But he could not come as he promised. At first, his father was sick. Being an only son, he was unable to leave his ill father. When Dad died, he was busy with his father's business empire. Mother chose a girl, his would-be wife. Ayon got married.

But Lily's face remained unwashed, unchanged. When he saw her first in front of a ten-storied building buying flowers, Lily turned back and saw him. And a refreshing smile immediately put a long-lasting impression on him. A face! A picture imprinted forever. Lily suddenly turned her face, and her gaze was long and deep. A classic view of the Old Masters. With masses of hair blowing in the wind. An unforgettable moment.

Rupsa was quite a good girl. As beautiful as some flower. She was happy. Loved him truly. Then who knows why Lily was appearing now and again, fresh as he saw her the very first day.

After twenty years, Ayon came to Paris again. That picture is clear in his mind and alive. Lily is buying flowers from the florist. Her dark hair was playing in the wind. How old was Lily then? Nineteen or twenty. A teenage girl from a broken family. Being separated from her mother, she was living in her own small flat. Though it seemed she was free like a bird. But something about her was not very clear. Ayon was not sure what it was.

Ayon found the house, but Lily was not there. Lily Roy. No one in the building knew where she was. No one knew when she was there and when she left. Ayon was looking for Lily everywhere, mostly the places they visited... That obsession with spending a day together still haunts him.

Where did Lily go? Where? Finding someone without an address in the city of Paris is as difficult as finding a needle in a haystack. Her house was very close to the Bel Air metro station. Now there had been a lot of changes, but still, there was that ten-storied tall white building.

Days in Paris are nearly finished. Lily could not be found anywhere. Ayon got on the train from the Danube metro station. He had to go to Victor Hugo Station. He was wondering where his Lily got lost. He was deep in his thought; Suddenly, he looked up in wonder. Good Lord! That's Lily. A black band is tied around the head, and another band is tied around the wild masses of hair to protect it from the wind—a ringlet on her Mahjabeen forehead.

As soon as Ayon ran towards her, the train stopped at Danube station. Lily got down. A heavy bag on her shoulder. A bouquet in her hand. She was strolling. Ayon was looking for her. She was going up on the escalators. Ayon did shout and called her name but could not. She was just keeping on walking fast. Ayon knows that Lily can walk very fast. Walking fast, she crossed the road and went to the other side. Ayon ran and soon reached her, then stood beside her. Taking the things from her hands, he uttered with a sigh of relief, 'Lily, Lily, I've been looking for you everywhere for the last fortnight. Oh, dear God, I have found you!'

The lady turned back. There was noon light on her smooth forehead. Infinite wonder in two eyes. Black big eyes, masses of dark hair now in a big bun.

'This is Lily!' Lily was looking at Ayon's face. Then smiled sadly. Then she just uttered, 'I'm not Lily.'

'Who are you?'

'I am Shivan.'

'Aren't you Lily?'

The girl said, 'Let's sit on that bench.'

The bench was under a huge tree. Shivan put her shoulder bag and flowers on the bench too. Then she uttered, 'Oh! You are Ayon, isn't it?'

'I am Ayon. If you are not Lily, how do you know I am Ayon?'

Shivan was smiling again. A kind of smiling and sobbing together. 'She said in a calm voice - 'I am Shivon. Lily was my mother.' The same voice as Lily's, sweet and assuring. Bit husky.

'Mom gave me a picture and the notebook. The picture of you two getting on a boat on the river Seine. My mother kept the picture very carefully. And the whole incident of going around with you was written in that notebook as much as possible. I know my mother has been waiting for you for a long time; it might be till the last day of her life. Do you know something? In fact, I was with you two that day.'

'Were you there?

'A few days before, when you see my mother, someone left her mercilessly. He thought that the French girls were just things to be enjoyed. My simple mother did not understand the brutality. Because of that man, my mother had to end her relationship with her mother because of me. She wanted to keep me, but my Nanny did not like it. And my mother lived the rest of her life on her own. My mum was carrying me when she met you. That man threw her in the garbage and vanished forever. She met you with her blistered raw heart. And what I gathered, she was so bruised that she needed a shoulder to cry. Then seriously, you two fell in love.'
But she didn't ...
'Though she said nothing that day, she would have if you come back. Since then, she has been a single mother. She didn't want to have any relationship with anyone else.'
Ayon is listening to Shivan. He was trembling a bit.
After that, she was silent for a long time. Then she said with a long sigh, 'Do you know which day is today?'
'No.' answered Ayon. 'I am going to put flowers on my mother's grave. On this day last year, my mother died of cancer.'
The pain again hit Ayon like a sharp needle. Shivan said, 'Everyone says I am my mother's carbon copy. No need to be ashamed of making a mistake.'
Ayon bought lots of 'Lily of the Valley .'He wore the Vincent blue tie that Lily had given him. He wore it with a matching suit. A red rose in his buttonhole. A proper gentleman came alone to pay his last respect. That tie was carefully kept for such a day. Lily's grave was in a secluded place. There were trees, and there were flowers

and a garden all around. This place did not seem to be a tomb but a shrine. Lots of flowers in spring. Lily always wanted to have a big garden. He remembered it.

What did the tree say to Ayon softly, 'You got back late, Ayon? I have been waiting for you all these years. ?' A branch full of flowers was swaying or trying to touch Ayon. Spring was always lovely.

Ayon's handkerchief was getting wet, and he whispered - 'You are always with me, Lily.'

Nasrin Jahan

Allen Poe's Cat

When the cat meowed, Ratri felt that she started to sweat, and her fever subsided. The young woman opened her eyes. The girl usually spends her nights holding the bedsheet with her fingers like a claw. Holding on to cotton sheets and staring at the ceiling, she sees the shadows of many things on the ceiling as the night falls. Sometimes she sees the shape of a man, an animal, or a tree. She wants to tie the eyelids, which seem to be mortal enemies of one another; it was as if they had to be held together by force. Hours go by. She gives out long sighs, and her body sways, but sleep evades her.

The wet cat begins to cry in the cold. The girl forces herself to get down on the floor; she makes her way to the door groping the wall in the dim light. As soon as she puts her hand on the latch, she realises that the sound might wake someone up!

Night after night, she suffers like this. She remains within the labyrinth of insomnia; the devouring night rushes deep into her blood. Everything was a lot more intense for her- the itchiness on her feet, the thirst, the need to go to the toilet, and the coughing. As she tries to force herself to be normal, she feels the coagulated blood in her heart and the pain in her chest. Her days are often spent in breathlessness. Oh! How the head starts to pound as if someone was hammering inside, and it resonates in every vein in her body. She didn't want to share her suffering with anyone, so she concealed her peril under the veil of a smile during the day. Often, she runs to the balcony gasping for breath, but there is no breeze.

People who are so familiar during the day become strangers at night. Every time people sleep, it makes them isolated, cruel, and selfish. Why does she fear waking up the person sleeping next to her even if she suffers? Oh, why? What is this fear?

The perilous night gives the girl the strength to survive. The struggle during the night makes her smile in the midst of difficulties in life, and she fights the battle.

But in the meantime, the girl cannot cope with life at all; when she begins to break down, then her husband is surprised and asks, "Oh! What happened to you?"

The girl bit her swollen lips and said in a hoarse voice, "I am unwell."

"What's wrong?"

"I don't know."

"Strange! What do you mean you don't know? Do you have a headache? Fever? Chest pain?"

When the girl is bombarded with question after question about the various diseases, and she comes up with the answer "no,...no," the husband gets frustrated and starts flipping through the channels of the TV. The girl starts feeling guilty; she desperately wants to find a name for her illness. She felt a heavy pressure on her chest with no pain; shadows appeared in front of her eyes, and it often felt as though the blood was oozing out from the liver. "No, no," the girl shuddered. Then the daily routine begins; swallowing the pain and resting her weary head on her husband's shoulder; she exhales and says, "I feel so much better now."

The girl has never seen the mountains, never seen the sea either. So what if she hasn't seen the sea and the mountains? They were so indescribably beautiful in her imagination; they were such great mysteries that the mountains and the sea went beyond her imagination and started to form a multicoloured wave in her head. Just as a blind person sees the corridor of her own house better than a person with eyes, this girl also feels as though she has a keen imagination in her house. And if anyone ever asks the question, "What do you desire from life after death?" Just like a child in a fancy store who clutches the shaving cream tube and makes a meaningless demand to have it. Instead of asking to go near the magical garden, the mountains, the sea, or to the edge of the solar system, the girl goes around dreaming the same dream,

"Can I go out and roam around this city one evening? Can I have this one evening when I can be as isolated as a sleeping beauty, and no one will look for me? Where I am, the kite is flying free in the sky. I am like the snow-white cloud."

Hey, kite! Fly away! Fly away! Only God knows how many such things the girl says to lull herself to sleep; she counts a hundred to one backward that she could hear before the wind and a few lines of memorized poetry.

"Not wealth nor fame nor creature comforts—/There is some other perilous wonder/ Which frolics in our very blood./ It exhausts us—/ Fatigues exhausts us." Reciting these lines, the hours pass, her mind ebbs and flows near the shore of sleep, and suddenly, a demonic hunger rumbles in her stomach. Immediately, she feels the need to go to the bathroom, or the curtain rustles with the sound of the wind.

Every single night, she witnesses her sleep falling like a chandelier! The precious sleep that she weaves carefully like the tailorbird. The girl walks as if she had cotton under her feet lest she wakes the isolated, sleeping man beside her.

Alas! On a hostile night, even with a thousand precautions, the sound of pouring water into the glass sounds loud, her feet colliding with the shoes lying in front of her, and even the bathroom light switched on makes such a sound that the hammer beats in the girl's soul. Clenching her teeth, she stands in the darkness like a living statue until the half-sleeping man falls back into sleep. Then again, lying in bed, she feels like Allan Poe. Allan Poe's black cat walks on her empty head. The girl feels that the bleeding cat lying inside her head becomes one with herself.

It has been a year since the wedding.

The girl has spent the entire year giving up everything she called her own. She did it with passionate warmth of love for her husband. She had such intense intrigue and excitement when she first saw him a few days before the wedding. As a result, the girl did not turn to look inside her own self for an entire year. After waiting alone each day, when he returned in the evening, the girl approached him with the steaming cup of tea. The self-engrossed husband would take the cup and walk into the study room and repeat the same question every day, "So! You are at home all day or not?"

"Strange! Where else can I go?" The girl was also surprised every day. Do I have anywhere to go? After finishing his work and leaving the study room late at night, the husband came to bed, and the girl waited for him eagerly. She tried to understand her husband's likes and dislikes diligently. She sensed if she said a few words more, her husband would be upset. She knew some topics would be frowned upon by her husband. She also knew he wouldn't tolerate it if she ever left the house. Incessantly taking care of all these things, time after time, she asked her husband for one thing only. That they sit face to face quietly, for some time, with the steaming cups of tea in front of them - She said this to her husband right after their marriage. Husband replies, "It is only a small thing. We will do that one day when we have time."

She eagerly waits for that time. She believes him.

However, after six months, a very dissatisfied soul asks him once more.

"No worries; we will do it," the husband repeated.

She keeps her hopes hidden in a box for the whole year. This evening, when the girl playfully repeats her wishes, the husband gets irritated, "You have only been concerned with yourself since the first day of our marriage. You have only been wandering in yourself. You haven't given me anything." the girl is dumbfounded and immediately falls from the sky hearing this.

She never saw herself in the mirror. When she is in front of it, she thinks about how to dress herself to impress others. She never thought about the fact that other people's favorite pendants and garlands of flowers got in it. Tonight, after the cat cries out, she realises that she didn't give anything to anyone. Day after day, she sliced her heart open to make others happy. What did the heart gain by that? When did she not spill blood or cut herself? Whose worldly needs were met? She rather felt utterly alone and in grave danger as a result of doing that. She has lied to herself, which was the worst crime she has ever committed.

She was dreaming before the cat meowed. The girl loves having nightmares. On most nights, the electricity fails, and she loves load-shedding. When she had a wonderful dream, suppose two people were sitting face to face, and there was a smoking cup in the middle, or she was walking with someone in the evening. She was fond of such dreams. But things in the dream feel so alive that she sinks in pain immediately after she wakes up. "Alas! This was just a dream! it wasn't true." But the nightmare, let's say she saw she was falling from the roof of a huge building or that her husband's body was laid in the grave. Such dreams. Seeing these, she wakes up with an immense pain in her chest! And then, "Ah! It was just a dream; it was not real." It gave her immense peace of the world! "What a bliss it is! What a relief!" As she drifted off to sleep, the girl thought, "I'm so lucky. Nothing has really happened!"

She feels almost the same even when the lights go out. The tranquility of having the lights could not be felt if there was constant light with no outage. This is how the girl had sieved tranquility and peace from her life.

Her sleep was interrupted, or maybe she wasn't asleep at all, as the cat's meow nearly numbs or inebriates her. Yes! She was relieved of the tension of giving anything to anyone since she had been told that she had not given anything to anyone. She found it much easier to get out of bed now. She jumped out of bed and was shocked to see Allan Poe's shadow, who had died a hundred years ago, on the wall; he was holding a pipe.

"That's why I say, why is the cat crying?" The girl feels agitated and reaches out to touch the smoke of Allan Poe's pipe. He disappears into the endless night after a fleeting glance.

"Where is the cat?"

The cat has vanished.

The girl boldly puts her hand on the latch and realises that there was no sound today. She feels so relieved. Looking out on the balcony with light feet, she inhales the cold cheer of darkness. It's as if the tongue of the night was dripping its saliva and not the dew of the night.

"No! No! There was no meowing of the cat! But why is there so much sleep on her nerves? Why is there a smell that intoxicates the blood?" As the girl turns to get back into the bedroom, the cat cries again. "Stop crying, please!" It felt as though she had taken a thousand sleeping pills when she heard that cry. The inebriated girl sits with her head on her knees on the balcony.

When she comes back to her senses, she sees the dark and deep night," You haven't given anything to anyone, girl! Now save the cat..." The girl listens to herself. "Your life hasn't been a complete failure. Today Allen Poe came and sat in your empty place." Saying this, the girl grabbed the long pole, found her way to the wall, and looked for the cat.

She knew that the blood-smeared body of the cat was buried under the brickwork of the wall; she just needed to find out its location in the huge white blank wall of this house.

The girl sniffs the walls with her cold nose and walks with the cat crying. Sometimes like a deaf person, sometimes like a person with sharp ears touching the wall while she was lying down on the wide floor, she again heard the meowing that came down from the deepest shivering night. The girl madly runs towards the wall of the balcony as if confused by the sound..., "Here is the clear sound... here!" The black mist was covering the body of the wall...! The girl, with her sharp fingernails, desperately scratches the wall to open the brick. By doing this, blood started to flow from her crumbling nails. Alas! The bloody cat was dying, and it was her husband who killed her and hid her under plaster in this empty house. The girl trembled–"What if the heat of the last slice of my heart can save her?" The girl could hear the cat's last coldest moans.

Now, lying next to her husband, she could scream out loud.

Translated by Md Sajjad Hossain Zahid

Mojaffor Hossain

No Man's Land

For about a fortnight, a woman is lying in the No Man's Land at the border of India and Bangladesh. Her attire carries all the proof she needs to claim mental imbalance. Furthermore, her one lame leg unquestionably places her among the masses of beggars crowding the sidewalks of Dhaka or Kolkata. The woman is prostrate on a mound, as high as a hut, in the wet gully that skirts the slopes of the No Man's Land. No one knows where she came from or how she ended up there.

On the day she was discovered, a swell of excitement ran through the Border Guard Bangladesh (BGB) and the Indian Border Security Forces (BSF). On the second night, the BGB snuck in at night to ascertain if she was an Indian spy. Unable to detect any identifying clues, they returned in frustration. The next day, the BSF bomb squad went to her. They believed that an Islamic suicide terrorist was playing a complicated charade to attack their camp. Somewhat convinced, they informed their superiors. Unfortunately, the woman did not possess a bomb; she didn't even conceal a suspicious nail. Thus, following orders from senior officers, the BSF jawans prepared for battle and situated themselves at a safe distance. They were eager to start shooting but became disheartened when they couldn't detect the slightest movement that would justify their actions.

On the eighth day, the sector commanders of the two nations sat down for a high-level talk. The meeting did not yield any results; rather, it ended with both parties blaming each other raucously. The Border Guard Bangladesh claimed that the BSF was forcing this mentally disturbed woman into their country. Thus, they deliberately left her in the same spot. On the other hand, Indian border guards belligerently asserted that the Bangladesh border patrol had pushed her onto this territory.

As a result of this meeting, the woman sprawled in the No Man's Land turned even more undesirable. Both parties heightened their vigilance and readiness. On the tenth day, the BSF concluded that the woman was dead. They sent a message to the BGB to take the body back to their country. At that point, the BGB became more resentful. This is how the Rohingyas have been dumped on them. No more! Dead or alive, it didn't matter.

Bangladesh was not going to get involved further. BGB responded in no uncertain terms: "This case doesn't belong to Bangladesh— but to India. India must assume all responsibilities."

This mild argument between the two border patrols inflamed the neighboring villages a bit. Who's going to accept this woman? If she were dead, the villagers could take a few measures. But to engage with the living is no joking matter! If the state had turned away, who would take on the duties of feeding and clothing her? Besides, she was lame, perhaps even insane!

In this situation, the only solution the neighboring villagers could think of was to seek divine mercy. But as soon as the issue of 'divine' arose, one had to consider religion. Who was this woman? Her age and identity were obscure. The people on this side scratched their heads and pondered, "Was she a Muslim'" The other side questioned, "What if she is not Hindu?" If it were a man, one could lift the clothes and check for circumcision. A decision about praying for "divine mercy" could then be made. But as she was a woman, that was not an option. No one could guess her nationality or religion from what she was wearing.

Perhaps all poor and homeless people in the world share the same religion and nationality. As poor people spiral down into deeper destitution, they lose religion and the honor of citizenship.

And then there was the issue of language. If she would talk, perhaps one could gauge if she was Hindu or

Muslim, from Bangladesh or India. But who could make her speak? Both the BGB and BSF had settled at a secure space with their rifles aimed at her. Neither wanted to take on a new role. Then there were the people of the neighboring villages who feared any new entanglement. Everyone agreed that this was none of their business—it was a matter to be settled by the two countries.

"In 1971, during the freedom struggle of Bangladesh, you left your elder sister at a Pakistani army camp. Don't you remember?" In the cover of darkness, a wife in a border community whispered to her husband. "Shut your mouth, bitch!" The husband reprimanded her and turned his back to her in bed. All was settled in the dark.

"One of your younger sisters was lost in childhood. Isn't it true that girls were snatched to be sold in India? Why don't you go check?" During an afternoon, a mother pleaded as she coated the abandoned wood stove with cow-dung paste. "Don't you dare say that to anyone?" The son admonished the mother. From then on, the mother's wistful eyes clung day and night to the border sky.

Gradually, the fact that a disabled and unidentified woman was laid out in the No Man's Land lost its surprise for the local people. The phenomenon turned into a habit. Somedays, when crows and vultures flew toward the field, people presumed she had died. Even though the woman was a nameless and sans nation, and even though she had never troubled anyone, some carelessly exclaimed, "Good riddance!" But now crows and vultures routinely hovered over the field, so even that guessing game was over. The two patrolling forces of the two nations zoomed in through their binoculars and observed that the crows, vultures, and women were fighting over their share of food. No one questioned who had transported the food to avoid unwelcome responsibilities.

There are still some people in this world who come forward to seek individuals like the woman. They deal with entities like hers. Hence, such persons and their related miseries are manufactured by a tiny sleight of hand. The villagers had no awareness of such people. They couldn't figure out if, indeed, there was an ethereal signal that had instigated the woman's deprivation.

On the twenty-fifth day, a leading media organisation broadcasts a human-interest story on the woman. Worldwide media caught onto it within a few days. Once the news became global, the Bangladesh Government received a strongly worded communiqué from the UN Headquarters. In the missive, the United Nations stated that it reviled the situation thoroughly and requested the Government to provide the woman with holistic care. A similar letter was dispatched to the Government of India. Subsequent to receipt of the letter, both BGB and BSF called a second flagship meeting. It was decided that representatives of both parties would jointly approach the woman. First, they will search for citizenship papers or other documents that could establish her nationality. Then, they would try to find out if she possessed any money. With the help of these clues, they should be able to confirm her citizenship. Whatever it might be, both teams agreed to abide by the outcome.

The meeting ended at 3 p.m., and the joint force arrived when the woman was around five. After a few days of scorching sunshine, it had rained and stormed mildly the night before. The woman was welled in mud. The area was horrendously filthy as she had urinated and defecated right there. One of the representatives vomited at the sight of her. The woman was looking at them with eyes that saw far beyond. No sound emanated from her. No one could fathom from her body whether she was forty or seventy. The party of representatives from both sides included a couple of women soldiers. They covered their noses and began their search. No papers. She should have had some money, but none was found. There might have been a paper, but it would have dissolved in the rain and urine. The team came back disappointed.

On the tenth day of the publication of the international news, one local and two foreign NGOs arrived and established their temporary agencies in the town. Since the woman was homeless and an asylum seeker, the United Nations Office for Refugee Resettlement, UNHCR, sent their representatives. As she was characterized as disabled and deaf, the World Health Organisation shipped two Autism Specialists to the area. Because the victim's gender was female, international women's rights organisations loudly voiced their protestations. Human rights workers also showed up.

In the beginning, the villagers did not cooperate with these workers. In his Friday sermon, the imam had clearly professed that their activities emerged from a conspiracy by the Jews and the Christians. The woman was their spy. The infidels were setting traps to destroy the integrity and creed of Muslims. The Hindus of India were also linked to it. If this was allowed to go on, soon there would be white women in shorts walking about the village. Alcohol shops and nightclubs would appear. The youth would face ruination. Women would go astray.

'We can't let that happen on God's green earth. Currently, they are globally oppressing our Muslim brethren. The Jews are collectively bombing Palestinians. We must proclaim Jihad against these malicious forces. Only then will we effortlessly cross the slippery bridge that all mortals must pass through on Judgment Day? God willing!'

After heeding this oration by the leader, the galvanized villagers set fire to the first tent that was pitched in the field near the border. They broke and destroyed the camera of a local journalist working for a foreign channel. Then, who could tell how the workers curried favor with two foreign nationals and the local chairman? The chairman called for the imam. The villagers were not aware of their discussions through the night, but after the midday prayers, the leader changed his tune. He announced that the last Prophet of Allah, Hazrat Muhammad (PBUH), had materialised in his dreams. The Prophet had remonstrated that Muslims must attract infidels by their conduct. 'Muslims must present themselves in a way that non-Muslims are mesmerised and compelled to inquire about the fundamentals of the religion.' The Prophet elaborated on the rights of nonbelievers. 'If a Muslim is unjust to an infidel, He would side with the latter on Judgment Day.' No one could debate this statement.

'If nonbelievers are still unable to accept our guidance, we could oppose them. But remember, Allah is the only one to bestow rules. Thus, as humans, we may not impose them on fellow humans. Come, let's accommodate our non-Muslim brothers. Let's show them our higher moral standing.'

People's minds reeled at the leader's words. The next day, when the imam's son became the coordinator of the local NGO, everyone praised his leadership. A few other jobless young men also found employment. More and more visitors were coming to the border. A few tea stalls and small restaurants, where one could get rice and fish, popped up. A political leader financed a lovely coffee shop and named it Las Vegas Resort. Young couples from cities traveled there often. A large hoarding went up in front of the resort. The display featured a beautiful young woman with a mobile phone in her hand. The legend in large letters announced: '4G Network—It's in every corner of our country—No place to hide!' To transmit 'live' news 24/7, three TV cameras were installed in the location, and the central station posted news crews.

In nearby villages, several had turned lucky. In the beginning, many had insisted that the anonymous woman should be sent back to India. Those people went silent. The numerous organisations that had come there to observe no longer quibbled about returning the woman to India or Bangladesh. The United Nations representatives called a press conference and declared that the first item on their agenda was to protect this woman's human rights and to make sure she receives needed food, potable water, and healthcare. If necessary, they would construct a small house in the No Man's Land and take care of her. After that, in accordance with UNHCR policies, they would garner support for her and help her return to her own country or persuade the governments of India and Bangladesh to rehabilitate her properly.

One foreign official and a local one from Amnesty International assured everyone that they were scrutinising the situation critically. Undeniably, human rights have been violated.

'We will work our utmost so that the woman can enjoy her human rights to the fullest. We have noticed that the woman has been deprived of her basic rights. She is struggling with a dearth of lodging, drinking water, sanitation, healthcare, and food. She is suffering from a complete lack of safety. We hold the governments of the two countries answerable for why she has not been provided with a roof over her head to shelter her from rain, sun, and wind. They have badly violated her human rights. This is unacceptable. The woman is homeless and without suitable protection. We will ensure her human dignity and rights as an asylee.'

Due to the enthusiasm of the Rights advocates, the remote locale was humming with energy. The BGB, as well as the provincial administration, became anxious about the situation. One couldn't really trust the Rights Workers, and the international media were breathing down their neck. Any slip of the tongue could embarrass the Government and land it in a heap of trouble. BGB came to a final decision. If, within three days, no family came forward to claim the woman, they would hand her over to the International Committee of the Red Cross (ICRC).

As soon as the decision became public, the neighboring community broke out in an uproar. The chairman and his party workers ran to the MP.ii Because of this incident; the local economy was shifting. If they removed the woman, many a person would be bankrupted overnight. Some had paid exorbitant amounts to buy land or had leased at a high price to set up their shops. So many had serious financial investments and obligations! After the petitioners promised to donate a particular sum to the party funds on a regular basis, the MP agreed. He cautioned that the matter had gone to higher-ups, but he was certainly going to give it a good try. The people got a glimmer of hope at this reassurance. They believed that the MP could accomplish anything if he so wished.

It was the month of June, and the monsoon had broken. It rained relentlessly for four days. Following the new diktat, the BGB kept sending food to the woman. Now the foremost problem was that No Man's Land was sinking into the water. A tiny knoll was still visible, which might not be there after another night of rain. The woman should be moved. But if she were relocated inside the country, they would have to stop pressuring India. Also, if she was from India, why should Bangladesh accede? After many such reflections, they resolved to build her a scaffold with the help of nearby residents.

The rural people zealously chopped down bamboo and clamored to build a platform for her but returned in a couple of hours looking glum. The foreign and national workers also reverted, seemingly downcast. The media people and talk-show intellectuals were crestfallen. The woman's body was still visible in the water. Everything that goes down must float up.

The fourth momentous meeting between the border guards of both countries on whether she should be cremated or buried was about to commence.

Translated by Shamita Das Dasgupta

Notes
[i] In Hindi 'Jawan' means a '[strong] young man.' Recruits of Indian army are called 'Jawan/s.'
[ii] Member of Parliament

Moom Rahman

Urmimala

Kudrat was staring at the fish. It seemed as though the fish was also staring back at Kudrat. At least, that's what it seems like at the beginning of the story. Kudrat and the fish are looking at each other. The fish is called 'Tilapia.'

No, that's not entirely correct! Tilapia is the name of a species. There are billions of Tilapias in the world. Every one of them is called Tilapia. So, let's give a name to this particular Tilapia fish. For the story's sake, let's name the fish Urmimala for now. Tilapia do not live in rivers or seas. It lives in tranquil ponds. Nowadays, it is also grown in waterbodies on farms. So, there is no Urmi or wave there. But the body of this Tilapia fish is slightly wavy. Moreover, as far as I know, we don't need *aka* or registration for naming a fish. So, let's call this Telapia fish, Urmimala.

It sounds good.

Kudrat is looking at Urmimala intently. The more he stares at it, the more he is in love with Urmimala. Well, there is lust, wish to enjoy.

Just by gazing at Urmimala, his mouth has become watery. She seems to be a mature fish. A fish that has good taste in every layer of it. One would have to respect her dark and oily body. Kudrat touches Urmimala softly. He feels a sensation of excitement. He decides he would prepare the fish with a lot of care.

Urmimala's weight is precisely one kg and two hundred grams. Four to five times larger in size than ordinary Tilapia. If Urmimala were a human being, we could call her overweight. For a fish, she is perfect. Had the fish been more significant than this, it wouldn't be so soft; and if it were smaller, it wouldn't be that moist. Fish is the cleanest soul on earth that lives underwater. When you touch the fish, you feel like floating in the water, just like the fish.

Touching is an act that initiates someone with a feeling which may spread all over the body and remain in their mind forever.

Kudrat caressed Urmimal's body yet again; now, he was paying much attention. He stares at her, and Urmimala stares back! But alas! Urmimala is dead now. She was bought alive. She was still jumping up and down with great strength. She was like a skilled acrobat of the fish society, or maybe even a dancer! Who knows? But Urmimala is dead now, for she has been ashore for a long time. Yet her eyes are wide open. With those eyes, she was looking at Kudrat. As she was dead, she couldn't see the Kudrat. Or, who knows, maybe she can see him.

We are not yet confident that death stops us from seeing everything. Mr. Kudrat here believes that Urmimala can see him. He caresses Urmimala's body once again.

Kudrat begins his work by saying Bismillah; in the name of Allah, he picks up a spoon and starts scaling the fish. He uses his fingers to pick out the stubborn, left-out fish scales. This is an important step. The work has to be done slowly and carefully. No fish scales should remain in the end. Urmimala looked naked after scaling. If Kudrat knew how to paint, he would immediately start drawing an oil painting of the fish and title it the study of a nude fish. Kudrat always feels disrupted after scaling a fish and taking out the chicken feathers. Somehow, they remind him of naked girls.

Kudrat bathed Urmimala under the flowing tap water. It was as if this was the last bath of her life. The atmosphere in the kitchen became solemn, like that of a ceremony. Kudrat had already lit two candles before he began the work. It's one of Kudrat's rituals. Whenever he cooks fish or chicken during the day or night, he lights up candles. Now we don't know why he does this.

However, due to scaling and washing her properly, Urmimala's dark skin looks fairer.

And we know that it's an advantage to be fair in a country where women use Fair and Lovely, the skin-lightening cream.

But it's better not to talk about the feminists. It can be simply said that Urmimala now looks like a bride-to-be.

This feeling was bound to become the truth in a moment. Because in a little while, Urmimala's whole body will be smeared with turmeric. Then Kudrat will be adding ginger, lemon juice, and whatnot! You can say it's like an absolute spa; manicures, pedicures, and so on will go on. A little music was needed for Urmimala's Gaye Holud ceremony. Kudrat played Nusrat FatehAli's Damadam Mast Kalandar; on his phone. The entire video is 16 minutes and 43 seconds long on YouTube. Kudrat will need exactly 12 minutes to prepare Urmimala. There will be five minutes extra. It's always better to have some spare time.

Kudrat kept staring at Urmimala; he gently said, "Sorry baby!" for once. Then he cut Urmimala in the middle with a big knife. He then throws away the intestines and cleans the gills. He washed Urmimala again for three minutes in tap water; it seemed as if Urmimala was bathing in a cascade of flowing water. He scratched Urmimala three to six times on both sides with a knife. These scratches are a necessity. In this way, just as the spices will blend into the body of the fish, three deep lines will act as an adornment in the monotonous flat body. These lines, these folds have an aesthetic need.

Now the actual work will begin. It's time to mix the spices. He needs very little spices. But everyone knows extraordinary things happen in an ordinary situation. Two pinches of turmeric, juice from a large Colombo lemon, a little ginger-garlic paste, and the right amount of salt - these are the ingredients to decorate Urmimala. Kudrat first squeezed lemon juice on Urmimala's body and turned it around.

Then he applied a light coating of ginger-garlic paste to it. Kudrat arranged small ginger pieces in six deep cuts on the body. Finally, he sprinkled salt on her body like throwing marigold petals on the bridegroom.

Fish, ginger, garlic, turmeric, and lemon – all together produce an aroma that was somewhat familiar to him. A flash of old memory comes to him; it was Lina, yes, probably it was her, she smelt like this. At a very intimate moment, it seemed that a little salt and turmeric were smeared on her body as well. But as soon as he told her this. She lost her temper. As if the smell of fish, ginger, lemon, salt, and turmeric in the body is a sign of being smelly. Women spend their entire life cooking and scaling fish, yet they do not understand the greatness of a fish!

At last, the complex job of mixing spices was done. Because there is no biblical measure of this complex chemistry. Exactly how much turmeric, ginger, lemon juice, and how much salt is required, and how to mix is what you need to master. After that, it can be said that.

Urmimala is almost ready.

Kudrat put Urmimala in a concave tray. Kudrat brushed olive oil all over Urmimala's body. Now he cut the carrots, potatoes, and cowpea in the shape of fingers and put them all around the tray.

He slices dark red cherry tomatoes into two halves and spreads them around the tray. Lastly, he sprinkles green chili and a handful of minced raw corianders. Red carrot, tomato and green cowpea, green pepper, and coriander leaves together make an excellent composition of red and green. This artwork would now be refrigerated for a while. It must be covered. In this way, the spices and herbs, and vegetable extracts will be gradually mixed with Urmimala's body. The most important thing about baking a fish is that you can't rush it. In fact, Kudrat believes that being hasty in any preparation is not good.

He puts the tray in the refrigerator. The fish will be kept in the refrigerator for three hours.

Keeping Urmimala in the fridge, Kudrat switches off the Fateh Ali song. He doesn't need that song anymore. He took off his apron. He has three hours in his hands. That's enough time to pay attention to himself. He will shave, take a shower, and sleep for almost an hour with the alarm on.

2.

There are two types of Lakme iconic liners. One lasts for 22 hours and the other for 10 hours.

Mithiya buys the one that lasts 10 hours. Kajal, which lasts for 22 hours, will only be useful for movie stars. You need everything extra for movies. For Mithiya, 10 hours of eyeliner is good enough. The spelling iconic in Lakme's iconic kajal is very interesting. The big companies are clever with naming their products. Instead of writing `Iconic, they wrote` Eye co nic; She liked all these tiny details.

Mithiya put the liner on both of her eyes very carefully. One's hands need to be steady, as steady as a surgeon, the hands cannot be shaky, or you can't draw any even lines. Not only the hands but your mind also needs to be stable and calm. Kajal helps to highlight the shape of the eyes perfectly and profoundly. Ah! The eyes are an amazing part of the face. Someone said, perhaps it was Maulana Rumi, "No matter how tiny your two eyes are, with these two tiny eyes, you can see the whole universe." This stayed with Mithiya all her life. Firoz told her that. Firoz used to crack funny jokes while caressing Mithiya. Firoz is the only man who has touched her entire body. He used to say- I don't want to leave even an inch of your body untouched.

Firoz liked Mithiya's eyes, nose, tongue, and especially her ear. He used to kiss her nose, ears, tongue, and eyes. He loved to lick her ear with his tongue. Firoz would say-

listen, baby, you listen with your ears, and I talk with my tongue .my tongue in your ears. This is, in fact, lovemaking.

That man was so witty. All of a sudden, he died one day. he left no words, no messages; he just died falling down the stairs. He just fell and died instantly!

No, now is not the time to reminisce about that. Mithiya has to go out. He promised Kudrat that she would go to his house for two hours at least. They will have lunch together. Kudrat, however, wanted her to have dinner with him. But it's not always necessary to accept the invitation. A wise person is one who knows how to keep control of everything. You can give privilege to someone, but you need to have a grip on it. She feels a sting in the corner of her eye. She wasn't careful enough. She doesn't know why she was being inattentive. Having lunch or dinner with someone like Kudrat is not a big deal for her. Rather she can eat them up alive; she is capable of that, absolutely.

Mithiya feels like caressing herself while looking in the mirror. After doing her eyes, she concentrates on her lips. Men usually pay attention to three things, women's eyes, lips, and breasts. If he is that sly, he will look at the buttocks. For the time being, Mithiya pays attention to her eyes and lips.

There was no need to look at the other two parts now. By now, Mithiya already knew that she was good from the lecherous looks men gave her.

She put on matte lipstick. The biggest advantage of matte lipstick is that it does not dazzle much; the colour does not give a different sheen. For Mithiya, anything that shines too much is not good. But the problem with matte lipsticks is that they are a little dry. The solution is to mix matte and moist lipstick together.

Aishwarya Rai wore the moist and matte lipstick from; Loreal Paris at the 2014 Cannes Film Festival. Since then, it has been Mithiya's favorite. The price of the lipstick is a bit high, but it is certainly not more expensive than her lips. The biggest advantage of this lipstick is that it does not keep the lips dry or wet. It gives a natural colour to the lips. Loreal makes the lips look pleasant for 6 hours.

Earlier, Mithiya used to apply Boby Brown cream matte lipstick. That was kiss-proof. As in, it stays if you are smooching lightly. But it costs more than Loreal. And Mithiya doesn't use it nowadays. At least not for someone like Kudrat.

3.

Tilapia is considered the fish of the poor. Maybe because the price is low. The price of Tilapia has decreased due to widespread cultivation. Shing, Magur, and Pabda are also cultivated, but their nobility has not diminished as much as Tilapia. The people of this country have not learned how to eat it. The Bengalis have killed the dignity of this fish by making the curry with eggplants. Bengalis don't know that Tilapia is one of the best fishes in the world in terms of taste.

But we have ruined its actual taste by cooking curry with it, by putting too much spice also. One has to keep the original taste of it by using fewer spices and slow cooking so that when you put it in your mouth, it feels heavenly. Tilapia fish tastes best when it's baked. Marinate it properly, then slowly bake the fish. If there is no oven, it can be done on the stove. You have to put water in a big pot and lay the fish in another small pot of that water. Then the Tilapia will be boiled in water vapor.

No, this fish cannot be mixed with water. The taste of the fish will remain the same if no water is added to it; this will change its taste entirely. You can bake or even fry. It is also good. An entire Tilapia fish fry is no less tasty.

"But by calling her tilapia repeatedly, I am disrespecting the name Urmimala." Kudrat thought to himself.

Today Kudrat will dedicate Urmimala to Mithiya. She is very arrogant. If she sheds her pride a little, she will be much more beautiful. Pride has a different beauty; modesty has it as well - in fact, everything has its own beauty. But you have to understand where and how much. The beauty is, like salt in a food, it cannot be used even a bit more or cannot be used a bit less either. Kudrat has adorned Urmimala for Mithiya. Let her see and learn that the ultimate form of beauty is devotion.

Mithiya is devoted too. She devotes herself. But there is pride in that devotion; there is a need, and there is also a kind of audacity. Kudrat doesn't like that audacity. He works as a chef at a three-star hotel. Mithiya is a regular customer there. She sometimes has dinner and drinks with different people and finally spends the night with them. Kudrat met many women like her in his workplace. He really couldn't care less about them. But one day, Mithiya called him from the kitchen. She pointed her dark red nails at the one-kilogram red sniper and said,

"Are you the chef? What did you cook?"

Kudrat was professional enough not to let the incident of that day go too far. He replied in a humble voice and said,

"Sorry, madam, I am changing it for you."

After eating the red sniper for the second time, Mithiya said, "Hmm, it's good; see, if you concentrate on your work, then you can do well."

"Yes, Madam," Kudrat didn't say more than that. Kudrat realised that day, Mithiya liked savory food.

After that, they met several times. They just said Hi, exchanged looks, and that was it. One day he got a chance to say

"I wish I could cook for you someday!"

"You already do that."

"No, not like that."

"Then, how?"

"I want to cook for you at my home."

"Really?"

"Yes, I will only cook for you."

"Why all of a sudden?"

"Just like that, we can drop the idea if you don't want it."

"No. It's alright."

"Then, we can have dinner next Thursday.

"Right away, dinner? No, Lunch. Let's start with lunch; if it's good, then we will have dinner as well."

"Ok, done."

"What will you cook for me? You didn't mention that."

"Keep faith in me. I will cook something good."

Mithiya kept faith in him. The bell rings. Mithiya is standing at the door. She looks beautiful! Just like Urmimala. Simple, naïve, and beautiful.

4.

"Come in; thanks a lot for coming."

"Why are you so formal? Wow, your house is very neat."

"Come on, let's go to the dining room first."

Kudrat also decorated the dining table with a lot of care. The main course is Urmimala. It comes with soup, brown bread, salad, butter-fried vegetable, and mojito. Candles are melting on the silver candle stand on the table. Purple and pink carnations adorn a brass vas on one side.

"I heard about candlelight dinner but never heard about candlelight lunch.

"Well, you got to see it today, then."

"You arranged the table nicely. What are those flowers?"

"Carnations."

"Do they have a smell?"

"Not all flowers have a smell. God created some flowers to be so colourful they don't need any smell. Like Shimul."

"Are you a Philosopher?

"Indeed. Cooking is the biggest philosophy of the world."

"Really?"

"It is also art and science, you can say."

"Explain, please!"

"How many senses are there in a human being?"

"Five. Some people have six, I heard."

"Now tell me, when do you use all of your senses altogether?"

"Am I to give an exam here?"

"No, have the soup, please. It's pumpkin soup. Soup made of pumpkin. I added prawns to it. A little sweet, sour, and spicy. Let's chat over the soup."

"Hmm, it's very tasty. It is a little different. I didn't even know there was something called pumpkin soup. Tell me about your cooking philosophy or art."

"Let me give you an example. Suppose you take today's main course. I named it Urmimala."

"Urmimala? The name of a fish?"

"No, it's Tilapia by its species.

"I don't like Tilapia, sorry.

"But you will today. I guarantee it. She is no longer a tilapia. I transformed her into Urmimala. I cut her myself, cleaned her, and washed her. I mean, she has a touch of me. Then I used this tomato and cowpea to decorate, so I used my sense of sight for it. Then lemon and ginger - worked as functions of the sense of smell. While baking, I tasted it a bit with my tongue, which means I also used my sense of taste. And the fried vegetables you can see as a side dish, they are very crispy. Butter Fried. If you put it in your mouth, your ears and even your brain will play a crunchy melody. So what stands out, the feeling of touching, seeing, smelling, tasting, hearing -is a matter of using all five senses. Now tell me, is there any other work like cooking that deepens all the five senses so deeply?"

"sex?"

It is true. But it didn't have to come out that strong. Kudrat feels a bit shy. Mithiya was busy eating, so she didn't notice.

5.

Mithiya didn't do any injustice to Kudrat. Just as Kudrat has cooked exclusively with all five senses, so Mithiya also eats and enjoys the food using all five senses. These very simple daily chores of cooking, and eating, seem different to her today. She got different tastes while having different items. It seems she enjoys the music of the soup and the melody of the vegetables. Mithiya licks her lady's finger-like fingers while eating Urmimala. Kudrat kept watching Mithiya and Urmimala simultaneously.

"Is everything alright, mam?"

"Absolutely. I enjoyed my food with all my five senses, maybe the sixth one as well.

"Hail! Hail to all the senses."

"It has to be!"

Although Mithiya came for lunch, she stayed till late. She thought that dinner might be good as well. Most importantly, Kudrat deserves a dinner as well. She also thinks using all five senses can be done in a different way too. Besides, she wouldn't mind lying down for a while.

Mithiya walks towards Kudrat's bedroom.

Translated by Maliha Tasnim Tithi

Nahar Alam

Pohela Boishakh and Rodela

Today is Pohela Boishakh[1]. It is full of joyous mood all around. I remember my sister Rodela badly on this day every year. Rodela, my dear cousin, was two years senior to me in the department while studying at the university. She had a love marriage that took place very secretly, without the knowledge of their families- only a few close friends from the university campus were aware of this. They were from different religions. Sadiq Arfan came from a very rich Muslim family based in the central area of Comilla. Both of his parents were teachers at a private college. Rodela was from the Ghosh family of Barishal, a vast joint family on its merit. Her father was a businessman and her mother was a high official in the Family Planning department. Sadiq and Rodela were classmates on the Arts faculty of Rajshahi University. They had a court marriage just before their Masters Final examination took place. Both of them continued to exercise their respective religion aftermath of the marriage as agreed beforehand. So many activities were taking place on the campus as usual to celebrate the first day of Baishakh. The picture of the Arts faculty getting busy drawing alpana[2] on the streets was a very

---

[1] Pohela (1st day) of Boishakh (the first month of Bengali Calendar)
[2] Alpana is a folk-art style of Bangladesh, consisting of coloured motifs, patterns and symbols that are painted on

familiar one. Sadiq and Rodela were also involved in all the fun like the previous years.

Rodela was smart and lively with a constant friendly smile on her face. Her physical appearance with bright and fair skin colour was exquisitely charming. She used to croon a lot. Sadik had a so impressive appearance with his fair skin, good height, and physicality which could be noticed from a distance. Anyway, finally, there came the eagerly awaited moment, the Mongal Shobhajatra and all the activities surrounding it that took place all day long. Rodela, who was an excellent dancer presented her solo performance for an hour. Once the programme finished, Rodela and Sadiq visited Madumathi Park to spend some time together. Sister Rodela liked to go around a lot carrying her bag full of painting materials like brush, paper, board, etc. They spent a long time chatting sitting in a very quiet place until it got dusk.

They were so engrossed in chatting without realising that it was night already although this park used to be so crowded even at late night with the people taking part in different activities. It was around nine o'clock. Suddenly, from nowhere, a group of an armed gang of four/five people stormed in and tied Rodela and Sadiq to a tree to their utter shock. Then, right in front of Sadiq, they brutally raped Rodela in turn multiple times. Those animals gagged her, tied her hands and legs, and tore apart her numb body mercilessly. It was a flood of blood

---

floors, walls and streets on special occasions.

all over the place. They thrashed Sadiq heavily when he tried to scream. It was an unbearable scene. Sadiq could not tolerate this barbaric torture and humiliation of her beloved one right in front of his eyes. He somehow managed to wrestle them and kicked heavily on the private parts of one of those miscreants who screamed and fall on the ground. Other members of the gang became furious to see Sadiq attacking their mate. Out of rage, they left Rodela alone and started stabbing Sadiq savagely nearly to death. By then, Rodela managed to get up with his blood-bathed body after a lot of trouble, dressed herself up, and shouted for help removing the gag.

That group of rapists ran away when the traffic sergeant on duty nearby blew the whistle. The wounded rapist was still scrolling around on the ground in pain. The traffic surgent followed by a team of four/five police officers arrived on the scene in the next twenty minutes. After a few minutes, an ambulance turned up as well. Sadiq was lying in a pool of blood whilst Rodela managed to get closer to him limping. She attempted to stop the flow of blood by pushing her scarf on his wounds but failed as blood was oozing out from the wounds all over his body and then it started raining all of a sudden. Rodela was utterly confused whereas Sadiq was speechless. He was trying to say, "Are you alright?" so hoarsely that Rodela had to struggle to understand it. Sadiq was lying on the grass all along with his head on the lap of Rodela although she was struggling to sit properly with the wounds on her body. She was screaming with all of her strength, "Please, please, could anybody save my Sadiq's life." Cloud-rain-storm and the noise of shrieking got mixed up in the sky and the air then. Sadiq kept looking at Rodela silently without a blink as he was dead by then. Police took both the dead body and the injured rapist away. An autopsy was carried out on the dead body. There was a further autopsy- the live one- for the marks of rape on Rodela's body. Rodela was silent, traumatised, and never responded to anybody, rather kept looking blank.

In a blink of an eye, both families came to know this bad news with utter shock as if everything had turned upside down. What a sin and anarchy! Everyone was shaming such a disgusting act. Who would take the burden of this sin? Although Rodela's family was ousted from society her parents did stand by their daughter arranging treatment for her. Police interrogation did not progress as such due to her unstable state of mental health. In other words, she was behaving like a half-mad person by holding the sandals of Sadiq on her chest all day long- not letting anyone take them from her. It's been nearly two years now since that tragic incident happened but

Rodela's mental state is worsening as the day progresses. She is in a badly insane state now and does not want to keep clothes in her body. Her parents are unable to continue her mental treatment due to their destitute situation.

Within seven months of this incident happened all the rapists managed to come out of prison on bail in a befitting manner with big smiles on their faces and garlands around their necks. Immediately thereafter, they threatened and warned both Rodela's and Sadiq's dads to withdraw the rape and murder cases. Those two families were forced to leave their respective homes and take shelter in a relative's house in Dhaka. The corrupted representatives of the system of law let this debauchery act of political leaders' children go unpunished whilst their wallets are getting thicker with the illegal money they beg from people.

Rodela has been in a completely insane state for three years now. She must be chained when her madness gets uncontrollable. On this specific day of the Pohela Boishakh, she starts running around on the road randomly, without any direction, and with a sigh. There were joyous processions for the well-being of people. Roads are jampacked with participants creating a colourful environment with the loud noise of Dhol-tabla-madol[3] and singing.

It is during these processions, a goods truck stormed in from nowhere and drove away after running over Rodela. At least in this way, Rodela, who was raped and tortured mercilessly not only has a peaceful death but also gets redemption by liberating this frail society of crooked spine from sin on the very first day of a sin-free season.

From that point on, although Pohela Boishakh brings the message of good luck to every home, the families of Rodela and Sadiq have to experience the glory of silent

---

[3] Dhol-tabla-madol are Bangladesh musical instrument.

mourning. I always remember Rodela- my cousin on this very day. I haven't seen a decent human being like my sister Rodela who had such a beautiful heart. I have also seen the other side of the coin- four people who look like human beings in their appearance but are not human by any means, rather animals by nature.

Translated from Bengali by Shuvra Bhowmik

Kazi Rafi

The Moon of the Mountain

Only after crossing the highest and last hill will we reach our destination. There is an antique and ancient temple and a few aesthetically pleasing recreation rooms built in modern times. Several springs can be found by trekking around there. There are also many stories about how the mountain's moon looks on a lonely night from those bungalows. As they feel the moon of this mountain and go back from here and they spread the story on Facebook, so many people are now visiting this inaccessible mountain. But even ten years back, there were very few people coming here. The huge difficulty of the road. More than just hill-temple, those who came here told tales of hardships they endured to get there. When conditions are established in the presence of more people, people tend to find heroism in the midst of sorrow. The memory of conquering a hostile environment rather than suffering grows on them.

I believe that the creator created this lovely environment so that he might experience the pleasure of seeing human presence. In the presence of people, the being of the mountain is flourishing, the heart of the spring is a rumble, the spirit of nature is looking forward, and the heart of the river and the sea is trembling! Because nothing else – nature may contain human feelings within itself. That is just reflected in the presence of people. That's why the hidden soul of this universe is solicitous and anxious to understand the language of human dreams, so the musical note of the lonely mountain at night is unique.

Our bodies have been really worn out and drained from traversing the mountains for the past five days.

Our bodies almost collapse from exhaustion in this uninhabited silent, silent nature close to the sky and this green circle of grass-trees-vines. It awakens with a vitalizing need to move on after a little rest, spring water, and nourishment. I think to go forward with a strange and unique motivation; there is nothing but vines and grasses and mountain trees in front of me - but what else to pass such a difficult path with the addiction of seeing new things? Moreover, while getting a new degree in medicine, our life plagued by the cruel whip of strict punctuality seems to have attained nirvana. The pleasure of the completion of the study mingled with the susurration of these halting leave. Looking at the clear blue sky in the quiet night and looking at the moon washed by the light coming down next to the head, what so much I feel - how can I explain it in words?

Several other groups of people like us are also running to elevated land in search of this mist of illusion in life. Running too higher. The human soul, most likely, is satisfied by being bathed in the natural interactions of the world. Without looking at the boundless horizon, their creative being becomes worn out. That's why the addiction to getting up high and seeing the distant horizon is hidden in people's blood. Maybe it is. Even a philosopher, in my opinion, would not know what to answer to such a query. The group of people may therefore be running to the mountains to look back at themselves. They will become a moon by washing themselves thoroughly in moonlit. Looking at their eyes and faces, it seems as if they go and get something like the touchstone, or they are close to discovering the secret of the relationship between this world and God that is hidden there. This is a tragedy of human life.

When I saw the full moon on the Earth before dark, all these phantom sources of life together sparked my emotions. Let's say that the crooked mountain road is a little stiff after coming so high. I glanced at the low-lying plains in the distance. As we left, I stood weary with my hands on my knees. However, it is not quite a map; even then, it seems the location of human habitation appears to be designated by various lines that cross the little hills and are embellished with green carpets and water fountains. Even though the Sun has lowered its veil before sunset, the body is sweating more now than in the afternoon due to the intense heat radiating itself in nature. I said the word 'frowzy' and the word frowzy of the plains and the word frowzy of the mountains have a little difference in adjectives. I may not be able to explain it exactly, but every time I say the word 'frowzy' or think of the word, the fragrance of mountain wildflowers surrounds me as well.

And immediately, with strong thirst, dry lips, and thirst, my esophagus wanted to be wet with water. And if you believe it, do
it or if you do it—something more with these words— is lulling me into an immersion of unmindful dreams that I'm hesitant to say. But I can tell you this - I mix the scent of mountains with this word and imagine a dreamy girl whose sweaty body smells of wildflowers and the gentleness of mountain plants. For an instantaneous such imagination evoked in the cooking smoke rising from a house in the plains and diving into the taste of my mother's dishes. This memory peeked into another memory. It was nothing but a rainy and lonely-weedy afternoon in my village. How magical the memories become when looking far, far away from this high land!

Do people come to the mountain to see, there at the bottom, under an infinite sky, the impermanence behind the harmony of happiness and sorrow in the life-adaptation of people, the greatest creation of God? Did the creator create this universe for the same purpose? In the midst of all kinds of life and animals, people with unbridled conscience-intelligence tied to the reins of a nomad called 'Time' and tied them to their backs, watching the eternal fun, making their own infinite time wings to fly. None of these possibilities seem very appropriate to me. And even no thought seems to be absolutely pointless. The purpose of life in the midst of impossibility - who knows better than me because of the study of medicine?'

I feel that none in my group has enough time to focus on this life and its impermanence, the ups and downs. They are moving toward their destination. Or they are so hungry and tired that they want to reach the summit quickly for the peaceful fantasy of the hilly restroom. But looking at the plains left behind, I no longer wanted to move forward may, be due to some nostalgia. To take the support, I put my body on the branch of a tree lying on the ground and took out a bottle of water from
my backpack. And yes, that's when I saw her. In the fall of the day, the moon of that mountain rested its tired body on my posture by my side. I forgot to open the water bottle. The delicious aroma of herbs and apples that emerged from her body was so priceless to me at the time that I got fascinated with the worry of losing it due to the efforts of a thirsty sense of gratification. The girl looked at me with tired eyes. She smiled sweetly. Then suddenly, her smile disappeared as soon as her eyes fell on the water bottle. The sensation of sweat under her eyes, near her throat, made my thirst double though,
but I asked the girl as I offered her the drinking water, 'You seem extremely thirsty?'

Without any hesitation or objection, the young lady took my water bottle in her hand and started to pour the water down her throat and gulp, and suddenly she stopped. However, half a bottle of water she has consumed within this time. Looking at me pleadingly, she said, 'Sorry, I'm so thirsty that...'

Before she finished her sentence, I assured her, 'Well, you can drink the water till your thirst is quenched. The young lady didn't hesitate to call me as like as we call our friends. She said, 'But, you….';

'I am not very thirsty... I ate a while ago.'

Now she took a pause before pouring the rest of the water from the bottle into her mouth and saying,
'Now you say 'ate,' then you say 'water-drinking'... your head is fully gone mad.'

Then she gulped down the rest of the water with such gusto that I wanted to stick my beak inside her mouth and wet my tongue with a little water while she was drinking. Oh, if only my mouth were a bird's beak! I didn't know there was so much wonder in the world through the drinking of water. I am looking at the girl in surprise. Actually, I'm not at all embarrassed to admit that I'm not looking at her water—rather, I'm staring at her rosy lips and red little mouth cavity. Where the waterfalls, but the fire is not extinguished! I felt a little ashamed to see a lady like this so closely for the first time in my life. The girl held the empty bottle towards me and said, 'Are you really not thirsty? I ran out of my water four hours ago. I asked many people for a gulp of water. Everyone says that their water has run out... And you have saved a whole bottle of water! Your wife will be very lucky….'
'Why?'
After hearing my question, the lady went to the high part of the branch and sat on it. Waving her legs, she said,

'Because you have so much patience. OMG, what a cruel place the mountains are. Today I can feel it…

'You can see how a full bottle of water became just one gulp of 'water'!'

She was fascinated by my words and looked at me in a shy manner, making a barricade before her eyes. Just then, a soft and sweet breeze blew past the scorching heat. No, it's not just in my mind; I was clearly felt in my body. That beautiful lady was still looking at me in that position. Her steadfast gaze seemed to divide me in two with a saw. I became from one to two, from two to four, and finally into the billions number and merged into the trillion's particles-atom and dissolved. I dissolved from the palms to the cheek, from the body to the heart with the smooth breeze that carried the sweet wind. And on the wings of the wind, I spread my wings and flew with that young lady looking charmingly at me to the last border of the blue sky where a point of white cloud stood in the shape of a hut.

A feeling of intense thirst brought me back from the Infinite to the million. Brought me back to this human body. Thirsty, I looked at the water bottle. A few drops of water at its bottom. Oh, if only I could wet my tongue with those few drops of water! The young lady turned the cap anti-cloak on the
bottle and closed and handed it back to me. I looked once at the drops of water and several times at her sweat on the young woman's shoulders and neck, under the eyes. It seemed that a few drops of holy dew were

clinging to a reservoir of all the beauty of the world like a drop of God. Rather than thirst for water, it increased the heart's thirst so much! As much as I wanted to live by drinking bottled water, I don't know why I wanted to die loving the girl more. The whole of my life, I
have read and learned-nothing that is greater than living. But today, I learned—for the first time—that there can be a cause in the world for which there is no greater artistic pleasure than surrendering oneself to the will to die. After death, I want to be the sweat spots under her eyes like the best blue
water canal in the world on her goitered mounds. If she embraces me once in her long-fingered arms, all the thirsts of a lifetime's imagined dreams of mine would be resolved in no time.

The girl then looked at the deep-black cat's-eyes-like watch on her wrist, and anxiously seeing up but finding none anywhere, she said, 'I can't see anyone from my team. They seem to have reached the resort by now.'
'No, at high altitudes, even faraway objects seem quite close.
Evidently, my group hasn't yet arrived.'
'You know, I've always wanted to...'
I couldn't hold my interest. I asked in an impatient voice, 'What would you like?'
'I'll stay there if one day I can find a hut on a hill with a beautiful sky and clouds, clean and lush grass.'
I'm not sure what happened when that girl said those things to me. I have a stronger urge to find such a hut

with her now. However, my thirsty body of mine was unable to cope with the weight of this desire. I saw darkness in my eyes. After that, I could not remember anything else.

After regaining consciousness, I found myself lying on a bed in a hut. There is a strange earthen lamp on a small bamboo-made basket that stands next to me. It is like the desire of a little light from the lamp to spread the luminous viva of the woman leaning towards my face. My heart was burnt by the full
moon blazing on a hut in the sky mountains. The mystery of the moonlit night in the mountains has spread a fog of illusion up to the far horizon through the gaps of the bamboo fence house. I looked at the beautiful lady. She breathed a sigh of relief and said, 'I was very scared. You will lose consciousness like that; I don't understand. While opening your mouth and giving water, I realised that you were about to die because of me...'

I wanted to tell her, 'No, no… but for you, I live anew. I always imagined such a life. Near the sky clouds, outside there is the silver lining of the moonlight, and inside, next to an earthen lamp, a moon fairy descended from the sky like
you!'
But nothing I could say. I just surprisingly stared at her face.

She kept saying, 'You were so thirsty, but you gave me all the water to drink. Listen, fool, and girls understand their own needs. Why don't you understand yours?'
I don't know how to answer this question. Again I wanted to tell her, 'I really wanted to enjoy dying like this. When I thought about how you were also separated from your team, like me, on this mountain, I thought that there must be a God somewhere. Otherwise, how could the spirit of this mountain know my cherished words that I kept within me all my life, and it not only provoked here but also made it true?'

But so many words inside me remained inside as all trembled words. She asked me, 'Do you forget to speak? Don't you remember anything?
I looked at her in affection. As soon as I touched one of her fingers, I came alive again. I said, 'I don't want to remember the past if my eternal life began today! It is not the life that I left behind; only the endless horizon of mountains will be ahead and...'

By now, I remembered that I didn't even know her name. I looked into her eyes, restless to know her name. Her blue-black eyeballs watched me intently as if trying to grasp the meaning of my words. Three letters of a word slowly played on her lips, 'A…n…d…?'

Without hesitation in her question, I told her, 'Here is you and your sky-clouds a hut! But look, I don't even know anything about you, your name or place of birth.'

'I am Yagmur Marvy. You can call me Marvy. I was born where two continents meet at one point. My birthplace is at that point in the world where sometimes the snow plays with the Sun
during the day and the moonlight at night.' 'In the midst of such beauty, the people of your country find
more meaning in life by diving into paintings, tunes, and songs, don't they?' 'That will not happen. People in all corners of the world have lost all the beauty of the soul while contrivance to doing business makes the people the products. Do you feel better now??'

'Yes. It feels great. But here I am…?' 'Yes, while you went faint. The Sun was getting down. I screamed for help. A resident of this hill went to the plain to market two days ago. He was returning home. I took water from him and poured it on your face. Then leaving my team's destination, we are now in his own guest house. We are fortunate enough that he had built this house so secluded as to rent to guests. He named the house Jumghar.' What a surprise! It felt like I was listening to the story of an episode of a film she had just completed an actress, and my heart beat so fast as I wondered who the hero of that actress was that I began to sweat. Many people flee the human universe of the world and come to this quiet and secluded abode of peace called 'Jumghar' 'Do people really run away from people?'
'no…'

'So then?'

'The people with whom one lives for a few days in this 'Jumghar' - they actually discover each other. Find back. What is the joy of finding a loved one and getting lost in it, tell me?'

This is the first time in my life that I realised that it is more peaceful to stare it in her eyes than to listen to the meaning of life or philosophy in the mouth of a fairy of heaven named Marvy. So instead of paying attention to her words, I looked at her eyes in an embarrassed manner seeing the elegancy of her hair that was scattered around her ears, crossing her forehead, and a lot I imagined. I imagine spending many colourful lives with her in one moment. I wanted to tell Marvy, 'I'm in love with you.' I could not tell. I am frightened.

My youth began in a country where peoples are more accustomed to foreseeing their downfall than to dreaming. This seems to be what happens in the habits of an uncertain life of blaming others for self-interest and missing out. Before getting her, the fear of losing seems to have started an agitation inside.

Marvy got up to leave. She returned a little later, along with the owner of the 'Jumghar.' The sons and daughters of the owner came behind them with hot food. They arranged the food one after the other on the scaffold next to us. Marvy took my hand and lifted me to stand. My dead hunger rekindled sharply.

Two of us eat on full stomachs with absolute satisfaction. Then we left the hut and came out. Sat on a wooden bench at the edge of the hill. Even though I was facing the higher mountains of one another country, all my attention was actually on Marvy. I am thinking about how will be my proposal for love to Marvy, seeing the love-offering technique of the hilly nature falling in deep love amidst whispering conversations with the blue sky descending in the moonlight.

Whether the mildly blowing wind that cools the soul and mind but spreads the fire of love in the body, floods the eyes with the dream, and spreads the shiver of tremor over the grass leaves giving me a hint? Why the sound of the leaf is 'murmuring' - today, I can feel it in the resonance of the soul. Is it the edge of the hill that spreads moonlight's wings? Or after my death, God sent me to heaven?

Marvy took my hand. The touch of the cold air became hot and burned me as she came closer to my body. Without any hesitation, I hugged Marvy. The scent of Marvy's skin and hair spread as if the soul of every grass and shrub on the mountain and mixed in every molecule, in every bend of the path of the rushing wind from the blue of the sky. Marvy hugged me. Nothing in the whole world is truer than her glorious face in the soft light of the moon.

Before I wanted to become unbound, the touch of her lips drowned all my dreams together with the agitation of emotion. This time not only her beauty of face but Marvy took off his t-shirt to burn down this mountain night by spreading his own light. I hesitated because of the open space. I immediately felt that I was on this mountain with a foreign lady! If, in a few days, the newspapers spread the news about her 'missing'? I became excited and worried, thinking that the identity of my boyfriend-girlfriend would come to ash and I would be lost by some force. Then my t-shirt was held by Marvy in her hand. She said, 'You ruined me by using the scent of my favorite brand on your body!'

I immediately remembered the t-shirt with a world-renowned magnolia-scented perfume that my uncle had brought for me while back from London. Three months after coming back to the country for marriage, my uncle is no longer to be found. My aunt became a widow soon after their marriage. My mother becomes mad because of the disappearance of her dear brother. And now, if something happens to me, my mother may not be able to be alive. This thought increased my anxiety so much that I lost all my sense of 'love.'

But nature has become so intoxicated by Marvy's manifested, wild beauty that the random change of direction of the wind makes Marvy's short hair crazy too. In the meantime, Marvy made me lie down on the small bench. I gently touched my finger on her lips. She bit. Instead of getting crazy, I calmed down and allusion her to calm down. She was surprised and looked at me for a long time. 'This is my first time,' she whispered,' and as far as I know, there is no such thing as a 'period' in boys' lives.'

I play with her hair.

'Oh, good boy! Feeling uncomfortable outside? Let's go inside. But I dreamed, and I promised myself that if I ever found someone loveable in the mountains, I would fully offer myself to him.'

Saying the words, Marvy looked around in astonishment, as if she were looking for a creator with her eyes. And she said, 'What a surprise, the creator fulfilled my request in this way! Just like the visual of my imagination. No other moment can be better than this moment of this night to give away my light carefully cherished within myself. And I want to devote myself to you that all the events of today and such mountain nights have been determined by God's indication.'

How do I make Marvy understand how a family member feels when a lively person suddenly disappears, and even the body is never found? I hid my inner anxiety from him. I said with a sweet smile, 'I want to get you by burning myself up.'

'What?'

'If I ever underestimated the celestial maiden like you who I am getting so easily. You are very extraordinary, Marvy….'

She sat up and managed all of the clothes she had removed from her body. Tied up the loose locks of hair and said, 'I'm sorry!'

She bowed her head. I realised she still couldn't handle the emerging larvae inside. The word 'sorry'; in her mouth became water for her erupted fire - I understood that too. I sat up and went to catch her, but she didn't let herself be caught. As she fastened her hair with a clip, she hurried to the other end of the bench and said, 'First, be expensive for me. I'm very extraordinary….'

I was silent for a while. Marvy once said softly, 'There is a very big difference between the love of God and the love of humans. He has not been able to convince people even by arranging this world so freely for love; He didn't give his creature enough times to commit so many crimes, to conspire, and to make laws to remedy it and to go through it!'

After saying this, she hurriedly went home. She turned off the lamp and lay on a single bed between the two beds, wrapped her body with a blanket, and fell asleep. It is not known whether she stayed awake or not.

We spent the next day exploring the surrounding mountains. Collected mountain fruits and bathed in the shower. As I fed her the lunch by my hand, she looked at me with gratitude and deep affection and said, 'It is very true; there is a great difference between the love of God and the love of Satan.' I repeatedly expressed my admiration and love to Marvy. I proposed to her.

Without saying 'yes' or 'no,' she reminded me again and again that - you don't have to get something extraordinary; you have to earn it.

As it was the night, I could not control myself at all. Even though Marvy just allowed me up to her lips, I became frantic. She gently placed her finger on my lips and asked me to calm down. The more she told me to calm down, the more restless I became to have her. Finally, my volcanic larval energy was extinguished by her one sentence, 'Not tonight. I'm sorry.'

'When then?'

'After a few days. Even if they do not have to men, ladies have to go through the word period.'

Tears rolled down her eyes as she spoke those two sentences. And she again said, 'Time and God… I was accessible to you that they wanted it. However, we have to shrink due to the indication of time.'

Before noon the next day, I laid eyes on a wall calendar of last year hanging on the wall of the hut – looking at the letters of the dates with the passage of time, I have been restless and bored. Rather than showering with Marvy beneath the spring water, then my desire was as mad as the smell of wild mountains in my blood to see the thing that goes away called a date.

But this call for blood came cold with sweat before passing the three days of a wall calendar. Three days later, the sweaty members of Marvy's team arrived at the hill with a sweatier team, the police force. They took cover on the lower slopes of the hill and called out to Marvy. The policemen also take up positions behind them with arms and ammunition, as if Marvy has been hijacked by the mafia, and while they come closer, he is ready to open fire as soon as the hijacker pulls out an AK-47. I could see all their activities through the gap in the window.

The thin shout of a woman's voice froze my blood, 'Marvy, we know you're staying here with a terrorist. Military helicopters watch your every move. Ask the devil to surrender. If he attempts to hurt you, he will never live.'

When did the army helicopter reconnaissance figure out Marvy's location – we were so immersed in ourselves, immersed in the unblinking gaze of each other's eyes, that we didn't notice any of it. I also told Marvy my secret in response to the question of why I was so startled all of a sudden. That's why Marvy may have been afraid of the police. She said, 'A country is never freedom until the soul of its people is subjugated. I don't want them to know your location. Escape through the toilet door to the back. Stay well. Take care of yourself. Even if you are leaving, I will remain in this light-washed mountain nature. Remember, I will keep you in my mind as the God of this mountain.'

Marvy walked slowly to the door. Pausing and pretending not to understand anything, she moved forward with a carefree pace, as if she had awakened from a peaceful sleep and was glad to see her people. Every step she took distanced me the more, and I embraced all the arrangements of meaninglessness in the meaning of this small life.

My team didn't even come looking for me. Once the missing culture is introduced and the fear of talking about it is created in society - that society will no longer create a situation where people lose themselves while looking for the missing person; this is normal! If someone is rather lost, it becomes easy to make excuses for not looking for him, even against inhumanity.

The people whose names were registered in the missing book became too touchy.

When Marvy left, the owner of this unostentatious hill resort came and took my hand and said, 'You did not go, Sir? You ran away here, didn't you?'

Looking into my tearful eyes, he said restlessly. 'Don't be upset. Everything will be fine. By walking, we can reach our town before the afternoon. I will keep a chamber there for you.

Patients come day by day, and patients return back. A doctor remains. Looking fascinated at the mountain moon, he talks to the moon, but nobody knows what he says. In lamplight with the pencil, he desires to sketch the moonlight on Marvi's body, but instead of it, he spreads Marvi's glow in the moonlight. After then, while he thinks of touching that abstract body, he remembers – falling in love is a prohibition for him! He draws Marvy's voice. He draws the joy of the two's exuberance bathing in the spring. Draws the sound of the falling spring water. Suddenly he stops as he touches Marvi's beautiful fingers - those fingers are not to be touched with a bound consciousness that they are beautiful and a symbol of unlimited freedom.

No one else in the world came to know that a medical man in love with whom it is forbidden to fall in love, looking for that woman in the nearby spring, thinking of the moonlight for every moment after moment - touching the heart of pebbles and stones. Only this unblameworthy nature - Hills comes to know after thousands of years – even if a doctor understands the human body, why and how an artist, in search of the soul and being one day merges his soul with the eternal being called by the rattle of Brakhand!

Translated from Bengali by Ashraf ul Alam Shikder

Tareq Samin

The Girls of Bengal

Nilay is a 24 years old young man. Medium height, blackish-complexion, the head is
full of black curly hair. Big eyes and eyebrows are like a crooked bow. Sharp-straight
nose. He always has a smile on his face.
He is standing in a sports jacket, jeans, pants, and boot shoes. Today is the 19th of
December. One year ago, on this day, their love affair started. In the afternoon, five
Shila told Nilay to wait near the public library circle.
From the 1st day of Paus (winter in the Bengali calendar), it started to be chilly in
Dhaka city. Shila is coming by a rickshaw that one can see from a distance. Shila is
also 24. The classmate of Nilay in the university. Shila is medium in height and in good
health; she is neither slim nor bulky. Full of long dark smooth wavy hair. Brief forehead,

circular health, deer-like beautiful dark eyes. A dimple shows up on his cheek when
she smiles. Light yellow with a three-part pink dress, she wears a golden pink Kashmiri
Shawl.
As the rickshaw stops, Nilay goes forward and opens the money bag (purse).
'No, you'll not spend any coin of money.' Saying this, Shila hands over thirty takas to the
rickshaw puller.
Such a unique sweet, and beautiful girl is his beloved, and Nilay takes pride in that.
'Hello, the people are wonder-stuck to see you,' Nilay says. This is a naughty sensation.

From Shahbag to Dhaka University T.S.C., beside both sides of the road, many
temporary shops are installed. On the van, a young man takes many 'vutta' (maize). In
a big pan in a burning red fire, he sells those burnt maizes.
'Hi, let us go to taste maize,' Nilay hurriedly said. Then he asked the maize
seller—'Mama' (maternal uncle), how much the price of maize is?
'Twenty takas.'
'Fifteen multiplied two means thirty—if that would be—then please give,' Nilay said.
Looking towards Shila, the young maize seller said—'Okay, take these.'

Shila stares standstill at the burning fire. Nilay stands to keep his hands in the jacket.

Shila catches his triangle-folded hand and stands up with him.

With the help of a fan, the Maize seller burnt the maize for 5 minutes on all sides

, and then he mixed salt, 'morish' (pepper), and lemon juice.

They started to eat it by walking.

'Do you remember our love affair completed a year?'

'yes,' Shila releases a big sigh.

'Happy Anniversary! Now say why your mind is not well?'

'Nothing .'Shila replied.

'Do you feel physically unwell? Are you in the Red signal?' smilingly tells Nilay,

'Jah'! Shila patted his back.

'Tonight I'll go home,' Shila says and becomes silent.

'Suddenly?' Nilay asks him to move his neck towards Shila.

'Mother is not well at all.'

'What happened to Aunt?'

'Okay, let it leave. But how are you?' Shila turns the context and questions.

'Even in hell, 'I'll be happy if you are with me.' — Nilay said seriously.

'Yes, I know'—saying this, Shila keeps her head on the shoulder of Nilay.

Suddenly a warm sense of love moves Nilay's heart.

'Do you love me?' Shila questions Nilay in a serious voice.

'No.'

'Really!'

'Yes, really. See that mad woman covering a sheet on his body lying; I love her.

Now Shila smiles. With a soft sensation, Shila rubs her face on the back of Nilay.

'On my back, you mop up your cough!' Nilay is pretending to show his anger.

'Jah–just mop up my face'—to say this, Shila becomes morbid suddenly. Then she

kisses on the cheek of Nilay tenderly.

The wintry evening enters gradually into the night. Nilay ended his maize and then

discarded it.

A poor little boy was collecting polythene from the roads. Shila gave her maize to him.

Delightedly the boy has gone away.

Let us go; I'll feed you 'chatpati'" said Shila.

'On the way, if your stomach feels upset?' by saying this, Nilay laughs cheatingly.

'I'll go by train.'

At the roadside shop, Nilay takes Chatpati, and Shila takes Fuchka.

Then they shared their plates with each other.

'I'll miss you much,' Nilay said deeply.

'Is it really?' Eating fuchka Shila asks. Her eyes are then moistened with tears.

'O mama (uncle) has given so much Chilli in Fuchka, why?' Nilay said nervously.

'What Aapa (sister) much chilier?' Chatpati seller asked her.

'No, Okay, it's all right'—in a hint assured Shila.
'How many days you'll be at home, don't you tell me?'
'Don't know.'
'Don't you know?' Nilay wonders in his eyebrows.
'Examination has ended; I don't prefer to be in the university hall,' Shila irritably says.
Taking a spoon, Shila pours some sour in the 'fuchka.'
She is looking very anxious. Her two beautiful eyes are flooded with tears.
'Hei, what is the matter?'
'No, here is something chillier!'

By train, Shila is going to Chattogram. The villages are covered with fog. In the
distance, sometimes, one or two blinking lights could be seen. Now it is 3:00 AM at
midnight. Tears burst and flooded her cheeks.
The day after tomorrow, there will be Shila's wedding with an unknown man! Her
parents had fixed everything even without asking her anything! She is a young woman
without a voice, like many other Bengali girls.

AKM Abdullah

A Piece of Soft Fair Hand

Small coils of smoke still billowing from the wreckage of the building that was destroyed in the airstrike, and rescue workers are tirelessly working. There were only a handful of survivors, most of whom were injured. Someone's head is bursting with blood, some have lost one leg, and others have lost both legs or arms. The bodies were removed in trucks, and there is no fire now.

The rescue team has been working for almost thirty hours, and now a few fire crews are performing one last job of removing broken walls and checking various small holes to see if there are any survivors or dead bodies. Asif is also part of this group, and he has been courageously cooperating with the rescue work for many days as he has been working in the fire department for a long time.

On the other side of the rubble, where the wall of the building has been broken, lintel rods are sticking out. Slowly, Asif checks a little in that direction when he suddenly sees a small, soft, fair hand hanging on the rod. Asif goes closer and takes the hand with deep emotions, and his chest trembles. This was the first time he saw such a sight, and he broke down, having difficulty controlling himself. A little arm from the elbow to the finger was severed from the infant's body, and all the blood that was in this piece of the hand had been drained. Asif's eyes get wet, and he kisses the hand. His breathing becomes thick, and he sits down on the broken stone, holding the little hand. He does not want to find the rest of the baby's body and attach the severed arm, and he cannot think anymore. He falls down on the rubble, and his colleagues call an ambulance.

Asif is lifted into the ambulance, and he still holds the piece of the fair hand tightly, but the hand is slowly becoming rubber.

Part Four

Prose Poems

Poems by David Lee Morgan

The Rules For Busking In The London Underground

(back in the day)

The first rule, of course, is there are no rules, there are never any rules.

The second rule is that the first rule is bullshit, there's always rules, especially when there's no rules.

The third rule is that the first one who gets there starts playing, if someone else comes by they get the next hour, if someone else comes by you start a list, an hour per person, a duo gets two hours, but no group gets more than two hours, in theory, although who's gonna argue with four speed freaks who have a better idea on Saturday night? Morning pitches last till 10:30, no matter what time you start, except for Green Park and Oxford Circus, which last until 11:30, although every now and then you come across someone who doesn't know that and thinks you are cheating them. Then you have to be assertive.

Rule number four is never let anyone bully you out of your pitch.

Rule number five is if someone comes along with a shopping cart full of plastic shopping bags and reaches into one of them to pull out a carpenter's claw hammer and starts pounding it into the wall, sending sparks flying and gouging out chunks of concrete, and if he is screaming, "I'll kill for this pitch, I'll die for this pitch," rule number five says: give him the pitch.

Rule number six: you don't have to be good, you just have to be determined.

(The golden rule for busking worldwide not just in London is never ask permission – it just gives them a chance to say no.)

Rule number seven: the more illegal it is the better it pays.

Charlie Savage

Kings Cross. The kitchen was on the second floor. Charlie Savage destroyed pretty much everything on the inside and then started to work his way out. He broke the windows. Then he tore out the window frame. Most of the wall came with it. Jeanette stood frozen in the middle of the room holding the baby and saying, "Why are you doing this?"

Charlie couldn't answer.

Kreutzberg. Charlie Savage told me about London. It sounded like another planet. He said everything was done by keeping a list. There were just so many pitches and every pitch had a list. You had to sign up then fight to keep your place, but he said you could make a lot of money. He said there were violin players saving up to buy houses in the country. I was sure that was bullshit.

Brixton. Charlie and his brother grew up in an orphanage in Brixton where his daddy who was a Cornish nationalist fascist had dumped them. Charlie said that busking in the London Underground was what had cured him of insanity – and that staying there would have driven him crazy all over again.

I met Charlie in Berlin, 1983.

Krakow, Poland. 1989

I got off the train and followed the crowds, I knew they'd be headed towards the center. I could see I was in a different part of the world: peasant women were hawking wool on every street corner at giveaway prices. Lots of uniforms – nothing new for eastern Europe – but some of the uniforms looked like their wearers had just finished cavalry patrol in the eighteenth century. The narrow street opened onto a giant medieval square ringed by market stalls. I walked around, checking out the stalls and the soldiers, watching the crowd flow –

the usual mating ritual between a busker and virgin territory. When I'd sussed out the best place – and worked up my bottle – I set my pack down against the wall and started to pull things out. Suddenly there was the blast of a trumpet from a high church tower – it happens every hour on the hour in memory of a lookout back in the middle ages who sounded the alarm and got a Mongol arrow through the eyeball for his trouble. Quickly, I set up the amp and got the backing tapes ready. When I turned around to open my saxophone case there were about a hundred people gathered around watching me.

Who is this strange looking guy and what's he doing here?

Choo Choo Ch'boogie.

Poems by Gauranga Mohanta

Solar Geometry

Solar geometry manifests as the brilliance of the day melds with the radiant clouds. I move into few quivering mlliseconds and liberate twenty pairs of Eurasian collared doves as a tribute to Aphrodite from a sandy shore or a breezy balcony. I keep Commelina flowers, steeped in the timeless current of a river, ready to spear the tentacles that voraciously devour moonlight amid an illusion of stillness. The sweltering flames of the desolate desert excluding regolith stir a sense of anticipation in the hearts of humanity. I persistently discover that no path extends wide enough. The breath's game of hide-and-seek must be prepared to raise its sail on the mast of a schooner. Rain descends from the horizon where the day merges, carrying with it the unchanging fragrance of the stream.

The Fundamental Blossoming of Lotus

Recognizing the impossibility of defying gravity, the wind gracefully spreads its ahiri, intertwining with the vibrant hues of solar radiation. Gradually, a dampened sound stirs within the aesthetic realm of the flesh. This wild orange jasmine reveals how Ocampo experienced the essence of pagan flaccidity on the banks of Plata. As I stand beneath the coconut trees, where 20.95% oxygen is generated, a boat adorned with Gustave Doré's brushstrokes attentively heeds the words that mimic the flow of water currents. Before Charon helms the craft, I yearn to witness the fundamental blossoming of the lotus in the serene domain of border-dwelling.

Simorgh at Dibrugarh

Having cleansed his coppery feathers in the waters of Bharali, Simorgh took flight, soaring through the sky before touching down at Dibrugarh. The radiant glow of the Sakya monastery, illuminated by golden letters, emerges from the poet's secretive sigh, igniting dialectics within his musings. His plumage bear the hues of the swarna champa blossom. A multitude of hoopoes traversed seven valleys to grasp the essence of luminosity, while Lucretius perceived life as an enduring struggle in the darkness. Armed with this understanding, they firmly believe that the brilliance of words unveils the recognizable nature of the struggle.

Poems by Maria Starosta

Reflections of a Woman 01
The light of hope, like the eternal moon, will guide you even on the darkest of the darkest nights, even when you lose faith, but the one to whom you owe your life and without whom there would be no light or darkness will believe in you. ..

Reflections of a Woman 02
Life goes in a certain direction. We are just fellow travelers who met at one of the stops. Impressions are different, but we walked side by side. This moment is unforgettable - poetry was born.

Reflections of a Woman 03
You can touch hand, take and lead it, no matter what,…. you can touch the heart, excite the blood, upset everything lived and see the new; you can touch the soul, penetrate the invisible into the invisible, fill the void and give new life…

Poems by Sumana Ray

Time's whims

No longer able to embrace a new dream, I seek refuge in the garrulous pages of history. My prophetic vision will dissolve in memory fossils to wipe away the accumulated fatigue. Unalloyed moments falling from a quiet time show the decaying reflection of a mirror. Silence-fostering living is now hugging the unreflective arrogance of last spring. The murmur of the decaying leaves reverberates all along the mind's basin. The kingdom of flight remains unknown even today, the deeper lessons of psyche become more elusive. The noiseless river therefore continues to record the simple lessons of life against the estuary. The cardinal needs of life begin to dissolve in the soft light of the ephemeral evening. The quivering flame is deposited in the sense and being of emptiness. Now only way of owning myself is to be alone with myself. The most daring conviction in this decadent time is the spirit to re-assert oneself in the dissolution of pain and pleasure.

Water-hymns

The joys and sorrows embedded with life touch the uncontrollable equation of translucent complexity. Shattered visions paint the tragic nemesis of slumber. Shaking off remnants of drowsiness, night lays bare the courtship of the moon and the sky. The greeneries being clad with stark colourlessness reflect in their own mirror a melancholy loneliness. The sounds and echoes deserted by the twilight come and mingle in the infinity of darkness, as the fair maiden, the lion and the ring master mingle in the circus. The messenger of clouds is now harbouring tirelessly the canopy of moonlit. He can only witness the hymn of undulating water playing continuously on the body of doleful piano…

Fragmented Cockpit

As the warning bulletin for public-interest sags wearily, Nemesis gauges the winds of gloomy geography's proportion and its acme. By opening the anchor, the river gets bifurcated in loss-gain hiccups – dissipated time and troubled hours come to the fore. In worn-out time, trust can never dwell in human hearts. Who knows where and how ailments outspread harmful virus! Young desires touch the sky of Ayurveda by erasing the howling lines of happiness and unhappiness. The melody that has not yet touched the lips of the flute, enthralls me to embrace it in the atrium. I tie a genial kite in the decaying feathers of a bird, oblivious of pouring its full heart in profuse strains in waning warmth of ribs. Now I just pretend flying in the cockpit of a fragmented plane.

All of them translated from Bangla by
Dr Nitai Saha

Poems by Sudip Biswas

My Margarita

Thoughts will create your swing.Stand up, you forget, before my eyes. Play the venu close to the chest, play the venu away. Margarita came dressed in shame and fear. I hear this in the sky, what I see in my tears. One is the harmony, one is the pain. Only the good lasts forever. In the trembling chest, what do you know, it does not feel happy, can't understand the untied Greek pearl dreams.

Run Away

The mist of the old man incapable of perception. Protection of community rights, the Bhog Aarti Expectations of the princes right to Voting. Screams are heard Oh! Lord. You are close to sleep. Tied the racist to the sexist house. At the height of ruling axiom tied collapsed, Humanistic doubts in busy outlets! I am the kingmaker. Wilderness Make a difference, make an opportunity is my right. The ranks of the people made up of the labor force. The signal is black. Transcendence is the light of civilisation. A deed is not a document for escape. Join the organisation, brother. Hold the fisted hands. By taking away the right, however, the light on the haunted face, Wake up the silent Rajakini room, Shame must return to the deep roots of racism.

The Scrapes

The deer-neck accumulates the spirits of music. In search of memorandum, I grope in my pocket, The vowels are emerged in the heart of the Gitabitan. It also rollicking the Golden boat. Separation doesn't exist in the imperium of the Moon, Also cultivated domains persuade to preserve some personal scars in the lonely full-moon night.

Poems by Lipi Nasrin

I Kiss The Puffy Clouds All Around

The desire intertwines with the sun, as it meets the spadix of an arum flower. Delonix pollen fondles the hue of a cuckoo in yellowish light. Eternal spring is absorbed as it comes into contact with longitudinal bark. The dream magic's kiss causes the puffy clouds to flourish. Grasses create ornaments with a little touch. The flame-of-the-forest falls in love as it smears with the feathers of a dazzling golden shower that is awakening in the lap of noon. A bondmaid on mercury-coloured Mount Ida receives the golden robe of puffy clouds; terrified and humiliated, she snuggles close to the feudal lord and turns into a babbling gully. In the conference of tweeting birds, the touch-me-not swings to the vibrant shoots. Andromache then twirls her safron-streaked scarf while black pearls pour from her eyes. All of the frangipanis on earth awaken in rows as the honeycomb is bewitched by the waking leaves and spreads fragrant breath.

Midday Amidst Nothingness

As I wandered through the lifeless foliage, a sense of emptiness accompanied me. Above, as I passed by the uppermost leaf of a burflower tree, the void dangled from the cornice beneath the white clouds scented with mango blossoms. Uncertain of their sentiments, the nothingness entities brushed against the black mole on the partially exposed back of a woman, all while keeping pace with my footsteps. The gentle midday embellished the delicate leaves with glistening adornments. Not far away, the intertwining branches embraced the serenity of the hills cloaked in cascades of weathered leaves. In the sweltering sun, the sweet midday melodies resonated against the colourful walls, shrouded by coconut fronds. Leaning into the void, I encounter an unfamiliar face bearing your name. Afternoon descends into the void, transported by the swaying wings of egrets in formation. I feel submerged and captivated by an enigmatic presence. Like an arrow shattered by the force of a crashing wave, I easily succumbed to fragmentation.

During That Particular Night

My existence remained entirety undetectable that particular night. My present moment turned out to be nothing more than a dark bumblebee, lying on its back and aimlessly meandering, adding a night's tale to the vast expanse of the sky. The foliage had stripped away all hues, imprinting a watermark on the balcony, and only the fragrance of fresh green leaves graced the earth, ascending towards the sun and creating a sweet and desolate morning within the roofless loft of the house. Soon after, a chill from a distant epoch descended from the sacrosanct city of Illium. It was a time when a swarm of sheep grazed in the lowlands of the mountains, amidst fields that lay at the fingertips of a grand poet.

All of then translated from Bangla by
Gauranga Mohanta

Poems by Borche Panov

Essay of Uncertainty

My friend once told me that his wife was like a giant sleepy cat that purrs in the bed in the middle of the jungle in which she rules - fed up with his impatience to finish the books around him, in the moments in which he couldn't resist fantasising in the middle of the sentences. My wife suddenly told me that she had always known about my madness and that she could kill me on the fine line with the genius while I was telling her about how Ionesco had perceived the world in both: fascism and Marxism, but that the time today is like a fridge and then I gulped back my bite from the lunch abruptly having thought about the woman that had butchered her own husband and kept him in the fridge for a long time and also about her friend that had confessed her that she no longer had feelings for her husband and that all of that was like the habit. The habit that is a smelly monster, according to Block; as I said to her, and the love is just a hell of a center of all heart bumps - unexpected surrendering to the opposite wind against the destiny when Daniil Kharms, as well, is painfully near his final destination and with his last breath fed up with soil, asked God not to deprive him of the heavens' letters that are being inhaled instead of air in the Promised Land and what would I tell her now with the mouth of Kis about the writing down here from the edge of the despair where a town falls down, pushed by the sigh and stretches on the nerves with which, like a marionette, I write down on the snow a dream that types automatically on the keyboard because the true experience of the truth is the personal experience itself but the harsh Sylvia Platt is pressing my pupil's loop and tells me that I am me, too, but it is not enough, oh not enough to finish fantasising about the end of the sentence as a way of surviving therefore, I ask her how to be wise in the uncertainty in this two-faced world while God is continuously writing the dark book that I will never be able to read and I constantly pray and ask him to write something nice, as well, for which I could fantasize without knowing it. Without knowing it while I am reading the whole time, what has been written since the day that touches me blindly to recognize my madness just like Borges, that penetrates the labyrinth of the world with his fingers is stretching the nerves of the whole time so he could see what could never be seen when I am getting blind by the burst of the fraud on the edge of my eye nerve. Oh, dear God, let me finish my fantasy about the unknown in what has not been read yet and help me not to judge before I understand that the bone of the bad is after the bone of the good by getting undressed and I'm - still uncertain in front of the two-facet world of Tarkovsky and protected by the incompleteness of the knowledge, naively fantasizing that I could be killed by my wife's jokes one day, because it is really hard to live in a world with strict boundaries between the good and the evil in which Kundera, too, suffered in silence

Cat Times

We have been raised by altar bread. Our childhood was grapevines for us on which the young wine was ripening in our sky. We grew up in a time when we could buy fresh chickpea bread or we could visit the ivied summer cinema at night. We watched Tornatore's movies and we were kids with the kids from the movie. We didn't know what fascism was, we thought communism would last forever,
and we loved to play mobsters. Our favourite scene of all was when we were staffing the fat Ollie's mouth with hunks of white socialist bread, and he wasn't complaining about it because he was always hungry. On the summer provincial movie screen, America was Marilyn Monroe for us – Marilyn Monroe rising up into the Statue of Liberty. Under the wind of her little dress, she was revealing to us the colonization,
Mad Horse, Sitting Bull as he is acting himself and swearing in the circus that rises up to her panties
in which there is no place for the children of Cheyenne raised by their mothers so they could be killed as little shooting targets in the air. There wasn't a place for the civil war, too, nor for the prohibition, and the gangsters with automats, but there was a place for Chaplin's toothbrush mustaches
and his two fingers with which he blocks his ears to prevent the lion from awakening, for Buster Keaton's frozen face and the house that spins the storm, and he can't get through the door in any way,

and for Orson Welles' Martians with which he performed a radio invasion with the same fear as the fear of the Cold War. There is no place in Monroe's panties for the helicopters Flight of the Bumblebee in the apocalypse of napalm, nor for the underground hangars with intercontinental rockets, but there is a place for the Jedis from Star Wars that hold the torch of liberty with their thoughts in the middle of the darkness of the universe. We have been raised by altar bread, we have become Democrats, too, and we have spent nine cat lives so we could survive, but no one wants to remember the death between them. I was left only with the memories when my grandfather Carlo, the emigrant, returned from America with a black limousine and a blond girl, Marilyn Monroe, he said she was, and we were just kids, so we believed him without any questioning, because we recognized her for her panties when we stumbled on purpose and fell under her little dress.

Milk Of Mercy

A ragged and toothless old man and a young woman, like two rings of a chain, grey for centuries, hovering in an embrace of a breastfeeding woman and a martyr thirsty sucking from a breast full of milk – two rings, like two destinies – convicted twice, but why, amidst loud thoughts in concentric circles, they are swirling again, I hear an echo saying what a pitiable image of a shameless old man and an easy woman that entices and lures in a bizarre manner this is, and I wonder why nobody perceives it as an act of merciful love in which a young mother – a daughter or a granddaughter, with warm milk refused by a nursling, is fiercely struggling to keep a prisoner alive, sentenced to thirst and hunger in a prison cell, in darkness, in a gulag, a bastille or Treblinka of death and why, in the middle of that swirl that is contracting and sifting life and plucking everything, rarely would someone think that the painter the gentlest story in front of our eyes – behind our licentious pupils has painted for us like lips that are sucking thirsty the milk of mercy that each of us has innocently tasted at least once in a lifetime

Poems by Louise Whyburd

Surf the wave

When you realise that happiness is found within, that's when true freedom begins. It's not in the next destination, but here in the now, It's not found within another person, a material object, nor money, It's found within yourself.

The only limitations to happiness are the boundaries that are the prison of your own mind, so don't be your own life sentence. Seek the beauty in small things, the feel of fresh air softly blowing through your hair, listen to the infectious laughter of a child, take in the smell of fresh rain on a summer's day, embrace the smile from a passing stranger. Because when you take in the beauty of the small things that surround you, that's when your soul truly breathes.

Raise your consciousness to a higher frequency so high it raises others around you and spreads that feel good vibe. Say no with no explanation or guilt, forgive, learn and grow from past hurt and mistakes. Accept in order to have the smooth you have to ride the rough, because you can't stop the waves from coming, but it doesn't mean you can't learn to surf them and let them carry you to your next destination.

Embrace her

Lay down on the bare earth and let mother nature tell her story, for she is powerful, she will blind you with her glory. Take a deep breath in and smell her sweet scent, she will show you the way, she will help you repent. As your energies intertwine, they align, you lose track of time, nature of a true kind, frequencies like no other as you feel the sense of discover. Trust her calling, she will stop you from falling, listen to her energy calling. It's in the air, It's everywhere, It's in the earth, It's in the trees, It's in the water, for she is your mother and you are her daughter. Feel her vibrations, let them resonate, she'll take over your body like an earth quake. Open your mind, let her in, She is calling you, It's a feeling within. For she is a sense, she is a feeling, she is the embodiment of true healing. She is a nurturer, a soul healer, the essence of earth's luminescence. She is there as the sunrises, by your side as the sunsets, let her power your body, she will never forget. Trust her love, trust her power, take her in like a gift sent from above. For she is there and she is healing, you just sense it; it's a feeling. Trust her judgement, for she is wise and she will protect you from birth through to your demise.

My Kryptonite

I'm not wearing a cape I'm wearing regular clothes, you chose to break me and a live in the lows. I was smiling through the bad times, but it was all just for show, saving my tears, because behind closed doors they flowed. I was a super woman, but I was not 'Super Woman', I was trapped in a prison, lost in a labyrinth of your lies that were hidden. What started off as a fairy tale of love ended as a dark story with lessons sent from my above. The charm and love you once showed me, was soon to be short-lived, once your masked dropped, my heart soon stopped. Our friendship returned into romance, I gave my heart a chance, but the words that once built me up, turned in to words of self-destruct. The softness you once showed, the tenderness, the affection, this was all just a show to lead me in a false direction. You left me confused, wondering "what did I do wrong?," when all a long it was 'you' that was not strong. Your mind was weak, stuck in your own prison, yet the way you treated me was your own decision. You carried your demons from childhood, came into my life like Robin Hood, you told me you were misunderstood but in reality you were not good. Your evil ways are now etched deep, like a hot poker brandished, but I was never yours to keep. You were my Kryptonite, but with you around I could not take flight, because you were a Villain, a fruit that should have been forbidden. I took a bite, at first it was sweet and delicious, but in reality the core was rotten and fictitious. You clipped my wings, but I still chose to fly, because I would not allow your abuse to drive my soul to wither and die. So I put on my cape and I chose to escape because I am a strong women and I know others can relate.

Part Five

Short Stories

Premendra Mitra

The Discovery of Telenapota

Saturn and Mars are the obstacles, and if there is contact, it is also likely that Telenapota will be discovered one day. Then you can find that if you suddenly take two days off from work after being swamped with people. This is if someone comes and says i t is the largest lake in the world. Despite their plain nature, fish are still eager to strike the heart at the first whiff of their water life. Unless you've never pulled anything but a few beads from the water, you may be surprised to find oil palms one day.

To discover Telenapota, you must get on a bus full of things and people one afternoon. Eventually, you will have a sticky body covered in sweat after walking for a couple of hours in Bhadra's intense heat—a sudden change. Even though the sun hasn't yet set, you will notice that the dense forest has become dark after the bus passes over a swamp-like area in front and disappears on the side of the road. In any direction, you won't see any people. The birds have departed. During this time, you will experience wet and humid weather. As the invisible hood slowly rose from the swamp below, a small crew of coiled water curses pulled it up slowly. The water pond is off the main road, so you must get off it and stand near it. It appears that someone has cut a muddy channel through the dense forest ahead. Also, this canal-like line travelled some distance before getting lost in bamboo groves and scrubby trees.

To explore Telenapota, you should be accompanied by two other friends. Although they may enjoy fishing less than you, they chose this expedition in Kezan over any other. As the three of them approach the stream, they eagerly anticipate it. When you read this, try to avoid being too close to the mosquito and stare at his face with a questioning expression.

Their faces were no longer visible in the thick darkness after a while. There will be an increase in the number of mosquitoes in unity. You will hear a fantastic sound from where the mud drain is hidden in the forest while deciding whether to take the bus back up the main road. In the forest, it seems as if someone is crying out inhumanely. You will be ready to wait as soon as you hear that word. If you fail to stay, it won't happen. A flicker of light will appear in the dark world, and then a dark car will emerge from the jungle in a slow oscillating motion. A car is a car. It looks like it came from dwarf land in the underworld, this miniature version of [1]Garu's car.

They will somehow find their way into the six cars without wasting words. They will solve the problem in the place where the three arms, legs, and heads can be placed most materially. The bullock cart will start moving back the way it came, either on the road or in the canal. It will surprise you that the dense dark forest is slowly revealing the path. At times it seems that the wall of black and darkness is impenetrable. However, a bullock cart moves steadily and slowly as if the way was spread by foot.

There is a reasonable chance that, for a while, you will be disturbed by the possibility of disruptions to the appropriate resources of the hands, feet, and head. Unintentional clashes occasionally occur between friends, but you'll learn to deal with them. In the darkness of the surrounding environment, even the inner part of consciousness is submerged. It has left the known world somewhere far away. In your surroundings, there is a fog of emotionlessness. There is no current time, only static time.

Time is frozen, so you can't tell how long this obsession will last. I awoke suddenly to a bell. Stars appeared in the sky, and a canes tart played on the coach. If you are curious about why, the guard will tell you quite calmly, Sir, the man has to dig the tiger. As you raise the question in a trembling voice, whether it is possible to drive the tiger away by the tin pot! the guard will assure you that a tiger is just a leopard. Its café's given nickname sets it apart unless it is entirely benign. How is it possible for a place like Leopard home to exist only thirty miles from the metropolis?

By the time you think about it, a bullock cart will cross a vast field. In the sky, the decaying moon of action has appeared. Due to the dim light, all the guards slowly moved on either side of the car. Ancient ruins - pillars, archways, fragments of temples - stand in vain as a testimony to the greatness of ancient times. In that situation, you will feel a tingling in your whole body by sitting with your head as high as possible. It will be thought that you have come beyond the living world into some vague memory of the past. You don't know how long the night is, but it seems like the night here never ends—intensive immortality. The museum is full of animal bodies imbued with eternal stillness. It is like being in an Ark.

The bullock cart will stop after turning two or three times. After collecting arms and legs from various places, you will come down one by one like a wooden doll. A sweet smell has been welcoming you for a long time. You will understand that it is the rotten smell of the pond. In the light of the crescent moon, a small pond can be seen in front. A colossal building stands as a fortress next to the newly renovated building with broken roofs, crumbling walls, and windowless windows like an eyeless hollow in a tree.

In these ruins, you will have to find a reasonably habitable room to stay in. The driver will bring a broken lantern to the house and put it inside, along with one pitcher of water. Entering the house, you will realise that after many ages, you are the first to join as a representative of the human race. Maybe someone has tried unsuccessfully to clean the house's dung, dirt, and dust. That the spirit possessing the house is angry with it will be evidenced by a faint musty smell. At the slightest movement, worn-out debris from the roof and walls will rain down on you like the curse of that rotten soul. Two or three bats will fight with you all night about the right of the house.

To discover Telenapota, you need a friend. One of your two friends is an alcoholic, and the other is a sleepwalker. On entering the house, some centipede was covering the floor. One would spread himself over it to snort; the other would fall. Immerse yourself in the beaker. The night will grow. The glass chimney of the broken lamp became darker and darker, gradually fading away. Upon hearing a mysterious radio signal, he sent all the able-bodied mosquitoes to the newcomers. Welcome them to the listening table. Congratulate them and establish listening relationships with them. Discreetly hang it on the wall. It is the giant mosquito and the unique vehicle of the goddess Malaria Anopheles.

Both of your friends are unconscious for two reasons. Step out of bed slowly, then use the torch to get some relief from the heat. You can reach the upper roof by climbing the broken stairs with your hands. Every time a brick or tile falls somewhere, trying to keep you from falling, you cannot rise above all evil attractions. There is a lot of broken and dusty roofing, as you can see if you climb up on the roof. However, in light of the weakest part of the moon, everything will appear magnificent as we demolish the building from the inside. If you look for a while, you will find that Susupti Manna is imprisoned in a secret cell of Mayapuri, unconscious in the dark slumber of Yugant, next to the wand of gold. A faint line of light appeared in a window across the narrow road far from the rubble pile. There will be a mysterious figure hiding behind the line of light. In the dark of the night, you will wonder who this shifter is and why he does not sleep. You will try to think, but nothing will make sense to you. At least it will appear that everything is an illusion created by your eyes. There is no shadow on the bed, and the faint light line is not there. Then you will return to birth, and sometimes you will share a small space with two friends. You will not know if you will fall asleep. When you wake up, you will be surprised to see that even in this land of night, it is morning, with the chirping of birds heard all around.

It would be best if you did not forget your true purpose. At one point, circumcision was performed sitting on the edge of a broken river covered in moss for fish worship and drinking green water. The fishing spear and appropriate offerings should be brought down. The time will increase. A kingfisher sang from the tip of a bamboo tree lying over there. To make fun of you, it will jump into the pond with a flash of colour in the air. It will return to the bamboo tip in the joy of a successful hunt and taunt you in unintelligible language. Terrifying you, a giant snake slithers from a crack in the broken gorge. He swam across the pond at speed like thin glass laced with sharp edges. A bird will wave at you and try to sit on your bed, and you will be bored, calling the dove. Be calm.

Then suddenly, the sound of water will break your surprise. There were ripples in the frozen water, and your fishing spear swayed gently. Looking back, you will see a girl with a shiny brass urn. The waves remove the pond leaves, and the water fills up. There is curiosity in the girl's eyes but no awkwardness in her movements. She looks at you straight on, notices your fishing spear, and then turns away before lifting the pot to her waist. You don't know how old the girl is. Her face is stern and sorrowful. She has survived a long and cruel life. Her long, thin, malnourished body looks like that of a teenager. It is as if she has been suspended from crossing over to adulthood.

When the girl looks back as she leaves with the urn, she asks,

"Why are you sitting here?" Pull it."

As the voice is so sweet and solemn that it is close to the voice of a familiar person, speaking to a stranger in this way will not be unusual. Due to the shock of sudden surprise, you will forget to pull the fishing spear. When the sunken fatna floats back up, you will see no more bait in the fishing spear. You have to look at the girl a little unprepared. She also turned away and calmed down. But it seems that at the moment when she turned her face, a glimpse of a bright smile played on that sad face.

The solitude of the riverbank will not be broken again. A kingfisher tried to humiliate you, but her innocent gesture has long since failed. Fish have a profound contempt for your strength and will not want to compete a second time. What happened a while ago will seem unreal to you. There is such a girl somewhere in this land of uninhibited sleep. You can't believe it.

At some point, you have to get up and get frustrated. You may go back and see how your fishing craft resume has already become your friends' conductor. Infuriated by their mockery, where did they find this story? Your drunkard should listen to a friend who will repeat it! Jamini saw this with her own eyes. Obviously, you are curious and would like to know who Jamini is. Then you may discover that the unreal cute girl at the riverbank is your alcoholic friend's acquaintance. At the same time, you will also hear that lunch is provided for them every day. In the ruins of a colossal building, where last night a shadow statue was the source of your wonder, the day will come when its wear and tear in old age will significantly affect you. The veil of night is lifted, and he is naked. You couldn't imagine that the ruins could become so decrepit.

You will be surprised to know that this is the house of Jaminis. You may have a room in this house where food has been arranged. It appears to be a modest arrangement, perhaps serving Jamini herself. You have already noticed there is no unnecessary shyness or awkwardness in the girl's facial expression. However, up close, only the pitiful seriousness of her face will be more apparent to you. Her face was shadowed by the silent pain that came from a world abandoned, forgotten, and uninhabited. Her gaze is still filled with fatigue even after she has seen everything. One day she will slowly disappear into this pile of rubble.

Even though she served you two or four times, she still got restless and anxious at times. A faint voice could be heard from an upstairs room. The shadow of pain on Jamini's face seemed to deepen with each return, along with helpless restlessness in her eyes.

After eating, you can rest for a while. Monida, listen here; someone desperately calls out from the door several times in the end. Monida is your drinking friend. The conversation that takes place after he stands at the door is not so low that you cannot hear it.

"Listen carefully," Jamini says in a very bitter voice. *"Mother is not listening to her at all. What can I say? She becomes restless until she hears that you guys are coming here."*

Moni will say in a slightly annoyed tone, *"Oh, that care is still there! Niranjan has come, do you think? Yes, just saying he must have come. Just shy of meeting me, I know. Call him. Why are you hiding from me?"* I can't think of what to do. Since becoming blind, she has become so impatient these days that she doesn't understand anything.

"Yes, it is very difficult. Even if I had eyes, I would have shown it to those who came. No one is Niranjan." Now you will also hear the call of a weak but sharp cross voice from above. Jamini said in a bitter voice, *"Come on, Monida, explain and cool down a little."*

"Well, you go; I'm coming." Mani will now enter the house and think to himself, *"This is a pretty big burden, but that is what it is. The old woman's arms and legs*

have fallen off, and her eyes are gone, but still, the old woman is sitting on the bed and will not die."

You might be wondering what's going on. In a tone of irritation, Mani says, *"What's the matter? During their childhood, Niranjan was the son of one of her long-distance friends, with whom she fixed Jamini's wedding relationship. Four years ago, that boy came and told her he would return from abroad, where he was working, and he would definitely marry her daughter. Since then, the old woman has been counting the days in this hope."*

You cannot hold back your curiosity, so ask: *"Does Niranjan still live overseas? He hasn't come back yet!"*

Moni replied, "He never flew abroad. Since the old lady is so stubborn, he makes a false statement to her daughter so he does not have to marry such a stubborn girl. He is already married to another woman. And make a family. But who will tell that to the old lady? She would not believe it. If that's the case, she will die immediately. Who will be responsible for committing such a sin?"

You asked: "Does Jamini know about Niranjan?"

"No, she is not aware of it. However, there is no way to tell her mother. Let's get the job done." Moni said as he stepped toward the stairs. At that moment, you have to stand up unconsciously. You might suddenly say, *"Let's go too." "You want to join!"* Moni will stand back and look at you in surprise. You reply, *"Yes. Have any objections?"*

"No objection," Moni said, and he will guide you in an extraordinary way. The room is reached by a narrow dark staircase that appears underground, not above ground.

An unopened window, also closed, makes everything appear blurry in your eyes until you realise that almost everything around you is falling apart; a thin skeletal figure is lying on a wooden bed. Jamini stood like a stone statue on one side of a wooden bed. They all seemed frozen after hearing your footsteps, including the old lady.

Translated from Bangla by Haimanty Chowdhury

[1]Garu's car - Bullock Cart

Syed Shamsul Haq

If We Met at Gabtoli

Gabtoli—an intercity bus terminal by the bank of river Turag in the west of Dhaka. A bustling hub—hundreds of long-distance buses are coming, going, or waiting. Vehicles are crammed with passengers, and conductors howl bewildered passengers to get on their vehicles. A great hullabaloo! The road was packed with rikshaws, motorcars, and vans. And in between, vendors, crippled beggars, and urchins are hawking their business.

The situation worsens when a Qurbani haat sets up nearby. With an erratic crowd, insane traffic, and startled animals fearing imminent slaughter, the place becomes unbearable.

But I enjoy it.

Whenever I come to this place, I get charged up. My friend owns a small eatery here. He sells rice and curry. I love to laze around here.

Most of the time, I sit outside the eatery with a chair. I watch people move. I watch their lives. That way, I get to witness many incidents. Many accidents too. Once, I saw a person almost getting under the wheels of a bus. My heart skipped a beat. I leaped up at once. Yes, it was me who saved her.

She was a new bride. She was draped in a cheap glossy red sari. The sari had golden floral embroidery all over. The bridegroom was next to her. They were crossing the road holding hands. The glittering sari caught my attention. They walked past me. A bus suddenly took a turn. The bridegroom jumped across the road. The wife looked flabbergasted. The bus was about to run her over. I rushed to the spot and pulled her aside. She survived.

Did she look at me with kindness in her eyes?

Well, as soon I pulled her to safety, she looked at me with reproach. The bridegroom was back by then; he glared at me. And then, the two of them hurried away, crossing the road.

She must have been a wife who couldn't imagine anyone but her husband touching her; she was surely startled, and hence she glared at me.

My restaurateur friend tells me, "I have seen such things so many times. Human life is very unpredictable. No one knows when the soul might fly away."

He continues, "Have you noticed that there are some beggars who sing and beg in the bus terminals, ferries, or railway stations? What kind of songs do they sing? Folk, spiritual. *Life is but a moment. God is summoning me.*

Do you know what I think—when people set off for a voyage, they harbor a strange feeling. They ponder over the great journey of life. It's a journey, indeed—from birth to death consisting of love, hate, infatuation, resentment, reconciliation."

My friend's name is Momin. He's from Old Dhaka. He has felt the rattle of the city's rise and fall in his blood for generations. Though he is a college dropout and I'm a university graduate, we get along very well. He, too, enjoys my company, and together, we contemplate life.

Momin says, "Since you write stories, why don't you bring out a book? If you need subjects, you'll get plenty of them at this terminal."

"Whether I find stories or not, just sitting here makes my day," I reply. "Where else would I get to see so many strange, unknown people?"

Momin encourages me. "You write such good stories. The world opens up before our eyes with such stories. Keep writing. Write more and more."

Momin's words flatter me. Do I really write well?

But yes, if Nila tried her hand at writing, she would be a better writer than me. She was such a good storyteller; you wouldn't want to stop her when she spoke. Time would pass by unnoticed. When I listened to her, I stared at her without blinking.

We were in love then. Nila had just started university. I was in my final year. She came from Jaleswari, and so did I. A connection united us immediately. She'd talk about Jaleswari all the time, and so would I. As we chatted about our hometown, we got closer, and Nila began to hold on to me, and I held on to her too.

It was here, at Gabtoli, when Nila first came on an overnight bus. She reached here at dawn.

"Sadhu, if we met each other back then, if we knew each other, then would you come to receive me? Would you take me to my uncle's house? Would you give me a ride?"

Nila called me Sadhu. It's my nickname. And I started wearing a blue sapphire ring for as long as I can remember. It is not a real stone, though. It's just a fake blue glass. But my love is not fake.

It was around this time that Nila first showed her mastery of storytelling. "It was dawn. I can still remember," she began. "the morning was shrouded in fog. The city looked like a pencil sketch. A few tall buildings soared high. People were wrapped in blue, red, and green shawls. The yellow lights of buses and trucks weaved through the foggy morning. Like yellow flowery dots on a grey bedspread. My bus reached the terminal. Passengers began to get off. A lot of people came to receive them. There was no one to pick me up. They were my distant uncles. I had yet to get a room in the dorm. Until then, I had to stay with my uncles, an arrangement made by my father. Would they come for me this winter morning? I looked for a baby taxi. I couldn't find one. I had no idea where this place, Shukrabaad, was or how far it was. If you were there, you'd have come. Wouldn't you? No matter how foggy it was, I'd have noticed your sparkling eyes. You would be standing there. As soon as the bus stopped, you would come to the door. You'd offer me your hand. I had already spotted you through the window. I wanted to hold your hand, but I felt shy. I'd look into your eyes as I get off the bus. Oh! My God! You had already hired a baby taxi; it was waiting on the sidewalk. You would help me cross the road. You would drag my huge suitcase across the road. Putting it on the footboard of the taxi, you'd say, 'You seemed to have brought the entire household. I'd reply, we'll have our own household one day. Won't we? Yes, of course,' you'd say with a smile. I wanted to prattle on in utter joy. But I stayed quiet. I gave a closed-mouth smile instead. You'd hold my hand. And the foggy town would turn into a bridal night. "If only you were there. Sadhu, if only you had come to Gabtoli that day."

I, too, get immersed in storytelling; I start to narrate. "If we met at Gabtoli," I said. "No, not when you came to study at the university. Not then, but when you were younger. You were ten or eleven years old then. Your father was transferred to Dhaka. When he finally got a quarter to live, he brought his family. You and your mother and your two younger brothers. I was probably living in Mirpur, Mazar road, then. I went to a restaurant in Gabtoli for breakfast. I was having a paratha. I was looking up every now and then—a bus stopped, then another one and passengers began to get off. It was a sunny day. The golden hue spread on the road. It was there, in that golden hue, you put your first step."

"What? I was a little girl then. Not so pretty, either. I was small."

"I saw a glow in the crowd?"

"A glow? Where?"

"In your eyes. The sleepy passengers were getting off the bus one by one. Puffy eyes. Unsteady steps. Untidy clothes. It was you, your mother, your two brothers, and your father. You were the last one to come out. Everyone looked tired after a sleepless voyage. You were different, though. Your eyes were shimmering as if you would see the entire city at one go with the light in your eyes. They were full of wonders."

"What a story you cook up! Did you notice my eyes? Or the hat? I got off the bus wearing a fiber hat."

"Yes, I remember. It was the hat that caught my attention. I forgot to put food into my mouth and kept staring at you. Momin startled me. "Finish your breakfast. Your paratha is getting cold."

Nila interrupts me, "No. Areh! Momin bhai didn't own a restaurant back then."

"Oh, yes. That's true. Momin was working in his father's fruit shop in Babubazar at that time."

Didn't I tell you? You can't just weave a story to Nila; it cannot be surreal only; it must touch reality. Like a white duck touching its wings on the water as it flies away.

"If we met that day," I continued. "If I were there that morning, I'd have approached you and said, 'Hello.' I'd have stretched my hand for a handshake and asked whether you were a Bengali or a foreigner. You replied, 'What do you think?' I would say to myself, Bah, what a smart girl. She looks like a small-town girl, but when she speaks, it seems she is not from this country. I said, 'I thought you were Spanish, a girl from Spain.' Surprised, you asked, 'Why Spain? I am a dark-skinned girl. Everyone is fair there.' I replied, 'They also have dark-skinned people. They have black hair too. The Arabs stayed in Spain for nearly seven hundred years; the lineage continues even today. Their girls look like us. Exactly like you.' Nila, you were so happy to hear this. A car from your father's office came to take you all home. You said happily, why don't you come with us?"

"And you were such a good boy; you didn't wait for a second to leap into the car,"

"Yes, I took the front seat. And you all huddled together at the back. I couldn't turn back to see you. I was a gentleman, you see."

"Ah!"

"But you smelled so good; I did get that. And you talked with my father in such a sweet voice. Where is the house? How far is it? What do the rooms look like? My heart flew around you like a bee. I fell in love with you the moment I saw you."

Nila protested, "No, not yet. Later. Much later. Not until I turned twenty-two. I was only eleven then."

"So, what? In Tagore's story *Postmaster*, the girl, Ratan, was exactly your age. Didn't she fall in love with the postmaster?"

"What do you mean? It was I and not you? I would fall in love with you at first sight."

"No, you wouldn't; I'd have made you fall in love with me," I said.

"At that age?"

"Yes, you see, even though my name is Sadhu, I am not that *Shadhu* at all!"

"Don't be so naughty! You are *sadhu*, *sadhu* and *sadhu*. How lucky I am!"

I loved it when Nila praised me. But I pretended not to like it. I shut her off with a gesture of my hand. "If I were so naive, would I have spotted you when you got off the bus? Would I notice a girl with eyes full of wonder and curiosity? I was so impressed. This is the girl! The first time I saw you in Gabtoli, I immediately knew my whole life was intertwined with yours."

Nila could weave stories far better than I did. "Back then, you would often come to our place," she said. "We had a huge rooftop. I made a garden with flowerpots there. One day, a rose blossomed on a pot. I wanted to show you the garden. As soon as we went to the roof, you plucked the rose and gave it to me. I was so angry. *Did you just pluck my flower?* You got nervous. Seeing your reaction, I burst into laughter. You got more agitated seeing me laugh. Weren't you dying to kiss me then? And you did too. No, it was not then. That came later, much later. You came to our house one afternoon. My parents were in my uncle's house. There was some programme. Someone's birthday, probably. I didn't go. I was slightly feverish. In fact, I had a feeling that you might come. You might put your hand on my forehead. And my temperature would go down. I was precocious even at that age. I knew about kissing. I knew such things happen. And then you really came. And you truly put your hand on my forehead. You were so eager to kiss me. Weren't you? It didn't matter that I was young. I was the young girl Ratan in *Postmaster*. You were not that old, either. You were only eighteen. Weren't you? You had back-brushed your hair. You wore a lemon green T-shirt. You were wearing jeans and sports shoes with white and blue stripes. Your eyes were sparkling as if you were not seeing me but a sea. A vast blue sea with stars shining on it. So what if the sea doesn't look blue at night? No harm in imagining! The stars scattered on the water were like a stone-studded blue scarf. You and I were there, by the seaside. We were at Cox's Bazar. We just got married. I was a new bride. We were walking on the wet sand. The waves pounded on the shore. And the sounds of waves sounded like your voice. You were reciting a poem. In fact, I fell in love with you when I was only eleven years old after hearing your recitation. You know, it was poetry that brought us together. I loved to recite poems too. But I felt shy in front of you. You helped me to get past my shyness. First, with poetry. And then with my body. Weren't you being a bit too naughty that day? You kissed me, and I was numbed. In those days, I had the notion that if you kissed, you became husband and wife. And since then, you have become my groom."

Nila's story captivated me; I added to the story, "If we met at Gabtoli back then, I wouldn't have to wait so long. I wouldn't have to wait for you to come to study in Dhaka. I wouldn't have to wait for the day when you pointed at a tree in the university and said, '*I had the exact same tree in front of our house in Jaleswari.*' No one seemed to know the name of the tree. Not a single girl in the class. None of the boys either."

"Is it an Arjun tree?" I asked. You were shocked. Instead of answering, you stared at me. I wondered what was wrong.

You asked, "Did you say Jaleswari? Are you from Jaleswari?" I said, "Yes." I never thought anyone would know the name of such a small town in a faraway district like Rangpur. You surprised me. You said you were from Jaleswari too. You wanted to know where my house was. Ours was Khondoker's house, next to the post office. You said your house was across the river in

Harishal. I said I went to Harishal once in my childhood. I went there to celebrate Eid at my grandmother's house. It felt as if we'd known each other forever. We bonded immediately.

"Ah! If we had met earlier, you would be in my arms for a much longer period," I said. "If we had met in Gabtoli when you were only eleven years old. Or even if I could meet you on any of those times when you came to Gabtoli by an overnight bus from Jaleswari. Suppose you were in your second year. Your father got paralyzed. Your family was finding it hard to get by. There had always been a shortage of money. Your mother could no longer send you money. You were returning from home; you got down at Gabtoli. You were thinking this was probably the last time you stepped into Dhaka. You thought you wouldn't be able to continue your studies. You had to go back to Jaleswari. What if we met at that time? I used to go to Gabtoli every day then to have breakfast in Momin's restaurant."

Squinting her eyes, Nila asked, "Did Momin bhai have a restaurant then? No, I don't think so. You went to some other place. I was getting off the bus. You saw me. You wondered why the girl looked so sad. It was not tiredness. It was something else. You found me struggling with my bag. You approached me, "Miss, can I help you?" I handed the bag to you without any hesitation. You walked with me and asked, "Where is your house? Where will you go?" I said, "Shamsunnahar Hall."

You asked, "Should I get you a taxi?"

I said, "No, the bus would be fine." You came up with an idea and said,

"Ah, it will be on my way. I will take a taxi. Why don't you come with me? I can give you a ride." I thought for a while, but you didn't even notice. "You fell in love with me at first sight. Didn't you?"

You called a taxi, put my bag on the footboard, and gestured for me to get in. I got into the taxi like an obedient girl. You were so kind. I was touched. You somehow realised that I didn't want to take the taxi because I wanted to save money. You were so understanding."

I told you, "You don't look like not someone who would give up their studies so easily." Your friend Shaila advised you to do tuition to meet the expenses for your studies. Where would you find tuition? Who would give you one? It seemed impossible. You had another friend called Lovely, a frivolous character. She said, 'You are so pretty. Why don't you allure someone into a relationship? Either marry him or leech him. If needed, sleep with him.' You were shocked. Lovely went on, 'What matters is your studies; it doesn't matter how you get the money. Let it come. You need the money. If you want, I can find a man for you. I know an old haggard. He has been after me for some time. This guy has a nest of beards, and he sneers. What do you say? Should I fix him for you?' How disgusting! You felt repulsed. Use a man for money! You were not that type of girl. You were honest and stubborn. You chose the option of doing tuitions."

Nila continued to narrate. "Suppose I had one tuition at Shewrapara in Mirpur and one at Siddheswari. I barely manage with the money I get. I go to Siddheswari after my class in the afternoon. Then, I walk to the crossing to take a bus, which I change again to go to Shewrapara. I return late at night. I am famished. Couldn't I buy some food on the way? No, I had to save every penny. The houses I went to served only tea. I drank only tea. It hurt the stomach. If you were there, if we met at Gabtoli when I was only eleven years old, or even if we didn't meet, then if we could meet when I came to study at the university. You would live nearby so that we could easily meet. You could wait for me at Shahbag and see me getting off the Mirpur bus after I finish my tuition. My eyes, too, would have searched for you as soon as I reached Hotel Sheraton. There you were, standing at the corner of the hospital. I'd get off the bus. You'd walk to me. Without saying a word, you would take me to a restaurant in Aziz Supermarket. You would order whatever I fancied. I was so hungry. You would keep staring at me. Girls usually feel embarrassed if someone watches them eating. But I hardly cared. What mattered was my hunger. My hunger and my stubbornness. I was stubborn to finish my studies. I was determined to do something worthwhile in my life. And you were there to treat me. You were not like that friend of Lovely who would want nothing but sex. I felt I could rely on you. I felt that there was someone for me."

My heart aches. If only we had met. If we truly met. I wouldn't have let you suffer so much. Suppose we already met and fell in love. Or maybe, we were just friends. By that time, I had finished my degree in Journalism and joined The Daily Star. I was earning well. I stayed with a couple of friends. Sometimes we threw parties. We spent quite a fortune on alcohol. My friends asked me to buy drinks since I was earning more while they brought food. Ah, I could have saved all the money. I wouldn't have touched a single bottle. I could have saved all the money for you, Nila. I wouldn't let you tutor two students. You wouldn't have to change the bus twice to go to Mirpur from Siddheswari. You wouldn't have to get off the bus in Shahbagh. And walk all the way to your dorm. I wouldn't let you go through any of those hardships. Wasn't I there? Didn't I have money? I was there. And I had money. But I didn't know you. Why didn't we meet? Why is God so cruel, Nila? You suffered so much; I could do nothing for you.

I couldn't even save you. My elder sister called me from Jaleswari. "A girl from our neighborhood is going to Dhaka. A smart, stubborn girl. She has just finished her studies. She came to Jaleswari for a few days. She has got a job in United Nations. She is very pretty, like a princess. Her name is Nila. Go and meet her. You might like her. I think it's time you settle down now. That's why I am asking you to meet her at Gabtoli."

I did go to receive her. I did meet her in Gabtoli. It was our very first meeting. And it was love at first sight too. But it was in Gabtoli. It was a foggy morning; after spending her Qurbani holidays at home, Nila came to Gabtoli; as she was getting off a bus, there she was; she put her foot across the road—a huge bus took a sudden turn. On that foggy morning, it took me a long time to reach Gabtoli.

My friend, Momin, says, "The journey of life and the journey on the road are not the same, Sadhu. No one knows when and where in which desolate place that crazy chauffeur of the sky would suddenly drop a passenger.

Translated By Marzia Rahman

Ashraf-ul Alam Shikder

The Alley Next to Gafur's Two-Story Building

I Gafur took two hundred takas from his wife and went to have his hair trimmed. Chan Mi's Hotel is located next to Tapan's Salon. The hotel is full of customers having breakfast this winter morning. Tapan is yet to open his salon. Police vehicles and officers can be seen scanning the three-way crossroad. Gafur's head will itch terribly if he does not trim his hair once a month. Gafur cashed out his monthly pension money and handed it to Maryam for household expenses, itching his head and adding, "Give me some money tomorrow morning; I'll go have my hair trimmed."

Maryam, his wife, was counting the money with spit from her tongue. "How many times have I told you not to count money with spit?" Gafur said mockingly.

"How much does it cost to cut hair?" Maryam questioned, skipping the words.
 "This is only a hundred, but I owe Abdul's store eighty-two taka."
"Hasn't the doctor warned you not to smoke?" screamed Maryam.
"Abdul's tea store is here. I didn't smoke; I drank tea and ate biscuits."

"I implore you; please don't smoke cigarette-bidi; there are already two rings implanted in your heart; if it hurts again, it can't be cured!" Maryam pleaded as she handed Gafur two hundred taka notes.

Gafur walked out in his official clothing to cut his hair at about 7:30 a.m., taking two notes into his pocket. It was at this time, even nine months ago, that he used to leave home for the office. It became his habit as he went to the office for fifty-two years till retirement. He believes that now is the appropriate moment to leave the residence. On such days, he would buy a cigarette at Sagir's shop and walk right up to Rajarbagh.

He debt Abdul's tea shop twelve takas, which he may pay later. He lit a cigarette and began heading toward Tapan's salon after paying the forty-two taka owed at Sagir's store. He remembered what Maryam said the night before. It was as though the words "If it hurts now, it can't be rescued!" resonated loudly in his ears. Gafur took a deep breath and thought to himself, "Who wants to live now?"

Tapan hasn't even opened the saloon yet. The scent of Nehari from Chan Mia's hotel fills the crossroads of three roads on this winter's morning. The heat from the hotel's tandoor appears to be warming the surrounding area. Two or four cops are wandering around their vehicles. It appeared to be less packed than on previous mornings. A tall-looking cop was spotted entering Chan Mia's hotel. It was not understood whether Gafur rushed to the hotel because of his interest in the news or because of the smell of the food. Gafur has been in this locality for twenty-five years. First, he lived after marriage in a rented house; then, for the last seven years, he built a two-room tin shed house after buying a three-katas plot. Now there is a two-story house on a bank loan. After allotting two floors to their two sons, the two elderly couples lived in two rooms upstairs. It cannot be considered a three-story building. The big emphasis can be said to be two-and-a-half-story. Yet it is two-storied in government documents. Two or three servers appeared swiftly in front of the police officer. Gafur is likewise keen to investigate them. Khabir, an older waiter, approached Gafur and inquired, "Would you want breakfast, sir?" Gafur didn't even pay attention. "hum," he said. "Today's leg bone soup is excellently made. Could I please bring you a bowl of soup with tandoori roti?" Gafur can't pay attention to anything else but instead understands the interests of the police. In order to say it in a different way, he said, "Don't bring rotis; not rotis; give me two parathas after seeing it swelling. Khabir, tell me what happened here. What's the deal with the cops walking around?" "Do you not know what's going on, sir? Fourteen maunds of onions had been discovered in one of the houses on the path leading to Sagir's residence." "Fourteen maunds of onions!" cried Gafur. He is aware that onions are in short supply throughout the country this year. Gafur was in government service; he used to take daily newspapers all his life at home. Now that he is a retired man, the morning paper reaches his hand around noon. Then he gets busy with the newspapers for the rest of the day. As he read yesterday, "Onion is being sold in the open market at Rangpur for Tk 250 per kg. And the rural market is selling at a rate of 280 takas. This instability has been going on in the country's onion market ever since neighboring country India stopped exporting onions. The abnormal price hike of onions has created intense anger and frustration among consumers. Buyers are concerned that the price of onions will soon reach 300 takas. Khabir pointed to a vacant table and stated, "Please have a seat, sir. I'll bring soup and parathas." "O yeah, a paya, a paya, and two parathas hot, quick," he said to someone in the air. Khabir became a part of the hotel's bustle. Gafur keeps attention on the officer's concern. "A cup of tea, very little sugar," the man ordered, pulling up a chair and sitting down. Tea was immediately brought to his table. Gafur got out of his chair and sat in the chair in front of the cop. "Sir, I am a retired government servant." The cop took a loud gulp from his hot tea and extended his hand for a handshake. Gafur inquires once more, "In which home was it discovered?" "Can you tell me where your residence is?" "The home next door to the first four buildings on Khanka Bari Lane is not far away." "Rent?" "No, sir, no, with your blessing, I have been at my own home for the last seven years." "Well, that's the home next to you at the end of Sagir's Alley." "Sir, did you mean Mr. Jabbar's house? "Sir, on which floors?" "There was a girl model living in a rental on the fourth floor." Gafur expressed amazement and stated, "Model? Girl? Fourteen maund of onions! Oh my god, why did the model start up a stocking business?" The officer was taken aback: "Fourteen maunds of onions?" "More?" Gafur said, yawning. "What are you on about, gentleman? There are so many of us here for onions..."

"Then?" Gafur said again. "Hey, buddy, fourteen hundred yaba pills have been seized!" "What! Fourteen hundred pieces of yaba? "Whichever one?" "On the fourth floor of Mr. Jabbar's building," "The model girl named Nasreen resided on the fourth floor of Mr. Jabbar's building; aren't you talking about her?" Gafur nodded. The officer's excitement had increased a hundredfold. "Do you know who she is?" "Yes, I have been living in this neighborhood for the last twenty-five years today. owning a house here, and I will not recognize the neighbors!" "Alright, good. Then join us; you must go to the police station." "But I have some job to do here," Gafur answered calmly. With a gruff, police-like tone, the gentleman said, "What's the problem? You must do everything in five minutes, and you will be required to accompany us to the police station. We hadn't even apprehended the lady yet." II Persons in government services recognize that the walls have ears as well. Because it doesn't take long for anyone in the office to reach the ears of someone else. This time, it turns out, the norms of society are as well. Rather, the wind in the air can be considered to have ears. Whoever needs it raises it to their own ears and passes it forward. Maryam went down to the grocery store, and the news was drifting in the air. Maryam dashed to home without pausing. Raha bin Gafur, their oldest son, is a chartered accountant. He had not yet left the house. Maryam leaped and halted in his room like a fully laden vehicle. She repeated all she heard in one breath, and her entire sentences were like explaining the paintings. 'When you listen to Maryam, you never think you're listening; it's as if you're seeing the action.' "Gafur had faith. 'But, as she described it, the usage of colours for her own imagination, thoughts, and service became more engaging and thrilling than the main event." This time, though, it is not of that nature. 'In the improper order of the police, think of Gafur as a stoker, and...... Raha, their eldest son, kept his calm and first inquired about his younger brother, Baha. "Where has Baha gone?" Baha Ibn Gafur is a lawyer by profession. Still a junior member of the bar council. He goes out to the office earlier. His office is in the court area. At that time, he could not reach the office; he had three to four bus stops left. His mobile rang in his pocket. Maryam and her two sons were at the police station within 30 minutes. As they arrived at the police station's location, there was no roofing on the larger level of the cement, but there were many green trees and lights surrounding the horizon, so the sun was not shining on anyone, even at midday. They appear to have arrived at a clean woodland. Maryam arrived with her two boys in her arms. Maryam cannot comprehend why two now-young boys are rotating with their mother's hand. Don't be concerned. A lot of police officers are seated at a table in this open police station, stretching the horizon. Numerous people are strolling around in circles. Hundreds of regular citizens are leaving the police station to go about their daily lives. They are exhaling rapidly. The cops are dressed in white aprons and wandering around. This appears to be a hospital rather than a police station! Maryam is searching for her husband in the forest-hospital-like police station, gripping the hands of her two boys. He goes for walks here and there. Suddenly, a spider, a Brazilian wandering spider, the world's most venomous spider, slid down from the air on her shoulder and whispered, "Come with me; I will take you wherever you need to go." It reveals them; some tables contain large journals, while others have massive ropes and shackles. A typewriter or computer is on another table, and a hefty cane is on another. On a table, there was a chessboard. An older police officer sat on one side of the table. He is chess-playing with a well-known politician. A lawyer raced rapidly from the opposite side, wanting to touch a young police officer, but the young officer guffawed and fled away, hiding behind a wooden shelf full of files. 'What must I do?' yelled a butcher from afar. A judge was beating a wooden hammer on his table on the right side, yelling, 'Order, order, how can I do work if you talk so much?' A man standing behind him with a large umbrella joked, 'If sitting and judging is a profession for you, then what am I doing?' Lady Justice, bearing a sword and scales symbolizing the judge's innocence and bound with a black cloth over her eyes, descended from above and smiled, "He has worked hard to master the art of passing judgment. If you total it all up at the end of your life, it may be equal to your entire life's effort." In the middle of all this confusion, a snake ludu playing board was spotted on a little square table in the northeast area. On one side, a fat police officer-doctor sits facing this direction, while Gafur sits with his back to this side, dressed in a prisoner's garb and wearing a prisoner's hat, as portrayed in the movies. The tall cop moves around them, his hands in his pockets. In the eyes, there is doubt. "Dad," the eldest son exclaimed, letting go of Maryam's hand and hugging Gafur from behind. Gafur swiftly turned around and smiled as he hugged his kid. As the younger son noticed the devotion, he rose up, took his mother's hand in his, and began meowing like a kitten. Gafur, the retired guy saw this morning, appears to be the same age as the children, and Maryam were ten or fifteen years ago. The tall police officer came to a halt. Furthermore, Maryam sees that, aside from the four of them, the surroundings appeared to be selfies snapped with cellphone cameras, static photographs of movement like a suddenly frozen fountain. Gafur unexpectedly inquired, "What happened?" "You're all here." "I have come to see your face," Maryam became agitated. "Why haven't you returned home yet?" "This officer, sir, has placed the snake ludo board here for your enjoyment. I've been playing; let's play two or three more games." The younger boy had likewise slipped out of his mother's grasp and covered his face in his father's arms. Gafur begins to explain, "I've erected a two-story structure for your two boys; give them both levels. Fixed Deposit is available to you. Also, you will receive the rent for Badda's four tin shades every month for the rest of your life." "How can you accomplish so much if you provide government services?" said the cubby cop. Gafur gazed at the game coat and understood that if he moved, he would fall into the large snake's mouth. That snake's tail leads straight into the flames. --- As his phone rang in his pocket, Baha Ibn Gafur got off the bus and took a return trip home; arriving home, he saw everyone in the house showering water on his mother's face in an attempt to bring her back to awareness. Raha, his eldest brother, was already at the police station. Maryam regained consciousness and gazed at Baha in front of her eyes for a brief period as if she had awoken from a dream. "Where is your father?" she inquired. Then she repeats herself from the beginning. Baha is a lawyer by profession. Thus, he must first go to the police station. "Did the cops abduct him without a reason?" Baha asks. "So what do you think your father used to do, store onions?" "But, at this time, it would have been plenty to return home with five to ten kg of onions!" commented Bahar's wife. Raha, their elder brother, assured them over the phone that they had nothing to be concerned about. They have brought their father for questioning. Everyone in the home is now at ease and unconcerned. "But why did the police take my father for interrogation when there were so many people in the neighborhood?" the lawyer queried. "Your father is not dead anymore; he is the one you posed the question to," Maryam answered after a little pause. She abruptly went silent after speaking. If you unexpectedly press the brakes in a moving automobile while it is full, the driver is stunned along with the passengers, the wheels shriek, and the interior of the chest-beating. Sadly, what did she say? She recalled a dream she had a while ago. Raha left the police station relieved after seeing his father and learning that the price of salt will rise this time as well. After an hour, salt became prohibitively costly as word traveled from shop to shop. On the way back home, he inquired about practically every grocery store in the vicinity where he could acquire nine kilos of salt for sixty takas on average. III Gafur returned home after the evening and was informed that the model girl from the next street had been arrested and that the salt crisis was not true; it was a rumor.

Taghrid Bou Merhi

Mother's Pain

It was a beautiful day in the small town of Maplewood, and Mary was busy preparing for her daughter's eighth birthday party. She had spent the last few weeks planning every detail, from the decorations to the menu, to make sure that her little girl had the best birthday ever.

Mary's daughter, Emily, was a bright and bubbly child who loved nothing more than spending time with her friends and family. She had been counting down the days until her birthday for weeks, and Mary wanted to make sure that it was a day she would never forget.

As Mary busied herself with last-minute preparations, her phone rang. She hesitated for a moment before answering, not wanting to be distracted from her task at hand. But something in her gut told her that she needed to take this call.

"Hello?" she answered tentatively.

"Is this Mary?" a voice on the other end asked.

"Yes, it is," Mary replied.

"I'm sorry to have to tell you this over the phone, but there's been an accident," the voice continued. "Your daughter Emily has been hit by a car."

Mary felt like she had been punched in the stomach. Her mind raced as she tried to process what she was hearing.

How could this be happening? Just moments ago, she had been planning a birthday party for her little girl. Now she was being told that Emily might not even make it through the day.

She rushed out of the house and drove as fast as she could to the hospital where Emily had been taken. When she arrived, doctors were already working frantically to save her daughter's life. But despite their best efforts, it was too late. Emily had suffered severe head trauma and passed away shortly after arriving at the hospital.

Mary felt like her world had come crashing down around her. How could this be happening? How could someone so young and full of life be taken away so suddenly? She couldn't bear the thought of going back to her empty house, where just hours ago, she had been preparing for her daughter's birthday party.

As she sat in the hospital waiting room, Mary couldn't help but think about the person responsible for her daughter's death. She learned that it was a reckless young man, the son of a wealthy family in town. He had been speeding through the school zone when he hit Emily as she was leaving school.

Mary felt a rage building inside of her. How could someone be so careless with another person's life? She wanted justice for her daughter, and she wanted this young man to pay for what he had done.

Over the next few weeks, Mary struggled to come to terms with her loss. She found comfort in the support of her friends and family, but nothing could fill the void left by Emily's absence. Every day was a struggle, and every night was filled with tears.

But as time passed, Mary began to find a sense of purpose in seeking justice for her daughter. She attended court hearings and spoke out against reckless driving in her community. She wanted to make sure that no other parent would have to go through what she had gone through.

In the end, the young man responsible for Emily's death was sentenced to prison time and ordered to pay restitution to Mary and her family. It wasn't enough to bring Emily back or ease Mary's pain, but it was a small victory in their fight for justice.

As Mary looked back on that fateful day when she received that phone call about Emily's accident, she knew that everything had changed forever. But even though her heart would always ache for her little girl, she found solace in knowing that Emily's memory would live on through all those who loved her.

Shakil Kalam

The Fair of Palashpur

'Where is my father?' Nishu asked his mother. Nishu's mother was silent. The black shadow of a cloud in the sky was in the mother's tearful eyes. Nishu repeatedly asked his mother, but she did not answer. Nishu got upset. He wanted to know about
his father again.

'Nishu, how many days have I told you when you grow up, you will know everything!' Mother angrily said the words to Nishu.

'Mom, how many years after I will know about my father? Why don't you tell me about my Dad?'

Nishu's mother's eyes were watered with saltwater. Mom pulled out a trunk from one corner of the room. It was covered with a layer of dust and had become a strange colour. Mother opened the trunk. There were various kinds of old clothes in this trunk.

The mother wagged for a long time and had taken out a flag. She had handed over the flag to Nishu. Mother said in a tearful voice, 'Nishu, your father is in this flag!' Nishu had
seen the flag several times.

Then Nishu said to Mother, 'Mother, where is my father? I can't see my father anywhere.' Mother became silent. Nishu did not ask his mother anything else.

The level five annual examination of Nishu was finished. Now he was waiting to visit Palashpur, where his uncle's workplace was.

Uncle had written to him many times about Palashpur. Nishu had drawn a picture of Palashpur in his mind.

Nishu had been waiting for a long day since his uncle would come home. Nishu asked his mother about Palashpur again and again. Uncle would take him for a walk this time!

Uncle had promised Nishu once before - he would take him to Palashpur. But could not. Uncle could not come home due to work pressure. Nishu still couldn't believe anything that he would come home!

This time uncle had come home just in time. Nishu was very happy. He wandered around his uncle all the time. I asked various questions. Which day would they go to Palashpur? When would the Palashpur fair be started? And much more queries. Once, Nishu told his uncle that he had to buy a lot from the fair.

The fair was held at Palashpur, three miles from his uncle's office. Hilly path. High and low. Crooked. The small hills and plains.
The sand glistened in the midday sun on the slopes of the mountains. It was as if someone had planted bushes

and trees on the slope. They would have to go to the fair on foot.

The day was Friday. Uncle's holiday. The fair was started in Palashpur two days ago. Nishu reminded his uncle to go to the fair. Uncle talked about the weekly holidays.

Nishu did not sleep well at night. Nishu was swaying in the swing of the fair; this scenery was floating in front of his eyes.

In the morning, Nishu and his uncle had left for the fair. They went ahead a little bit, crossing the dirt road. Two high hills were forwards. It was as if the body was leaning on both sides. Narrow road through the middle of the hill. Dense forest on both sides. Silence. The body became creepy. The wild
smell was wafting. Nishu took a deep breath. He looked around.

'What's the smell, uncle?' Nishu asked.
'Where do you smell?' Uncle said.

Nishu was silent, seeing the bushes at the top of the hill. What animals were playing there? Not recognizable from a distance. Seeing more, the body of the trees was wrapped by
the wildflowers. Colour could not be understood from far away.
They moved further forward. There was a dense forest near the road too. Squirrels of different colours were jumping. Nishu's eyes fell there. Nishu was surprised to

see a long tail like a cat. Trying to match the shape with the cat didn't match exactly. The tail seemed to be quite swollen. As soon as he had come nearer, the squirrels had fled away to see him. Yet Nishu wanted to catch them.

'What are these?' Nishu asked his uncle.

'Why can you not recognize them!'

'No, uncle. I cannot recognize it. Seems how are these different!'

'Didn't you read our National Poet Nazrul's khuku and squirrel rhyme?

Those are the squirrels.'

They crossed the dense forest. Nishu looked back, as well as his uncle also.

By then, the squirrels had started playing again.

Nishu pointed to the other side and said, 'Look, uncle, how beautiful they are playing!' They had reached the plains again.

Crop fields on both sides of the road. Small hills after the field. Thin shrubs on the hill.

There were different kinds of birds. They Flew from one bush to another. It was as if someone was shouting on the other side of the hill. A fox had hurried past them. Nishu was startled. Again a white rabbit ran fast and went away by the side of them.

The rabbit was sitting quietly behind the bushes.

Nishu kept an eye on the rabbit. Showed his uncle through the bushes. The rabbit ran away as soon as he showed his uncle again.

Nishu had told his uncle, 'Uncle, catch it and give me.'

'No, Nishu. It can't be caught now. You will get it a lot at the fair. I'll buy you one from there.'
'How do they catch it?' Nishu curiously questioned.

Uncle looked at his face. The young face had turned red in the sun. Sweat dripping down the forehead. Uncle understood Nishu was tired. They almost had come close to the
fair. Still, Uncle seeing Nishu's tiredness, sat down in the shade of a tree.

The large empty field was in front of it. The vision went far away. The sight was fixed on the head of a green forest, where the sky had merged with the ground. The trees of the
forest were standing intertwined. Three or four Palash trees were standing together here and there in the field. They seemed to be standing side by side. Nishu looked at the grass in front of him. Grasshoppers were flying and playing. A couple of birds called and flew away. Again came and sat on the branches of trees nearby the forest. Occasionally ate grasshoppers.

There were many flowers in the Palash trees.
What a colour! Gorgeous! The whole body of Palash trees seemed to be on fire. It looked very beautiful in the afternoon sun! None could turn a blind eye! Nishu looked at the trees with one glance.

Uncle told Nishu once upon a time all over the field was filled with Palash trees. That was why people named this area Palashpur as well. From then on, its name Palashpur spread out in everyone's mouth.

After harvesting the paddy, the field was fully empty. Isle after isle. Crooked. The telegraph post had gone through the middle of the pad
dy field. He is wearing a Chinese clay hat on his
head. As the rustling sound of the wire seemed to be talking to the soil.

Nishu's uncle had picked many flowers. Nishu had tied flowers together. The smell was dry near the nose. Nishu got a kind of sweet smell. He told his uncle to pick up more
flowers. Uncle gave some more flowers to Nishu. The dove called on the branch of the tree above the head. One or two birds came down close to the ground like an Aeroplan landing and flying. Went up again. The waves disappeared while playing the waves. Brown-coloured birds started digging grass in the field.

Then they went and sat on the bank of a pond. Clear-water. There were many big trees on the bank of the pond. Spread stalks all over the place. Thorns on one side of the pond. The smell of wildflowers was wafting from there.

Nishu told his uncle that he was hungry. Uncle took the food out of the bag. The two ate together. Then they leaned on the soft grass. Sometimes Nishu dropped his short legs and ran to catch the butterfly. Butterflies of different colours were flying. Nishu was desperate to catch them. But never. He
couldn't catch it. He came back tired and sat next to his uncle.

After a while, Nishu got up again. But at this time, Nishu caught a big butterfly. The wings of the butterfly were ash, and white spots were in the middle. Amazing beautiful. Nishu
showed the butterfly to his uncle. He threw small lumps of soil into the water of the pond. Now Nishu was very happy. He picked up the young grass and cut it with his teeth.
Through the gaps in the leaves of the tree, the sunray fell on the green grass of the bank of the pond and into the water. The fragmented sunlight looked very surprised. The leaves moved in the wind. The shadows were playing hide and seek on the grass and water. A couple of leaves fell into the pond water.

The fair had become almost glamorous. People were coming and going. Nishu chased his uncle to go to the fair. Perhaps his uncle seemed to be anxious. Nishu had been
noticing his uncle's situation since morning.

'Uncle, can't you go to the fair?' Nishu said the words in a soft voice.
'Yes, let's go.' Uncle stood up. Then he left for the fair.

Nishu and his uncle turned around and saw the fair. Nishu was riding on the merry-go-round. Uncle bought a rabbit for Nishu. Nishu again asked his uncle to buy a clay horse and a doll. My uncle also bought it.

A boy next to him said to his father, 'Dad, buy me a doll.'

Nishu heard these words. Then he remembered his father.

'Uncle, where is my father?' Nishu asked his uncle.

Uncle's face turned black when he heard Nishu's words. No talking. He looked at Nishu once and turned his eyes away. Uncle took a deep breath. Nishu realised that his uncle was

in trouble. Still, Nishu asked about his father.

'Uncle doesn't talk about father either. And mother doesn't say either. Where is my father?'

'Your father is here.' This time Nishu's uncle opened his mouth.

'Where?' Nishu wanted to know from his uncle.

'Your father is in Palashpur!' Uncle wiped his eyes saying this.

'Take me to Dad.'

Uncle left the fair with Nishu. Moved to an open space filled with green grass. There were many graves. The graves were paved. The name was written on the grave.

Uncle pointed to a grave and said, 'Your father is lying there!'

'My father is dead!'

'Yes, Nishu.'

'Uncle!' Nishu's voice sounded heavy to his uncle. Nishu's eyebrows twinkled.

'What happened to Dad, Uncle?'

'He died in our freedom war.' Uncle answered shortly.

'War!' Nishu was surprised. Nishu heard about the war. But he didn't know what it was! Why do people die in war even Nishu didn't understand?

'Yes, Nishu. Your father was martyred here when he came to fight for the liberation of Bangladesh.'

Nishu's face turned black, and he was drowning in thought.

Moynur Rahman Babul

Laura

Soikot was a bit absent-minded while talking on the phone. He pressed the clutch hard, although his hands were right on the steering wheel. The speed of the car started increasing like the pace of life as even before Soikot noticed, he turned out to be forty. It's very easy to calculate Soikat's age as it is the same as the independence of Bangladesh.

Soikot's found himself driving over a bridge, although he was supposed to take a different route. It had all happened as he forgot one exit while approaching the roundabout. He kept driving on a one-way road. The famous river St. Laurance, as the French called it St. Laura, was flowing with crystal clear water in it. A strong, stout bridge full of decorations connected the people on both sides in a civil relationship. That river of Canada was like an aristocratic symbol of the city of Montreal.

Soikot was also fond of the River Thames and Tower Bridge in London, so he liked the Kin Bridge on the river Surma in Sylhet. The moving car, crossing over the bridges, reminds Soikot about the bridges of his ongoing life.

Soikot was the adopted son of Miss. Hazel Harrison and Mr. Danzon. He was aware of the mystery surrounding his birth. In the year 1971, the Military captured a lady named Sushma from a bungalow at the tea garden in Sylhet. Sushma was the Dean of the Bengali Literature and Music faculty at a university. She was awarded the gold medal for securing the First position in First class in her Master's. She had prestigious scholarship offers for research from Australia, Canada, and the U.K. although, she went for the offer from the U.K. finally. She left for London before the frighting mass uprising of 1969 took place and came back to the country after two years to join the university at this post. After a few days, the liberation war started. The young students at the university picked up arms in their hands, leaving the books to join the freedom fighters. The cities were experiencing hellish situations following mass genocide, robbery, arson, and adultery. Sushma had to leave the city to relocate to the countryside. There she used to pass her time by humming Tagore songs, "*My King's* Road that lies still before my House makes my heart wistful."

But Sushma could not avoid the sharp crafty eye of the vultures. Kala, the Moulavi[4], passed this information to his boss, and then the Military camp came to know about Sushma. Just after one day, late in the night, the Military attacked the village, burnt so many homes, and looted numerous belongings of the village, even the chicken and goats. This onslaught happened everywhere in the village, in all the neighborhoods, even before anyone anticipated anything, as most of the villagers were in a

---

[4] Moulavi is an Islamic religious title given to Muslim religious scholars or teachers.

deep sleep. They picked up three/four young girls from the village, including Sushma.

Sushma was forced to stay in the Military camp for a few months. Colonel Nawazish Ahmed used to pass his days going around places as part of his war duty, but at night, he had a different duty- drinking alcohol in the company of Sushma.

In December 1971, the country achieved liberation from the invading forces. Those bunch of animals conceded defeat to the Allied forces and the freedom fighters, although women like Sushmas were left with so many stories- long and untold.

Soikot was born in February 1972. Sushma was hospitalized in December. Within three hours of Soikot's birth, Sushma managed to unchain herself from the bond with this newly sovereign country- in fact, from this world.

After completing his schooling in England, Soikot started to go to college, not in England though, but in Canada. Mr. Danzon had to relocate to Canada to continue his role as a Human Rights activist for his employer, and Soikot also accompanied him there. They used to live in Montreal City. Soikot traveled to places to gather various experiences as he was growing up.

Soikot met Tania while studying at McGill University in Montreal. Tania came for higher studies from Bangladesh. Tania, a sweet girl, happened to be Soikot's classmate studying the same subject. Tania's physical appearance, her movement, and her habit of humming

Tagore songs whenever she was on her own everything used to portray herself as a piece of Tagore's song.

Soikot had a neck of getting closer to Tania often by singing," With high hopes, I came to you, draw me closer…". For some unknown reason, Soikot used to feel a soul bond, a special match with her. Soikot could speak Bangla fluently, as Miss Harrison arranged for him to learn Bangla from a Bengali teacher in East London. Human Rights activist Hazel Harrison made sure Soikot learned his mother language very well and visited Bangladesh a few times, taking him with her so that he gets himself familiar with his root.

Tania became so attached to Soikot as she found a soulmate in him abroad, in an alien environment. They both obtained very good results in their respective courses. Now, when Tania prepared to go back home, Soikot was in an apathetic mood, aloof. Tania invited Soikot to visit Bangladesh with her. Soikot agreed as he planned to find all the information related to his mother, Sushma, in detail, anyway, taking his time. He would track down the days of his mum's childhood, adolescence, and youth. Soikot took the necessary preparation for a visit to Bangladesh this time as it was deemed to be different from the visits in the past. Nearer the time of their departure back home, Tania gave a brief introduction of Soikot to her mother and informed her that he would be traveling with her.

Once they arrived in Bangladesh, Soikot did not want to go to Tania's residence but instead went to a hotel.

Although Tania wanted Soikot to stay at her place during his time in Bangladesh, she did not make any issue about it.

Soikot started his research with whatever information he had about his mother, Sushma, from Hazel Harrison and Mr. Danzon. And then, he continued the task of collecting information.

Tania's father, Professor Minhaz, a teacher at a university, visited Soikot himself in his hotel after learning his life story from Tania. Sitting in the lobby of the hotel, he wanted to know every detail of Soikot and his mother's life story. The more he listened to his story, the better it matched his idea. Finally, when he found it matching perfectly, he hugged Soikot for a long time to feel the warmth of Sushma's blood which Soikot was carrying in his body.

Professor Minhaz and Sushma were classmates from College to University life. They used to spend hours singing Tagore songs together on their days off. It was as if their two souls were attached to become twin souls. Those two lives seemed to be in tune with the same rhythm.

At that stage, Sushma traveled to the U.K. for higher studies on scholarship, whereas Minhaz headed to Australia. Sushma went back home in 1971 and started teaching at a university, although Minhaz could not get back due to a delay in completing his course. Due to the communication breakdown, Minhaz never came to know the unwanted situation Sushma found herself in getting back home in those turbulent days of 1971. After returning to Bangladesh, Minhaz was not able to gather any whereabouts of Sushma, other than the incident at the Military camp. He continued to research and traveled around a lot looking for any news about her but failed to get any further information. Finally, he married Nasrin, and Tania was their only daughter. Nasrin was also a teacher at a university and a sociologist by profession. She was the Dean of the Faculty of Social Science. The salty water of the river that had been accumulated for so long was streaming down Professor Minhaz's cheeks as he was still hugging Soikot.

Soikot used tissue from his pocket to wipe his tears off. After gathering himself together, Professor Minhaz managed to convince Soikot to take him to his place from the hotel.

Later in the evening, a good number of people were called in and gathered in the living room of Professor Minhaz's house. And the storytelling began. Professor Minhaz started talking about one Shushma in detail and then recounted the tales of Tagore songs, the liberation war, the country, and so forth. Everyone listened to him with utter attention. There was an occasional attempt to sing Tagore songs by one or two attendees, either Tania or Mrs. Nasrin or someone else. Before anyone realised, a yellow ribbon-like slice of the morning sun ray entered the room through the window of the east by floating on the wave of tune and words. Everyone got up the way they liked, wiping their tearful eyes, not the sleepy eyes, though.

Soikot wanted to leave for Canada once the holidays were over and informed Mr. Danzon about everything. Tania wanted to travel to Canada with Soikot, and she had the consent of her parents and Mr. Danzon as well. Soikot also appreciated her decision.

Soikot married Tania before taking her to Canada. They had built a perfect family, exactly like the Tagore songs. Tania and Soikot had happiness across their entities, like" Joy and celebration in the winds of spring."

In the meantime, there arrived a cute little girl in their life, "Laura," who was named by the name of the river St Laura. Their time passes by in utter happiness amid work, family, and Laura. They miss each other so much, as if something's been lost when one of them leaves the other and goes away for a while. Their mobiles ring with the ringtone, "When you go sea bathing again, please take me with you. Will you?" as sung by Mousumi Bhowmik. And if anyone drives at this point. Naturally, the speed of the car gets to a different level.

Translated from Bangla by Shuvra Bhowmik

Ahmad Raju

Sleeping With Blue Lips

"You should not have said that to me in the way. It hurts to think that you didn't even understand me until now. However, do you think I have nothing to say? If you think so, then you did mistaken. I am human, A human made of flesh and blood. Only human is preceded by an adjective that is 'Woman.' And that's the difference between men and women. Let's not talk anymore about this; Yes, I am going; you stay with your household. Keep one thing clear in your mind that I'm saying while leaving, I will never return to your family again." Srabanti wiped her eyes and stormed out of the room before Kamal could respond. Kamal remained mute even though he didn't open his mouth to speak a single word.

Srabanti's leaving for her father's house has become everyday practice. Kamal does not know how long this family will continue like this. Always before leaving, she says, "I will never come back to your world." And after a few days, she returned to Kamal later than completing her turn of pique.

So for about one and a half years, Sravanti was in her father's house. Kamal went to get her back, but she did not come. Later, however, came alone. Not being taken to the fair this time, she heavily takes a wave of anger at him.

The Sun's blazing rays have just begun to enter the room through the window across the balcony. Little if any sound has come from the leaves. A few butterflies flit around a blooming rose. Kamal is busy with Lunch preparations in the kitchen. Cooking means potatoes are in the pot to boil, and an egg is fried. Nothing more.

He prefers to eat at home at noon, regardless of whether he ate breakfast at the hotel. Eventually, Srabanti remarked, "Avoid the hotel restaurant at lunchtime, as the food is subpar. And then she said, "I don't want to hear that you've ever had lunch outside the house." Despite the challenges, Kamal followed Srabanti's advice and cooked and ate at home. Kamal's way to work is shorter than usual because his office is only 200 yards from his house. He would never violate Sravanti, no matter how remote the location.

Srabanti quietly entered the kitchen and said from the back, "Stay it and don't have to knead the rice. Move away, and Now I'm here." Kamal turns back and is shocked to see Srabanti. He stared at his valiant sweetheart without batting an eye. A question posed by Srabanti: "What are you looking at?"
Kamal stayed looking the way he was looking and said, "Seeing you."
"What happened to see me?"
"It's been a while since we last saw each other. It seems like you dried up a lot."
"It's for you." Sravanti's eyes filled with tears. She rushed to Kamal's chest and said, "Why are you so

cruel? Tell me why you make me cry all the time. Don't you know I can't live a moment without you?"

Kamal wiped Srabanti's tears with his palm and said, "Do you think I'm a rock - I'm hard? I know how I live without you; my heart knows. How have you been for so long?"

"Did I want to stay?" Srabanti's lips swelled. "yes, I was s little egoistic. Why didn't you force me back home?"

It's five o'clock in the afternoon. Kamal got back from work a while ago. Srabanti came with two cups of tea that she had made and sat next to Kamal on the balcony. A postcard-size photo in Kamal's hand, which he is watching intently. Let me see, whose picture is it?" said Srabanti.

"No, it's okay; You don't have to see," Kamal said in a rough voice.

"Why are you talking to me like that?"

"How to say, you like me to speak?"

Srabanti placed her hand on Kamal's back and said, "Can't you tell me what's wrong with you?"

Kamal turned towards Srabanti. "May I ask you a question?" Kamal said.

"Yes, obviously, ask."

"Did you have a relationship before marriage?"

"Yes, it was." The usual answer is Sravanti.

"With whom?" Kemal's eager question.

Srabanti smiled and said, "Why; with you."

"With me? Or...."

"Why stop? What do you want to say?"

"Do you want to deny you did have a relationship with Hasan?"

Sravanti gets angry. "Kamal, I am your wedded wife; that doesn't mean you can't say whatever you want. We both got married for love. And you know very well what relationship I had with brother Hasan. You don't even bother to make such a nasty comment about such an angel-like human? I don't even know if the man is alive or dead today. You said the same thing to me seven years ago. He was the one who left the college bearing the burden of your slander and never came back."
Srabanti started wiping her eyes.
Why should I trust what you say?"
Why did you tie the knot if you don't think I'm telling the truth?
My most significant error was doing that.
"So what you're saying is that marrying me was a mistake?" Sravanti felt tears welling up in her eyes.
After shifting gears, Kamal asked Srabanti, "Can you deny this picture?" before extending the picture to Srabanti.
Srabanti took the picture. It's her and Hassan. The image is ancient. That day was the Bengali happy new year fair. Friends were all at the fair. Hasan tells Srabanti, "I don't think I will have a relationship with you for long. You go to Kamal's house, and I go to Mars. If there is no picture of me with you, how will there be a war in your world? You know, where there is no sorrow, there is no love."

Srabanti said in her heart, "Yes, brother Hassan, you said the right thing that day. But what you said was a little wrong; your pictures not only helped to start the war but also can start storming. It's storming inside-outside-heart." Srabanti covered her face and started crying. "Your picture is driving me crazy, brother Hassan. You floated me in the sea of sorrow! Why did you do this knowingly?" At this moment, Srabanti's tears began to beat even the monsoon rain.

Since this morning, rain has been trending downwards. Sometimes it rains intermittently; Sometimes, it rains all at once. Srabanti stepped out into the shower. Kamal did nothing to halt her. No matter Srabanti's anger, he knows she'll return to him alone.

Shortly before evening, the rain stopped completely. Now the sky is clear. Kamal was sitting on the balcony waiting for Srabanti's return. Suddenly the telephone rang; he quickly entered the room and picked up the receiver. A male voice from the other side said, "I wanted Mr. Kamal?"

"Who's talking? I'm Kamal Ahmed."
From Midford Hospital, where I work. Indeed Srabanti Ahmed is your wife, right? Now he is among us.
"What happened to Srabanti?" Kamal's devised voice.
"She had an accident. Somewhat healthy now. You should come at once."
Sravanti is lying in cabin number seventeen with her body covered in blood. And her eyes are covered with bandages. Kamal was rushed to Midford Hospital without delay.

"I didn't want to see you like this, Sravanti. Kamal's eyes widened. He slowly sat next to Sravanti's head.

Sravanti's lips, which had turned blue with pain, trembled gently at the touch of Kamal's hand—the contact of sleep on the lips that Kamal felt.

Translated from Bangla by Ashraf-ul Alam Shikder

Anindita Mitra

Water, Soil –Earth, and He

Neera could not sleep anymore but woke up instead of having an intense sleep due to the light rays' reflections from the house next door through the various gaps in the window. The room is dark; a single, weak blue bulb provides the only brightness. Since her last chemo session two days ago, Neera has been experiencing extreme fatigue, and the bites and stings of the fatal disease have become a constant presence in her life. Neera attempted a half-sit up, but even the slightest movement now caused excruciating pain. Neera finally opened the window, and the silver moonlight flooded the room, washing over her face. Palash flowers, a sign that spring has arrived, can be seen blooming on trees on both sides of the road. Mithu, the parrot, is chirping cheerfully from the small balcony attached to the house. She could barely muster the strength to feed Mithu chickpeas today. A stunning and glamorous family once adorned Neera. She spent time with her 22-year-old daughter Tanaya and her husband, Suman. The family was wiped out in an instant by the suffocating wave of disease. Suman works for a private company. It is impossible to carry on a considerable expenditure with this disease; all the land properties there are already gone. Tanya is currently pursuing her Master's degree while also working at a local cyber cafe. The light switched on, and in walked the cheerful daughter. "Where are the lights, Mom? By the way, I might have missed your call because I assumed you were sleeping." "When did you return, Tapu?" "A while ago, Mother. Would I feed you right away?" The tiredness on the girl's face is evident. Neera's heart filled with compassion; she held back her tears and said, "You people are suffering too much, darling, aren't you?" "Why do you say all this?" Quickly, you'll be well." Tapu said those words and then left immediately after. Neera is grounded in reality and truth, so she could never make a comeback. Nothing can bring back the past. She could no longer prepare polao-payes for Tapu's birthday, nor could she prepare tasty meals. Even Suman has avoided this room recently as he's nervous about Nera's awake and feels terrible. Suman sneaked in while Neera was napping. Neera can tell. She will wake up if he touches her, so he should resist the urge. The socially constructed myth is frequently twisted and broken; men also cry in pain, and so does Suman. People do cry. "Food and milk are here, Mom. Allow me to feed you." Neera can't feed herself any longer. Sometimes hands quiver, and dishes fall. "Tapu, I don't want to eat at all!" Tapu knows her mother's food supply is drying up; she says, "Oma! My sweet Ma, my sweet mother! I am giving you some small bites; please eat." Neera eats a little and leaves it. "You would rather give the milk. When will you eat?" "Just a few minutes. Mom! First, I'm going to medicate you and comb your hair." Neera says, "The hair is all falling out!" with a careless grin. "Every time I touch my head, clumps of hair fall out!" "It's time for the medicine; everything will be fine; don't worry, Ma. It's too late for you to sleep now; just wait." Tapu sprinted off to grab a book. I promise you,

Mom, you will enjoy this collection of short stories. "I'm not feeling well right now, so you should probably eat." "Oh well, at least the view is nice. Popular Bengali author Imtiaz Alam recently received the Sarnalata award for his poetry collection "Past, to You." Neera's voice cracked when she heard the name. "How do you spell that? Repeat that." "Imtiaz Alam. Have you heard of it before? Mother, the father has called; dinner is ready." Neera's heart was suddenly shaking; her chest was heaving. The familiar eyes can be seen on the last page of the book's cover. Neera is very sleepy after taking this medicine. Neera closes both her eyes and falls asleep. The past moments disappeared in the stream of sleep.

Neera sometimes wakes up late at night. Another time she remains asleep like a log out of fear that Tapu might wake up, but today she doesn't want to sleep. Backside being sweaty, Neera sat up. The window is half open, and the white moonlight makes the world outside look like it's floating. Neera, wanting to run to the balcony, suddenly exited the bed and stepped on the ground. To the balcony, she hurried. It wasn't as painful as it had been before—a peaceful environment floating in the air. In the bright light of the moon, everything seems to be alright. They say people experience a period of health just before they die. Potentially imminent death is now merely waiting for the passage of time. "Mom, aren't you sleepy yet? Why did you wake up without telling me? Isn't it difficult?" Tapu held the bandaged hand of her mother. "I want to say something." "Say. There's no need to be timid; just come out with it." "Mother, you are more than just my mother; you are my best friend. Since the day I developed feelings for Arindam, " Neera understood what her daughter was trying to say. "I felt like seeing your eyes and face that time..." Neera said, taking words from Tapu's mouth, "My baby grew up overnight, and now she can interpret my every facial expression. In any case, feel free to comment." "I'm asking you straight out: Mother, are you familiar with the author Imtiaz Alam?" A faint smile played on Neera's face. Tapu knows how much pain her mother has to endure after taking chemo once; it's darkening under her mother's eyes. "Mama, why are you being so quiet?" Until now, Neera kept the past carefully in the safe place of her memory and did not say anything to anyone. Doubts, conflicts, and fears of the unknown surrounded the mind; now, Only a few days of life remain. There is no need to tell your soul-begotten child imploringly about it. "Yes, I know Imtiaz; Imtiaz is a man of our Birbhum. I am a girl from a very ordinary family in a small town; Imtiaz was your uncle's friend. Moreover, we used to live near our house. There was a close relationship too. It has really been a long time. I did not know that Imtiaz had become a famous writer, but I heard it through your word of mouth. More than half of my life has been wasted by the demands of my family, and now, just a few days into our marriage, you've arrived. I made everything you see around you. At the end of this life, the unbearable pain of this illness sets in. "I know how much suffering you are in. Because I care about you and your father, I saw you writhing in pain, but I couldn't bring myself to look at you. Who else will take care of your father if you cry, Tapu? Don't be ridiculous! Neera shifted gears and suggested we try calling Arindam at home one day. Get in touch with me, and let's have a chat. Tapu's face flushed with embarrassment. "Today's youth, you have the right to speak for yourselves. We used to be too respectful of our elders to speak up when we were younger. There's a lot we have to keep close to our hearts. There is a lot of resigning to fate and adjusting to do. There were a lot of family decisions that we disagreed with but couldn't alter. "Come on, Mother, let's sit in the room; we can't stay here with mosquito bites." "Oh, yes, then let us go inside. But turn off the light. Let's sit together face to face in this dark." The history of the space in-between is stored in your eyelids, and the city is decorated with a bit of tinsel from the stars; the plaintive moon welters on the eternal dust of the light-n-dark..." "Very nice! Truly exquisite." "I told you a small part of a poem written by Imtiaz Alam." "Mom, why are you silent?" Tapu put her head on her mother's lap while talking. A few drops of tears fell on Tapu's cheeks. "Mom, are you crying?" "No. I learned to hold everything down when I was little. I forgot to cry." "Imtiaz would recite Jibanananda's poems with the ease of a native speaker. We were all childhood friends. How long has it been since I set foot on that soil? The cloudy sky of Swaroopdanga brings to mind Birbhum. Remember when you were a baby, and I would hold you in my lap? That was before my mom and our family uprooted to Chandannagar. Presently, hardly a few times we ever go there. Imtiaz was a man prone to insanity and frequented Baul's arena. In these last few days, I traveled to the Ajay River's bank in my mind. I ran along the riverbank in the Kash field in the fall. Beans would fill the surrounding areas in the winter, and I'd remove the fog cover and go flower-picking first thing in the morning. You can't even imagine such a childhood in this brick-and-shell town." "He used to write since then." "Imtiaz started writing in his school days. We've known each other for so long that we've become more than just friends; our thoughts are inextricably intertwined. We were both caught in the forest within the Sheetala temple just as it began to rain heavily. Then, suddenly, all was revealed. "Mom, you're in so much pain; it's hard to talk. Go to bed." "It's all over...." "Mom, lie down." Tapu forced Neera to lie down, and she also lay down next to her mother. The sleeping fairies brought a flood of sleep to the eyes of both mother and daughter.

Tapu has to get up very early every day. Since the mother's health has deteriorated, she has been doing household chores. Tapu saw his mother lying on the other side as soon as she left the bed following, stretching her body and rolling over in the bed. "let Mom sleep a little more; I will call her with tea." She went on just as she thought, and the sunlight came in as she opened the balcony door. "Mithu, say, mom, mom," Tapu's chest went cold as she approached the cage. There is no Mithu; the cell is empty. Tapu's mind was surrounded by unknown anxiety and restlessness. The water of the tea is boiling, but there is no sign of heat. He heard his father's voice. "Tapu, Ma gives tea." Tapu went to his mother's room with tea to his father. "Mom, have tea. Have to take medicine. Bringing food." No response. Tapu put his hand on Neera's head. Tapu shouted, "Father."

Neera is in the hospital, and saline is being injected into her body one after another. After leaving the ICU, Dr. Bhadra said, "Tanya, you go; your mother has realised this. It is better not to go to Sumanbabu; she is very broken." Tapu went to Neera's cabin; without making any sound. Neera looked at the sky through the window. "Mom!" When she heard the term, Neera looked up at Tapu and saw the girl with tears. "It's implausible that I'll be able to return home." You're going to be okay, Mom. What's wrong, Mom? When should I make an appointment with the doctor? You cannot communicate. "Nah, it's not hard at all. Please allow me to say one more thing to you. Okay, I'll say it. Neera pleaded for a chance to say goodbye, saying, "If only we could see each other for the last time!" Neera reached out to take her hand. Mrs. Mukherjee, please be quiet. You can leave now, Madam. Tapu recognized her mother's signal and exited the cabin to tell her father, "Dad, sit a while; I am coming."

Imtiaz Alam spends most of his morning reading and writing. Once, he goes to the garden for half an hour to water the thirsty plants. Now he is towards the end of a novel. Anishda, the editor of the newspaper, is in constant pursuit. "Dada, someone came and wants to meet you." "Who can come this time? No one said that he was to come." "A girl of about twenty came looking for you." "Any journalist? Let's see. You tell her to sit down. I'll be coming in ten minutes." Imtiaz Alam spotted a girl in a brownish top and blue jeans lounging on the sofa from outside the drawing room. Random strands of hair flying around. When the girl looked into his eyes, it was as if a memory from twenty years ago suddenly flashed before his eyes. A familiar face appears all over the girl's features. "Hello, are you representing a magazine?"

Please take a seat; I don't do interviews very often. "In reality, it's pretty different. I have a favor to ask on behalf of my death marcher mother. I have folded my hands pleadingly, feeling a little helpless now. It's not proper of me to show up like this. When those you care about are suffering, reason goes out the window." "But, sorry, I didn't recognize you!" "I am the daughter of Neera of Swarupdanga. Do you understand now? My mother has told me everything. She has taken a bed due to cancer. My mother wants to see you once." Tapu cried. "Sorry, I'm going; I must go to the hospital now. Dad is all alone. Let me go." Before saying anything more, the girl left, awakening his past.

Neera's face is still kept carefully on a rack of memories. The dark black ugly mark of humiliation sticks to every step of that memory. Whenever the memory of Neera is scratched, all the claws and cuspids come out. In the ups and downs of life, there have been many unpleasant situations, and the extreme insult done by Neera's father has not yet been forgotten. The orange glow of sunset illuminated the world, and the day was no different from any other day of the week. There were frequent power outages during that time. Neera's father and two brothers were fuming at each other in the eye of the storm. "Farooq, you are our family friend, and you know this relationship does not work; why didn't you stop your son?" Imtiaz has never forgotten the look of despair on his father's face. You know, we are Brahmins; the daughter of a Brahmin will be a heathen and move to a Muslim family. Will religion endure it?" "But love itself is a religion, uncle; people don't love after verifying religion." "Shut up, you rascals and traitors; you'll get burned if you play with fire. If you take one more step toward Neera, I will see the end of you. Farooq, make your son understand. I will destroy your life in this area." "Bipinbabu, I am going to say the last few words. Religion didn't come when we two families were socialized and stood in danger of each other; why now?" The explanation for this "why" eluded Imtiaz. His attention was drawn to the window that day as he left Neera's house. Neera's nose ring glowed softly in a yellowish hue. Neera's home was in a windy area close to the river Ajay's bank, and Neera's distance was expanding over time. He had never been so breathless in his life. Both Imtiaz and his father were deaf, so neither of them spoke. His father passed away a few days later. "Dada, what's going on?" Did you finish off the last of the refreshments? "Prabir, I have to go out right now; there is no time at all."

The hospital lounge is so crowded that it is impossible to push through. Imtiaz's mind filled with fear as soon as the hospital's chloroform smell entered his nose. "Sir, come, come. I am a fan of your writing. I have finished your novel, "The Shining Valley. " There are now yet ten minutes left for the visiting hours. Please come in." "Thank you very much, brother. It was a pleasure to talk." Entering a small room, the boy switches on the fan. " The hospital is well decorated; looking at the backyard garden, you can see that the flowers have fallen from the purple zari flower tree and that a beautiful flower bed has been made. "Sir, in which cabins will you go?" "Forty numbers. " " Go straight to the balcony on the right." As he approached the balcony, he heard a piercing scream: " Ma!"

Neera's body is taken to the crematorium, her rigid features and delicate hands tracing the eternal outline of death. Please assist me a little, Dad. A Baul likes me. When Imtiaz turned around, he saw a man in an ocher robe holding a monochord.

Many wonders what the cast Lalon occupies in the world;/Lalon, however, sought to see the specifics of the various casts, / and say, my eyes reveal nothing difference to me. / Many wonders what the cast Lalon occupies in the world;/When praying, some people use a tasbih, while others prefer a rosary./ To what end, then, does caste exist? / While going or coming / Whoever carries the mark of caste? / Many wonders what the cast Lalon occupies in the world.

A strong spring breeze is blowing. Neera's body is on fire, and soon all that will be left will be a few handfuls of ashes to crumble into the ground and dissolve into water. There are three people, one in each corner.

Translated from Bengali by Ahraf-ul Alam Shikder

Anukul Biswas

Princess of Valley

It's near about 5:00 a.m., and the light of the early morning is just coming out with rays of hope. Suddenly Bumchum awoke from her sleep with the sound of continuous firing. The girl comes out from her mother's side silently, as she does not want to raise her mother so early in the morning. Now she is standing in the window and watching the beautiful Valley. The first light of the morning Sun with the misty fog is so charming that anyone is in love with this scenic beauty. Though Bumchum is very much accustomed to this charming scenario, today she is waiting eagerly in the window side for the stopping of the continuous firing in the early morning. Every day the valley of Pumchum in the early morning is in a tremor of the firing for two consecutive hours. From 7 a.m. onwards, the Valley comes to its regular phase - normal life begins.

Pumchum is a small hilly Village in North Sikkim in India. The Village is situated on the bedside of River Chu, which is in the lap of the Himalayas, where only 10 or 12 families are leaving. This Village is surrounded by a boundary of hilly rocks on three sides and one by the beautiful River Chu. Bumchum, the princess of the hill, is a lass of 12 years who has been an inhabitant of this outstanding valley with her paralyzed mother since her early childhood in a tiny room. Her father deserted them for her mother's illness and started a newly married life in some distant village happily. The surrounding situation is totally different and not in the proper condition that Bumchum can understand so easily. She understands one thing that to earn two ends meal for both of them, especially for her mother, is the main moto of her life, and for that, she has to search for a job by which her needs would be fulfilled.

Sometimes she plucks the flower, sometimes search for firewood from the jungle, and sometimes fruits from the forest for sale are the sources of her earning. But those things are rare, and from them, the earning is so small, and also, the buyer is not available. So she is in trouble as it is a remote village. This is the reason for their starvation. Now Bumchum decides to do something by which she can earn two ends meal. The field of the Indian Army is very near to their house, which was constructed by cutting the hill. This is the field for the firing squad of the Indian Army. Every day from 5 am to 7 am is the practicing time of the soldiers to break the silence of the dawn. When the practice ends every day Bumchum 7 am runs to the field with a packet and an iron rod in hand and starts her findings of the empty shell. Then, with the help of the rod, she collects the lead in the field. It continues for an hour, and then, with tiredness and fatigue, she returns to her house with her collected things. Still, now her mother is in her sleep. Bumchum comes near to her and wakes her up, and gives her two pieces of bread as breakfast, and she starts her journey to sell the things. She had to walk 3 kilometres to reach the hilly Market Rongpo and sell the lead and shells, by which she would be able to buy some groceries and vegetables for them and starts to return home.

She is very much used to and happy with this type of hard routine, as by this work, she is able to give her mother some food, and with a blink, a smile on her face and the mother would feel better. Although she is able to give her food, but of no treatment for her disease. Every day she tries to lift her mother up in bed as she thinks that she might sit with her can walk, and if it is possible, then she will be cured soon. To recover from her illness, what her daughter is doing is enough, and her mother feels proud and is in tears. By removing the water of tears, the baby girl says that when she is fully grown, she must do whatever to recover her mother from her illness. The mother, with firm belief, keeps her hand on Bumchum's head and utters that she is not able to see the suffering of the child; someday, her wishes must work.

Bumchum's mother is very much fond of flowers. So every day before the coming of dusk, she goes to search for dahlia flowers. The forest is full of a lot of flowers like Rhododendron in various colour, Premule, etc., whose attractive looks takes Bumchum in the forest. After collecting such flowers, she comes home in a happy mood besides the Chu River, which, in this half-light dark shade, plays a colourful game with the sky and river that takes the heart in an ethereal world, and Bumchum is now afresh with this beauty and forgets everything thing hard and comes home with a blissful mood and with new vigor that will be the food of mind for next day to work more hard, and now she is enjoying the beauty with childish attitude. In her dreamy world, she only sees one thing, which is the recovery of her mother from the illness. By thinking this, the evening slowly comes down the hill, and she is in her mother's lap, and both of them embrace each other.

In this way, the unchanging life of the mother and daughter passes through days, months, and years. One day, when she was busy with her regular work in the army field, a man dressed up in full army attire came near her. Until this morning, she saw the army soldiers from a certain distance. But now she was in fear, as the man was standing beside her and asking her about her name and whereabouts...She replied in a choked voice - "I'm Bumchum, and you are our small hut." Then the man enquired about the search for the shell every day and who was in her family, and whether she was studying or not. Bumchum, in a trembling voice, answered that she was the only earning member of the family, as they were only two, her and her mother. Hearing such hard-core reality from a little princess, tears rolled down from the man's eyes. Seeing the man in such a condition, the little one called him Uncle and told him that her mother always cried like him and asked if he had the same kind of problem as her mother. She also told him that she promised her mother that when she would be a fully grown-up lass, she would remove all the problems and suffering of her mother. The man putting his hand on Bumchum's head was blessed and uttered that whatever she wanted to achieve must be successful. Bumchum, in a childish manner, asked the man about the reason for his crying and said not to bother. Everything will be good soon. The man with tears replied you are a real Jem, and you would understand why I'm crying, not now but afterward. Suddenly Bumchum starts to pack his things as she has to go as the time of her mother's rise is near. Before parting with the uncle, she asked his name as to what she would say to her mother about their meeting. "Baiju Uncle " is the sole identity and being in touch. Bumchum runs towards her home, happily calling the name Baiju Uncle.

In the month of winter, the valley is covered with white snow. The scenic beauty is so lovable than any of the time in hills. This small hilly valley is also standing as the queen of white snow. In the afternoon, the fog and snow play with each other, which is so energizing, charming, and engrossing the heart of people with joy and peace. But the practice of the Army is still going on in this scorching cold. Bumchum has to go to the field, but she has not had enough cold-proof dresses, as she is bound to go to the field, one day when she reaches the field to collect shells and lead, she finds not a single piece there and is very disappointed and sits in the field. With tears in their eyes, she murmured that she was unable to give her mother today's meal.

Manjunath was watching everything from the distance. But Bumchum's heart-rendering cry cannot keep him in his position, so silently she came near her and watched her. The child was crying because she did not get anything and how she would be able to provide food for her mother and also shivering in the cold. In a very low voice, Baijunath told her that as she was late in coming, he did the work for her. With astonishment in their eyes, she hugs her uncle, and both of them are in a state of happy crying.

Taking the shell packet from her uncle, she said that this is the only source of income to maintain their two ends meals. Such words are very heart rendering, and he was in grief and in a suffocating state and perplexed. Then he took Bumchum with him to the trench to give himself so relief from such a situation and as well as to see the smile of his princess. As he sometimes called her Princess of Valley.

Taking his princess, he gave her a beautiful Woolen sweater and asked her to wear it. The child is very much happy and wears it and looks like a real princess. Then he told her to return to her house. At the time of her departure, she, in a very happy and lovable tone, told her uncle that he was a very good man and the sweater was very nice, and she couldn't wear such a beautiful sweater in her life and thanked him for everything.

It has been raining cats and dogs since early morning. The firing practice time was over, but the rain was continuing. Bumchum waited for some time, but of no use, then she started in the rain. Seeing the girl in this situation, Baijunath came near to her and tried to save her from the rain by holding the umbrella above her, and Bumchum was astonished to see her Army Uncle there. She said that she was waiting for the rain to stop, but it couldn't. So she was bound to come in such a rain. The uncle gave her the umbrella and told them to keep it and to return to the house as she was drenched so badly.

From then on, each and every day, there are some surprises for Bumchum from his uncle as a gift. After getting the surprise gift, she was overwhelmed with joy and childish vigor and which is mental relaxation and bliss for Baijunath. To see her in joy is the only motto of his life. In this state of happiness, the sorrow for her mother is still shown on her face, which Baijunath could not miss.

Some days passed in this way. Suddenly One fine morning, a team of two doctors with an army officer came to Bumchum's house, and the team told them that Baiju Sir had sent them to treat her mother. They thoroughly checked her mother and gave her some medicine. Her mother started to recover slowly. After seven days, she was feeling well and tried to sit in bed and was successful. It was just a miracle after a five-long year for Bumchum, and both of them embraced each other and started crying in joy. Next in the morning, Bumchum reached out to her uncle to give him the good news of her mother's recovery; hearing it, her uncle was so happy and told her that soon her mother would walk and not to worry anymore. She would be all right soon. Bumchum requested him to come to their house to meet her mother as she was very much eager to meet him. Uncle replied by nodding his head positively.

Time is moving now with the progress of her mother's health. Both of them are now happy and taking Bumchum in her lap after returning from the field. The mother says that she was her mother in her before life, and she must have done some good for which she is her daughter in this life. She thanked the Almighty for everything and the man whom God had sent as their savior, the Angel, and also she prayed for the good of their Angel and to protect him from everything, and she uttered that for that man, her rebirth was possible. She was full of tears, but those tears were of joy, not of sorrow. Bumchum hugged her mother tightly.

Now it's time for Bumchum's fun and happiness as every day she gets a surprise gift from her uncle and returns home in a dancing mood. She is now not in her gloomy state before; rather, her mother observed that she was lively. The rays of hope are coming into this tiny room where once only dark was seen. After some days, with the support of a stick, her mother started to walk. That day was a memorable day for Bumchum. Her mother was very much eager to meet with her uncle and wanted to go to the firing field to see the Angel with her own eyes as her uncle did not come to their house, though Bumchum requested him a lot of times but in vain. So her mother decided to go to the field the next morning to meet the man.

The next morning the mother-daughter reached the firing field in search of their Angel. But they did not find Baijunath anywhere. After many vain attempts to find her uncle, she, holding her mother's hand, entered the

Army base camp and asked the duty officer about Baijunath. The officer replied that there was no one in this camp with this name. Bumchum was confused and startled and tried to tell them about her Army Uncle, who was probably inside the camp.

Both of them came home in a trance condition and did not understand what had happened to them and were perplexed. Bumchum was very sad. Her mother understood everything but was unable to say anything to the little princess. From the next day onwards Bumchum went to the firing field to search for her uncle, and sometimes she cried loudly with her uncle's name but got no reply, only the echo of her own voice scattered in the whole valley with Baiju Uncle. She returns home. After the night's end, the day breaks, the hero of the universe comes out with all its glory, and this is the law of nature. But to Bumchum it was really dark in their mind as she didn't find her Angel Army Uncle and didn't know where he was and whether he was a flesh-blood Man or Angel in disguise!!!!!

Aliza Khatun

The game

The train is slowing down. The last station is ahead. The general practitioner Jayanta will get down here. After getting down here, you have to take another vehicle to reach the village. He is going to be here in his village after a long time. Jayanta has a dream of being available in his village twice a month from now on to provide medical care to needy patients. This visit can be assumed as the first step of that today.

It is far from dawn. You will not find a vehicle at this time to go to the village. No motor vans or no auto-rickshaws, neither oil nor gas-driven, none at all. Although there are a few of them enfeebled in the cold outside the station, waiting to catch high-fare passengers. And even for no reason, why will Jayanta head out in the dark in pinching cold? Moreover, without knowing the condition of the roads, it is better not to get into any vehicle suddenly in the dark. Contemplating all this, he steps towards the waiting room with his luggage.

The late-night silence could not weaken the railway station. The uproar of the day is a little defused; that's all. Jayanta is walking past the homeless people sleeping in rows on grass mats on the right and left. Stepping cautiously into the empty spaces, Jayanta reaches a door to cross it. The empty space on the bench in the waiting room seems to be waiting only for him.

Keeping the luggage at his feet, Jayanta sits on the bench, raising his feet and covering them with a wrapper. He has to wait until the darkness is thinned a bit. It is going to be his visit to his village after a long interval; rather, the taste of waiting at the station is creating reminiscent of his childhood. Not that much has changed over time. A common scenario comprising the station's diverse characters is evolving daily. Only the faces have changed. The old man with frizzy hair he saw as a child sitting on the platform bench is gone. Through the half-open door of the waiting room, Jayanta's eye goes far outside. The light and darkness on the other side of the three-lane railway tracks just down the platform seem to draw his attention. Even at this night time, tea, betel leaves, and tobacco are not being sold less in the few shops far away on the other side. A little far away, the waiters in the restaurants selling rice are not relaxed. Over the blinking lights, railway tracks covered in thin darkness, and people sleeping in rows of mats, a knife-sharp cold wind is blowing toward Jayanta. Along with that, a sharp tone of the old days' song blended with the fog is waving towards him.

Meanwhile, Jayanta gets up and goes into the washroom inside. The moment he gets out from there after getting his eyes splash-washed with water, he notices a kind of noise behind him. Getting back, he takes his seat. He doesn't care much, but the noise remains to occupy his thoughts! How strange!

The tune of the song becomes louder while the strange noise is no longer perceptible. Jayanta feels a little drowsy, but his conscious eyes do not favor that.

A while passes like this. Outside, the darkness has started thinning, and as the dim light shines, Jayanta likes the dawn at the station. It is as if the whole station is waking up with stretching. Before the darkness completely dies out, one is folding his mat, one is hanging a pot of boiled eggs around his neck, while the other is walking from side to side with amulets, handkerchiefs, combs, safety pins, rosary beads, naphthalene balls arranging them on a typical wooden stand frame fixed with his neck. One by one, the traffic of peddlers carrying bread rolls, candy floss both of Indian and original recipes, sugar cakes, chocolates, and cane fruits begins while someone keeps walking around with a book of learning Namaz, the Islamic prayer, widely popular Bangla fiction books like Devdas, Laili-Majnu, Yusuf-Julekha and others with various pictures.

Meanwhile, the strange noise at the back of the waiting room has become more intense. Joyanta has to follow that direction on his way. He sets off with his luggage. Going down from the stoop of the platform, Jayanta's eyes get stuck at a corner of the square adjacent to the road outside. There is a circle of ten to twelve people formed there. What is wrong there? Can the yell of moaning be so intense? Who is moaning like that? It is natural at the moment for Jayanta to move that way forward with eager eyes.

Despite his hesitation after getting closer, Jayanta, out of his professional feeling, pushes one or two people aside while his sight goes into the center of the circle. What a mess! Both her bare legs are covered in blood up to the knees. Sitting, leaning against the wall, what a poor attempt she is making to stop the severe pain! Due to frequent twisting of the legs, the ankles are covered in blood-soaked mud. This is the first time Jayanta is watching the scene of a woman writhing in labor pain in front of his eyes! The people present there call her 'Mad Woman'; it can be guessed that she is not too aged. An accurate impression of a madwoman is present in her appearance and getup. With her hair tangled in dust, thick layers of filth on the skin, and gunk at the corners of the eyes, her skin around the knees-ankles-joints of her feet has become badly crusty. These fittings and outfits with multiple scraps offer her a seasoned certificate as a mad woman.

On the contrary, smashing all the features of the word 'madwoman' into dust, she intends to have her 'motherhood' written on the ground in the letters of blood! Meanwhile, the crowd is getting bigger. The circle is getting enlarged as people keep gathering around the madwoman. Finding no space due to the crowd, many have climbed up on the wall cornice, on the top of the human hauler, and the silk-cotton tree beside. Myriads of eager eyes from young to middle-aged people are staring at the madwoman. Not a single distracted eye will be found here.

Stepping ahead from the audience, an old guy holding a broom in his hand asks the woman, "Hey, crazy! Who is your baby's father?" The old man looks like a station sweeper.

Looking at the faces of people standing on her right, left, and in front, the sore eyes of the pain-stricken madwoman search for something at that moment. Her vision finds nothing and naturally sets back to a blankness. Finding the father of her child or not is nothing special to her; that's what her expression looks like. An unbearable pain is being thrown up through her downcast face, cheeks, and voice. Jayanta moves towards the madwoman. He puts the luggage in his hand against the wall, a little apart. It would be better to take her to the hospital, but looking around, he finds no pedal three-wheelers, locally called 'vans' at all. Although two or three gas-driven auto-rickshaws are standing in the distance, none has responded to Jayanta's signal.

Hiding, like an empty alley between two buildings side by side, catches Jayanta's eye. Jayanta appeals to everyone present there - "Please, one of you, come with me; she needs to be taken into a little covering on that side"! None of the adults moves forward. Two or three boys come, and along with Jayanta, they drag her under the cover between two walls. Following them, a few more people rush forward to the corner of the wall pressing on each other's back, but no one objects to being hurt at his back. This scene is a perfect example of adaptation. Jayanta persuades them to move aside. Even though the woman is a lunatic, she should be given a cover. Jayanta's words are being lost in the buzz while the words from different ones present there are being heard-

"Would have been better to send her to the hospital."

"Hey, somebody put her on a rickshaw van!"

"Look, despite so much trouble, she did not leave the doll from her hand!"

Along with some more words from the boys, Jayanta learns - the madwoman used to sit here and there at this station and arrange the house of dolls. Sometimes, some people staying at the station or the outsiders would jokingly play with her for a while and take pictures sitting next to her. For a few days in between, she was not seen; maybe she was at another station or somewhere else. Although she does not arrange her doll's family nowadays, taking the doll in her hand, she talks to it alone. And the daily game of these boys is to irritate the woman. Getting angry, as the woman chases after them, the game gets exciting.

Pushing the crowd, Jayanta gets out and looks for a nearby tea shop in the street. He asks someone – "Where's the tea shop around here?" The answer comes – "Bro, if you wanna have tea, go to the next crossroad, and you'll get excellent tea at Kalu's shop. Jayanta says – "Not for tea; I need some hot water." The man looks at him in awe. Entering another lane of that crossroad,

Jayanta finds a tea and snack shop in front. The kettle full of water has been put on the gas oven; the shopkeeper agrees to give him a pot.

As the water gets hot, Jayanta pours the hot water into a big pan with a broken edge lying in the corner of the shop. On the other hand, who knows about the condition of that madwoman?

It is pinching cold and misty all around. The sun is yet to appear. Still, the station is getting busier; the clock is ticking. Many of the people who enjoyed the fun and are now on their business opening hours at this time are gone. Those who are still here are not too small in number. Some are from neighboring slums. From the entrance of the hiding between the walls, the same question keeps coming- "Hey, crazy! Who is your child's father?"

In this situation, the typical way of irritating the madwoman seems to have changed! Everyone's expression is thoughtful. Who is the child's father? At the moment, in their eyes, 'crazy,' the identity of this woman giving birth is not prominent or dominant. Shouting, the madwoman raises her hands and says - "Get lost…get lost…."

The local kids are playing a little away. Getting stuck around for a while on the matter of the madwoman, they have got scattered on their own. They have gathered again on another side to play.

From the hustle and bustle, a middle-aged man attempts to chase the boys in favor of the madwoman. Groping at her back and both sides, the madwoman picks up a couple of pebbles and throws them. Sitting on the veranda, the way a family man raises her to stick to drive away the crows and other birds from the grains spread in the front yard; exactly in that manner, the madwoman raises the last pebble held in her hand. As writhing in intense pain, she eventually doesn't leave that one from her hand.

Jayanta brings the pot of hot water and wears a pair of disposable gloves taken out from his luggage. He asks everyone to move out of the way. Pushing himself through the crowd somehow, Jayanta enters the hiding from the mouth of the alley and notices that the condition of the madwoman is serious. Jayanta moves the legs of the woman to two sides. Freeing the lump of blood-stained flesh stuck to her thigh, he gently lifts it in his two hands. By this time, the madwoman is struggling to breathe; she is panting profusely. The buzzing people present there are dumbfounded to see Jayanta's activities. Jayanta dips the baby in warm water and indiscriminately looks in front and around for a piece of dry cloth.

With her crimson eyes, the madwoman looks at the people, picks up the stone in her hand, and who knows why she drops it instead of throwing it? Seeing the movement of the child in Jayanta's hands, she extends the fringe of her saree and spreads it on the ground. Wrapping in it, Jayanta places the child on the madwoman's lap. Jayanta breathes a sigh of relief. Trashing the gloves into the garbage bin placed nearby, he empties the pan by draining out the water mixed with blood into the sewerage line and hands the pan to one of the boys who helped him. He walks toward the place where he left his luggage.

Blood flows from the hiding to the mouth of the alley. Seeing that, the people standing there start to retreat. Shaking the sky and wind, the baby cries. Covering her with the fringe of her saree, the madwoman hugs her tighter in her chest. The children playing next to them suddenly stop playing and come to the child. Like the other days, today, the madwoman doesn't go into a frenzy to chase the boys away. Rather she is smiling at them. As the beads of sweat accumulate all over the face of the madwoman are dripping down, it seems like affection pouring from her eyes and face. Maybe, she is thinking that her child will also be growing up playing with those boys. The boys come one by one. One shakes the baby's hands, one shakes its legs, and one touches its head with his fingers and says affectionately - "Will you play?" Another boy says - "He just came to the world; is he aware of the world's game? Let him grow first!"

Translated from Bangla by Swapan Nath

Mridha Alauddin

The story of Sakhina

Halima Begum's husband, Sharaf Ali, was captured by Pakistani forces during the War of Independence. Two days later, Sharaf Ali's dead body was found beside a pond near the back of Bepari's Mosque. Half of its corpse, though, had been eaten by the foxes and dogs, and one or two foxes were still drinking water in a distant place. Seeing the people, the fox quickly ran away into the forest. At the same time, a weasel swam to the other side of the pond, and that created waves on the surface. The people who gathered there brought the body of Sharaf Ali home and lay it in the courtyard. The house was filled with people within a few minutes. Halima Begum fainted on the ground with a loud scream. The sky became heavy with the cries of her eldest daughter Sakhina even though there was a resonance of sadness in the barking of a dog.

Halima Begum regained consciousness and saw that everyone was waiting for her. Otherwise, the burial ceremony would have been completed earlier. Forgetting the presence of so many people, Halima Begum went near her husband's dead body and shouted again, Allah! What will I do now? Where will I go? What should I do? Someone among the mob grabbed Halima Begum and took her inside. But she was still crying and moaning; where should I go now? How do I survive with those kids? She screamed again, looking at the sky; in whose sin do you give me that much punishment? What kind of test is that? Allah! Where are you? Can you hear me?

A few weeks later her husband's death, Halima Begum took off her nose pin, earrings and left them in the trunk. The struggle began in her life. She started to sew people's clothes, cook rice, and wash dishes from house to house. She used to work with the pedal rice husking machine. One day she left all sorts of jobs like that and came to the ground and placed her feet in the paddy field. Working as a laborer in the paddy field, what she is able to earn in three or four days, she can buy food for her children for one day's worth. Someday there was no work, and there was no food, no rice, and no bread to eat. The family survived on raw vegetables collected from the field. When the male workers earned two and a half taka at the end of the day, the female workers earned half of it. But Halima Begum is the strongest among women. Her output of work was equally the same as a male one. When other workers took a rest in the middle of work, she continued to work under the Sun on the hot summer day. Her elder daughter Sakhina did some odd jobs at Karim Sheikh's house. Karim Sheikh's wife was a very good person. His sons were engaged in jobs in the capital city of Dhaka. Their family is affluent. Sakhina occasionally got food and drink from there, which was a great help for Halima.

Sakhina's mother has been suffering from a high fever for several days; she is unable to leave the bed. Sakhina's income was also stopped. Karim Sheikh went to Dhaka with his wife and children. His son married the only daughter of a millionaire. Wealthy people's marriage arrangements are full of pompous and almost like a competition. They spend tons of money on jewelry, sarees, golden ornament and bangles, and refreshments. Karim Sheikh was also spending money for the happiness of his son, and he was doing it extravagantly. Sakhina put a strip of wet cloth on her mother's forehead and washed her head with water in the morning and afternoon. Litton's widowed mother and neighbors rushed to see Halima Begum hear about her sickness. Litton is the only son of his mother. Litton's father died when his mother was seven months pregnant. He was raised by the uncles from his mother's side, especially the younger until he got married. After that marriage, all sorts of assistance from that uncle stopped. Due to drought, they did not get crops from their land, even throughout the year. Then he used to work on someone else's land as a laborer to buy food. In that way, you can say that the mother and her son were living a happy life.

Litton's mother came close and sat beside Halima Begum and put her hand on her forehead, and said, Sakhina! Do your mother has pneumonia? Sakhina's face turned pale upon hearing about pneumonia. She became speechless. While after she replied, I do not know about it, but she does not like to eat anything.

Do not give rice to your mother this time. Give her some bread or soup!

Rice? There is no rice in the house. I will make some bread.

It is normal for Halima Begum not to have rice in her needy family. Litton's mother was so astonished to hear that have no rice at all. She sighed and quickly grabbed Sakhina's hand and said let's come with me! They came out of the house in the yard, where two roosters were still playing in the yard. And seeing them coming, they were dispersed around with a noise. The dog barked and waged his tail and moved to a different place, and again sat there.

Litton came to see Sakhina's mother later in the evening. He called Sakhina by her nickname 'Sakhi' when he entered the house. Sakhina was a pretty 24-25 years old girl with good health. In the realm of poverty, Sakhina was not that much skinny due to half-starvation. She would look like a princess if she had expensive and fashionable dresses. Actually, Sakhina was a kind of terror in this needy world of Halima Begum. Fortunately, no vulture's eye had laid on her yet. Sakhina came out of her room in response to Litton's call. She said brother Litu! Come inside and sit beside mother's bed.
Litton replied, 'I'll not sit now; I just want to know how Aunty is. Let me see!'
Halima Begum almost cried out to see and hear his voice.
'Aunt, are you not well?' Tears came out in her eyes, and a few drops fell.
Aunty said, 'Oh! I am not crying! She attempted to hide her tears by lowering her eyes.
'I can see tears in your eyes!

Oh! What should I do? How many days I worked under the Sun of the hot summer season, but my tears did not dry up! Poor people's eyes never dried up!' There came down a silence of a darker shade in the dark room with that Halima's remark. Sakhina quietly went towards the door. There his younger brother was eating boiled wheat with vegetable curry. A lamp was there in that house. Litton is sitting quietly in the corner of the bed and in this darkness.

Halima Begum started to speak again after a brief silence. She said, Litu, will you take Sakhi to work tomorrow unless, otherwise, we have nothing to do except die of starvation? Litton was even more surprised and said briefly, 'Aunty!

She spoke out, 'I know people will gossip and make rumors, but I don't care anymore. People like to talk behind, but they will not give us food!' After saying that, Halima Begum turned her face to the other side, but still, she was holding Litton's hand. She had a fever, and Litton felt her temperature. Litton detached her hand forcefully and left the room without uttering a word. But he felt more pain when he came out of the house. He felt the air mixed with Sakina's cries. The dogs were walking aimlessly, foxes were barking, and owls were crying in the dark jungle.

Sakhina woke up after the call for Fajr time prayer. She came out of the torn blanket. She went back to see her mother and touched her forehead. Halima Begum's whole body was burning with a high fever. Sakhina was clueless about the reason for such a sudden strike of fever. Sakhina was confused and asked her mother, but

her mother was not responding. Sakhina was crying and pouring water on her head to bring the temperature down. She wiped her long hair after watering. Sakhina rushed to Litton's house to meet with him so that she could go to work with him. The dog followed her a little bit but stopped and returned to his place in the pile of ashes. Sakhina meets him in the yard.
Why are you here?
Yes! I want to go with you.
No way! You should stay at home! Litton replied straight.
What will we eat then? Mother is sick, and there is nothing to eat. There was a surprise on Sakhina's face.
After repeatedly hearing 'no' from stubborn Sakhina, Litton said, I will take care of you! Now go home!

Why didn't you say that earlier?
Well! I am saying now. You can go home!
I will go, but not home; I'll go with you to cut the soil, and that is final.
Litton didn't find anything to answer her. He was angry and muttered and started some kind of aimless walking forward. Litton was walking and limping like a half-slaughtered cow in agony.

The Sun was setting down in the west. They were walking back home. The workplace is far away from home. It was getting darker. The birds were returning to their nests too. They did not have any conversation on their way home. Both were quiet. Sakhina went to the kitchen with her younger sister Bela after arriving home. Bela used to understand her sister's pain and sorrow.

Bela heard from her mother that her sister went far away to do some odd hard job. She helped her elder sister to cook. After cooking, Sakhina went to the pond to take a bath. Nobody was at the pier except her and Litton. Litton was still rubbing his body on the plank of the pier. He had a small piece of torn and wet towel around his body. Litton saw Sakhina and jumped into the water, and that made a ripple in the pond. After a few frequent dives, he went home to keep Sakhina aside. Seem like two beings were never seen each other and were completely forbidden to speak. After she went back home, Sakhina delivered hot boiled rice and curry to her mother to eat and sat down with her younger sister. Sakhina looked at her mother's eyes were full of tears. Mother was not eating; she was sitting quietly with tears in her eyes. Sakhina came up to her mother.
What happened? Why are you not eating?
Her mother remained quiet. So Sakhina reminds her God does not like to sit idly in front of food.
Hearing the words of God, Halima Begum got up and said, where is our God?
I did not see Him in those sad days. Sakhina remained silent for a while as she didn't find an exact reply. She tried to say something. Mother interrupted her and said, Allah plays a game with the poor people. He let the young lady work in someone's paddy field to earn food and do hard work.

And at this time, Litton's mother entered here. Seeing her, Halima Begum quickly wiped her eyes.

She said; sit at the corner of the bed. She asserted I was fine but having a fever intermittently. It was so bad this morning that I was not able to talk.
Do you still have a fever?
Yes, Halima begum replied, putting down the glass of water.
Why are you eating rice, then? It will be better if you eat bread.
Halima Begum had tears in her eyes again, and she said without any slyness, Sakhina brings rice, and I will not eat? What does that look like?
I am here to discuss Sakhina. She came to the point. She is not going to cut the soil tomorrow! No! She must not go! There was an undeniable command in her tone. Again she said, where is the value of honor and respect?

Halima Begum said with a serious face, is there any value of honor and respect for the poor? After a brief pause, she said if she does not work, how can we survive? How many days can we go without food? We need to work hard to survive in that situation when there is starvation going on in this country. She added pain and suffering are not the same as hunger.
Halima Begum did not want to continue, and she was feeling sick. She was Annoyed and asked, is hunger here only for me? Why is hunger? For whom is the hunger here?

Litton's mother was not being able to give a thorough answer to Halima Begum's questions but asked one more time, is Sakhina going to work tomorrow? Halima Begum took a deep breath and said quietly said, yes.

The next morning Sakina got up early and went to work. The red morning sun shines like a hot plate of gold in the eastern sky. And just then, the wife of Malek, a sailor next to her house, came to Sakhina's yard and started shouting. She said, are the pepper plants planted by your late husband? Why do you then send your son to steal the green peppers? And where is your son? I will punish him if he is here. There was no response at all, and Malek's wife said again, oh! Don't you want to talk? No answer when the thief gets caught red Handed!

No response came from inside, and Halima Begum did not feel the necessity to respond to a couple of green peppers. Halima Begum even did not realise that her neighbor could be so harsh with a tiny thing. When Halima Begum and her family were in good shape, she helped her a lot. Malek's wife looked around and raised her voice, and said, you have started a good business; you have engaged your daughter with a male for work and engaged your son for stealing.

Meanwhile, Halima Begum came out almost in anger, but could not able to say anything, except that I did not send my son to steal. I sent him to get some chilies from you. But my son didn't find you there. That's why he plucked chilies from your pepper plant. Halima Begum stopped a little and said again, here are your chilies. Take it! Halima Begum was stopped, but Malek's wife was not. She said you lost your husband, your daughter will be pregnant, and you all will go astray! She cursed and roared like a wounded tiger and started returning home. However, before she left the house, Halima

Begum scattered the chilies at her feet. But she didn't take it. Instead, she stepped on it and smashed it, and deprived them of eating breakfast.

Sakhina returned home earlier today. She found her mother's condition was very bad. Mother was unable to speak; her body was shivering with high fever. Sakhina became scared and ran to Litton's house. She told her aunt about her mother's physical condition and urged her to come home and see her. Aunt Litton and neighbors came; some came from far away. They saw a lifeless body lying on the bed. Sakhina did not stop crying. Seeing her crying, the two younger siblings also started crying for a while. Litton's mother and some of the neighbors' cried. The only person who didn't cry was Litton. He was frozen, speechless, and remained standstill at the corner of the balcony. The ducks and chickens were on the ground. The dog also sat next to Litton with his head on the ground, as he used to sit next to Halima Begum and used to see her silence and tears. Meanwhile, the people of the village were leaving with the coffin, Sakhina screamed once again, and that made Litton's ears heavy.

Litton got up and started walking behind the coffin. Sakhina and Litton's mother also kept walking in a line. The dog was walking behind everyone. The dog walked at a slow pace. He did not know where he was going. He is just following the procession. He did not know the left or right of the way. They were following the river water but did not know where the ocean was. Besides the cemetery, a few weasels were jumping, two crows on a branch, and enormous seagulls in the sky. The flowers were bloomed and shaped, and the rays of the setting Sun were glittering on the leaves. They laid Halima Begum in the grave. Then all the people came back. Halima Begum was there in a silent grave at night, and Sakhina stayed at home alone.

Translated from Bengali by Tuwa Noor

Uday Shankar Durjay

The Tragic Turn of Fate

I woke up today, unlike other mornings. It was a bit early, but I couldn't keep my eyes closed due to unintentional sleep. The weather was still foggy, and when I saw Sheila, she was still sleeping, her face barely visible in the faint light of the morning sun. I quickly got ready because I had to go to work. I grabbed my bike and headed towards the elevator. Two people were waiting for the lift to go down. One of them said the elevator wasn't working. I was surprised and thought, "Why are you people waiting for the lift then?" Taking the cycle through the elevator was not possible as I live on the 7th floor. I tried calling customer service, but there was no answer. I had no choice but to risk being late for work if I waited for the lift.

I started pedaling faster, but I couldn't ignore the traffic light. I was cycling through Laindon Link when I encountered the first traffic light on the roundabout. I stopped riding and waited for the green signal. I moved to this area a few months ago from London, so I didn't know much about it. It seemed different as I heard a loud crowd of crows nearby. Their screams reminded me of the skies back home, where crows would shriek during ominous events. According to superstition back home, crows screaming meant something terrible would happen soon. My aunt used to tell us that we should prepare for an imminent loss in such situations.

I resumed cycling, realising I was running out of time to reach my job. I pedaled harder, pushing myself. Today was exceptionally busy at work with the beginning of the school holiday. My colleague finished his shift and left, leaving me alone to handle the more alive hours. Despite the struggle, I managed to cope. After a few hours, I received a phone call from Sajib. He was crying, and as soon as I answered, I heard his voice saying, "I lost my aunt. She had an electric shock." The call ended abruptly. I couldn't believe the coincidence. Sajib is my nephew, the son of Akhil. He is twenty years old. I wondered if I should call back and ask how it happened, but I thought it wasn't the right time to inquire.

A few months ago, I visited Bangladesh after a decade. I was excited to meet everyone, including my cousins, as we had grown up together. Our shared childhood memories are still vivid, like printed photos. When I arrived in my village, I was greeted with significant changes. There were many new faces, houses, roads, and landscapes. As I entered my village home, I noticed my cousin's wife, Rupa, sitting in the yard, attentively cutting fish. I approached her and looked at her face. She appeared stunned and speechless, as if she had seen a stranger. They had no idea I was visiting that day. It had been over ten years since I left the country. My unannounced presence was a big surprise for them. Rupa was a quiet and beautiful woman with a strong personality. She had three children, two girls and one boy. My cousin, Nikhil, was a farmer and a simple, family-oriented person. He loved taking care of his family and was motivated in life, despite financial challenges. All these memories came rushing back to me. I could still see Rupa cutting fish in the yard and talking to me. Her sudden death was not only shocking but also a great loss for her children and husband. Her eldest daughter, Nupur (15), might understand her mother's death as she tries to save her. The other two siblings, Sam (5) and Jhumur(8), how would they understand their mother is gone forever? How come she didn't come back from the kitchen with snacks?

Nikhil has a habit of having tea every evening, so he asks Rupa to join him. Nikhil and Mili, my other cousin's wife, were sitting in the corridor, separating the mud from the Bulbous root of the arum, while the children were watching TV shows. Rupa went to the separate kitchen to make tea and snacks. The kitchen is not attached to the bedroom building; it is an entirely different room about 15 feet from the main corridor. So, there is a gap between the two areas. Their houses and kitchen are made of bricks, and the roofs are made of tin. They are definitely on the ground floor. The kitchen roof is not as high as the village home; anybody can touch it inside. Electricity and other utilities are controlled from their bedroom.

While boiling the water for tea, Rupa realised she had left the sugar in her bedroom. She came out from the kitchen, standing on the veranda, and asked her daughter Nupur to get the sugar packet for her. Rupa was going back to the kitchen but needed to pick something from the nearby store. As soon as she touched the items, there was an electric wire attached to them. The wire leaked and came into contact with the tin, electrifying the entire roof. Rupa's right hand got caught in the wire, and although she tried to remove it, she was unsuccessful. Nupur came down to the kitchen veranda with the sugar and saw her mom lying on the floor. She screamed and ran to the TV room to switch off the kitchen electricity.

Nikhil and Nupur rushed to her and tried to remove the wire from her neck. They found Rupa unconscious, with her mouth completely shut. They were not even sure if she was breathing. All other family members and neighbors ran over to help. Someone called for doctors, but during the pandemic, they suspected that Rupa might be affected by the coronavirus and believed her family was lying about the electric shock. No doctors or nurses came to help except for family members. Finally, they found a van driver to take her to the town to see another doctor. Their village is two kilometres away from home. They arrived in town with Rupa, who was still unconscious. However, the doctor refused to see her for the same reason. They explained what had happened.

. As time passed, everyone became increasingly upset and shocked by the doctors' behavior. They decided to take Rupa to the general hospital. Still, they faced a challenge of how to reach there as the hospital was 25 kilometres away and ambulance services were limited during the pandemic. Sajib called for an ambulance, and after 40 minutes, the ambulance arrived and took her to the emergency room. Nikhil, Mili, and their eldest cousin Akhil went with Rupa. Tears streamed down everyone's faces as they wiped their tears and rubbed their eyes, exchanging indistinct sounds of grief. After a while, Nikhil and Mili wept and kept asking why Rupa touched the roof. Nikhil blamed himself for asking for tea, feeling guilty about the tragic situation. He wondered how he would forgive himself and survive alone with the kids. He questioned the fairness of it all, why God didn't give him a chance to save her. Nikhil lost control and screamed outside the emergency room, leaving Akhil and Mili in shock. They pondered how to explain their mother's sudden death to the children.

Nikhil looked at Rupa's face before leaving the hospital together. Rupa was an indispensable figure in their family, capable of handling all family matters. It was around 2 am when they returned home without Rupa, as her body was now under police investigation. The hospital would not release her body until the postmortem and police verification was completed. The report would then go to the district surgeon officer before Nikhil could collect the body.

Nikhil and his older daughter Nupur spent the entire night without sleep. They struggled to find a way to convince themselves and make their souls understand that this was fate and no one could prevent someone's death. As the morning sun spread its light, Nikhil and Nupur sat on the veranda where Rupa had been removing mud from the bulbous root of the arum just the day before. They were left speechless, tears flowing uncontrollably. Nikhil's other two children still didn't know anything about their mother, only hearing that she was hospitalized due to her poor health condition. The home felt empty without Rupa, filled only with sobbing from other family members. In just a few hours, they had lost their beloved family member Rupa. Her absence was deeply felt and unbearable for her sisters-in-law.

Jhumur and Sham sat beside Nikhil, their innocent voices filled with concern. Sham asked, "Baba, why did you leave Mom at the hospital?" Nikhil took a deep breath, trying to control his emotions, and responded, "I am going to bring her back. Don't worry, she is fine."

Nupur listened to her siblings' innocent voices, but her heart was anxious. Her heart raced, yearning for her mother's love. Nupur couldn't hold back her tears and started weeping again.

Akhil and Nikhil prepared themselves to go to the hospital. Nikhil's children also wanted to go with them, but they were reassured that they should stay home and would be back soon with their mom. Akhil and Nikhil entered the hospital and immediately noticed police officers walking around the morgue. Nikhil passed the main gate and walked into the corridor leading to the morgue. One of the police officers approached Nikhil and asked, "Are you the husband of Rupa?" Nikhil replied, "Yes, but what's going on here? We came to collect my wife's body." The police officer solemnly responded, "You must go to the police station. You are under arrest in connection with your wife's death. You are being accused." Akhil tried to explain to the police what had happened the previous night, but they disregarded his arguments. They handcuffed Nikhil and forcefully took him to the Kotowali police station.

Part Six

Prose Poems

Poems by Louise Goodfield

My Life In Trees

The Faraway Tree

Braeside Cottage, Dusyre, South Lanarkshire

I built a treehouse on you with nothing but a hammer, old nails and leftover wood. I remembered there was wisdom in my hands. You returned my inner child and I built a whole world for her under a canopy of green where she thrives, and thrives still.

The Threshold Tree

Valparaiso Parque, Palma Del Rio

Like two watchful Gods, you allowed me to pass as naked and bare as a human soul can be. I set everything down before you as you watched me pass through, ending up with less and less, still. You witnessed me step through your gates into a new phase and your silence was souvenir enough.

The Mother Tree

Seville, Opposite the Museo De Bellas Artes

You opened your legs to me, two huge branches extending sideways, and a raised hole in the middle that looked so much like a vagina about to squeeze something out I could not stare too long for fear of being called a pervert. The word dream comes back to me and whispers, 'Two Hands, a Tiny Poem', it keeps playing around my mind, like a riddle trying to be answered. Give me one more year, I plead, I have work to do. And not the kind you set your alarm at an ungodly hour for. The Mother in me is not yet like this Tree. Give me one more year, and then I am yours.

Poems by Rajashree Mohapatra

Without Fear

Between the dates of the month or the days in the calendar, on the wheels of time, I dared to walk without fear; neither I questioned nor I cared to know. In my busy moments or on dark lonely days, the oars of hope move back and forth and sway at par with the cadence of your call to all your dismaying attitude; I aimlessly bow. I hope you remove the illusion for a while and stop sailing it away with the ungentle wind. Now, the birds of the morning don't even sing, making me restless with my heart acutely throbbing. It makes me feel I have no option to play, and it better I wipe you from memory for good, I opt to say. Believe me, a dew_washed autumn is lost in a mangrove in tangles. As the gaiety of love is silent in your liplock shackles, wish that spread wings and flutter in the wind beyond my eyes swing and these illusions kept behind the screen in the silence of dusk ever cheering.

Passionate Enthusiasm

It was not surprising for me to trace myself whirling in a pool of evil eyes deeply stricken with jealousy and mistrust. No options left for me than to plan at once a rise from the vortex against a strong current of betrayals and social stigma. The wild wind of sneaky conspiracy engaged pinwheeling my concentrated hopes and aspirations, good moral conduct. Somewhere reverberated and rehearsed, emitting a voice of caution. The panic state of no option forced me to fix my lips and fingers on my flute; I started playing as another Nero at this hour of angst. Beyond my belief, the notes of my flute got harmonized as the mighty weapon that melted the frozen iceberg of jealousy, violence, and conspiracy and generated hope towards creating passions surfacing from an ocean. Patience and perseverance no doubt ablaze the will to raise the vertex of passionate enthusiasm. Of course, politeness with a stack of blended love may reassure humanism.

May the love rule and Jealousy drown into the blue vortex.

My Dreamland

I wish I belong to the land of my dreams, a trouble-free, fascinating, and imaginative but not mundane yet Promethean. Here the spring would be joyful like early youth, and summer would be rejoicing in pink to make me concerned about both innocence and burning passion. Autumn would be ready in time to be with a parody and try to evoke in me a sense of happiness and prospective positivity. The streets would be resilient and dazzle like the beams of the moon; the bluebirds flying with the cool breeze would often excite me by teasing, reminding me of Him who let me possess my dreamland as a boon. They would unbelievably whisper into my ears that I am not far away from serenity. I would love to transact, but soon, they would fly away, leaving me totally vexed and testy

I would keep on failing to guess where they come from and where they aviate. Instead that they knew me and my address, would my neighborhood try to propagate? I would wish those blue birds fly around me and sing for me the songs of my soul while allowing me to realise the veteran director who created me and my dreams as wormed ambrosial. My desires would provoke me to meet You. Oh, my creator! It never matters if I slip off the height of my urges, but I never quit, for I believe, It's not how far I fall but how high I bounce to inhibit.

Poems by Ataur Rahman Milad

A one-night trip

As I made my way into the elite club of the city, and saw, nobody from the town showed up. Some of the city's cunning foxes dozed at the tables and sold the day to embellish their night. A glacier of failures resting in cold, silent, and lonely exile.
The burner of the ferocious eyes of the night flickers. The moonlit's children float beneath the neon light and the night grows darker; guess the times I came out and leaned drunkenly at a ruined building in the city and looked out into the street, Abandoned sleep, tired clamor, lifeless environment. Mosquitoes music all around, and dogs are barking intermittently. A dog lying on the pavement across the road, wagging its tail to chase away mosquitoes, in a rejoicings mode.

Rubbing tired eyes, stepping forth, I saw a mad woman wandering in front of an elite shop in the city with uncombed dry hair, preparing to sleep on a cardboard bed. A uniformed janitor arrived at the fore, the traditional struggle of possession and ejection. I looked back to the chest of broken glass. Like the people of the opposite stream, I walk in the opposite direction, avoiding the red eyes of uncivilized traffic.

Measuring the distance of the road, wearing the grey clothes of the night, the dextrous guard measures the wave of insomnia. I did a lap around the neighborhood's roads and then waited by the front door. And I knocked loudly and repeatedly. Anybody from inside had not been answered. Is nobody at home and also you? So why don't you answer me? Those who reached out to me with open hands, hoping to pull me into their bosoms, are nowhere to be found. Have you attended their umbrellas?

The voiceless pic

After hearing the tiger's story, the kids dozed off on the cat's back. They share experiences; They made up tales, but nobody ever actually saw a tiger. They plagiaried them in the context of professions and uniforms.

Sleep after sleep increases the days. Children cross mountains in their dreams—a field on fire. Heart and youth grow in gentle darkness—the dying river of childhood.

They wake up to the smell of wet clothes given in the sun to dry. They opened their eyes and saw that they were lying on their doorstep. And a bowl of white milk instead of rice is seen in front of them. Children take a draught and turn it all upside down due to unfamiliarity.

Children avoid sleep time because they worry about having strange dreams.

After listening to the story of the tiger, the children, lying on the cat's back, forget their nature one day. They fall next to the feet of elders now and then, out of a vast carelessness, negligence...

self-sacrificing

She tied the key using the trick in the knot of the loose end of her sari and wandered around the house at her own will. She started her journey by seeing the face in the mirror of others. A kempt life, a masterly adorned layer-by-layer showcase. Secret desires hidden behind white glasses. Hides all painful mysteries and brown coffee stains smoothly. The joyful bath at the gathering waves. Has the mother voluntarily chosen the life of the golden fish in the traditional aquarium? Oh, fish! Your brightness increases, mother's life does not increase. In the triangle world, the mother is dying in the luxury dream!

Dad is a formidable magician! With the power of an ocean in his hands, he can wash away our suffering. His hairy hand extinguishes the dream of the lamp, and the circle of darkness accumulates in my mother's head side. My mother's miserly nature broke through the darkness and kept a comforter of affection in good care. An affectionate involvement in one another's lives. Mother, only one of us is calling; the fire's flame has reached the house, and there is a deep warmth in my heart for you.

Father casts his shadow in mother's bonsai world. Mother does not see her own shadow. On the day of faith painted, she keeps impeccable pride. The world is changing, the signature of continuous erosion. Divided around the line, open the mother's knot, do not see your face well!

All of them translated from Bangla by Ashraf-ul Alam Shikder

Poem by Laura Whelton

Inherent Space

How do I fill the empty pockets of erstwhile provocation the voiceless breaths gasped at sunrise, brilliant yet scathing guards of morning, stretching the day to yards of silence, wordless beauty echoed in birdsong on the rooftop in nature's way, sunlight whispers in slanting memory, illuminating the dark corners of last night's dreams, lyrical longing steeped in a Monday mood. All made sense by moon.

State of mind where you might find me (Massive Attack)

The servitude of these languished days growls like a hungry wolf. I've tasted sweetness and suffered pain; when the mind breaks, it never recovers, they said. Am I the broken one the damned infernal wreckage of wasted youth sucking on medicated happiness. I feel and think, the abhorrent human bereft and left to bore birthless children, the barren womb a cry to the Gods. Why me! I see the energy palpable in prospects doomed. What time is it again?

This heart is dying a little every day

stalwarts of non-love decaying in shrouded tomes. I eat my own putrid memories gagging on the fetid corpses of my rejections. If only the bell chimes just for you, an aching deep, profound, soulful song played every day until we fail inside cobweb quiet still now this beating drum, with feelings brimming, overflowing I drowned in pools so deep, the minute cause, a limp and torrid thing falling effervescent this thought, pulling ranched from tomorrow. Was it all worth it in the end?

Poems by Shamim Hossain

Shadow

As I walk, my shadow does the same when I raise my hand, it follows suit. Oh, how wonderful it is!
I dive into melancholy if I feel sad. But it doesn't...
It cries, too, when I cry. Alas, it makes no sound while crying.

Bird and Aeroplane

At the runway of the birds, feathers are dipping
I, picking those up in wide open palms-
Tucking those by the ears into my girlfriend's *shop*.

The plane takes off full of passengers in its belly. Feathers are dropping on the runway and falling and dropping down onto the outstretched palms...

Who knew birds and aeroplanes that day we were flying on the same runway!

Binocular canvas

The water city floats as far as the eye can afford—

Yogini's plaits in the dense forest
I have been tied by a mountain yogi. What is drawn on the canvas of naive clouds? Eyes are awake at the back of the binoculars! A deer-natured man. He hides like a bison chased into the chasm of spider-laid eggs. His body is suffering from mountain sickness, frees fingers of his hand—and to the distant dawn. Plants alien saplings into the ground.

All of them translated from Bangla by Hasinul Islam

Poems by Dayal Dutta

Diminishing Dreams

The depth of the dream The depth of the dream is decreasing gradually; Char woke up in Padma's chest. Wind dances in Kash forest. A touch of the city in the paddy fields Old Farmer I think and think, Now I buy rice regularly, Because trains run on my land now. I just keep asking And imagine the future.

Nature's Embrace

The golden crop is swaying in the wind The green wilderness catches the eye Burnt in the sun all around A thirsty traveler in the shade of a tree The shepherd's whistle stops. Farmers dream of new crops Common life waiting for rain; Leaving the city to the village People are running Running to the shade of the tree to take peace Abandoned childhood. The weight of litchi touches the ground He is a strange joy This feeling is on mango jackfruit Nowhere but!

You, Me, and the Rain

One day I, you and nature The blue clouds are dark, the rain comes spontaneously; The city of relief - vibrant. I, you and the rain! Ponds, ponds, rivers, reservoirs full of youth. Shy blackbird touched by the rain, The glow of the sun, Nature is colourful with rainbow obsession. I'm obsessed with you! Our perfect love - One day I, you and nature.

Poems by Sujit Manna

Zero

1.

Immersed in the dark smell of the night, I am still searching for a ray of breath. Failure is just like a thorn stuck in my eyes. Every sound that creates, every word that I start assimilates, and every vision that I foresee yields in vain.
I want to write about the lights, the sound of the leaves, and the affinity of my love, but everything ends in a circle of zero.
A zero feels like a parasite – clings like a leech.

This is a long waiting that stifles me in my every breath. I have been scrubbing here for almost half a decade. It feels like I have been pounding everyone with my sluggish day.

Immersed among the countless dizzy excuse, I have added nothing but a rain of promises.
Yet those words have failed me to prove.

2.

A sound that leads nowhere climbs into my head – a sound of nothingness – a sound of an eternal loser. It leans over my ear and says – I am falling down with all my finished hope.

In this time of broken darkness, nights full of unfaith – on the street, a dog shouts at its shadow. His brown head oscillates with a spin of sound. I am watching him in secrecy. A fear runs in my head – perhaps, an awakening whistles me from inside. If I could break the sounds of that dog – I wish it – in the darkness of this impenetrable night, I could recognize myself in him.

At me – just as the light goes by, everyone looks in an unfaithful way.

A row of nights – I have been waking without even knowing the endpoint of my route.

3.

On the ridge of my darkness, I go and sit alone – a row of chimneys exhales thousands of sounds – sounds of censure.

Yes, the clock is running without even leaving a mark. I have no urge to vindicate myself. It is eternal now – I have failed; I have lost my key in the promised land.

All the faith has been changed into boredom.

I am now sitting on the verge of the open window – it seems a large black shadow has covered my sky, and no bird is singing around. I lean over it, and I smell it; I exhale all my wounds knowing here nothing is mine.

Hope – a stairway that leads me nowhere, still I am thinking about rising.

Perhaps. Perhaps.

Poems by Mirela Leka Xhava

Sometimes... It Happens...

Sometimes..., it happens that the rains fall so violently inside the souls how they flood the fragile shores they liken it to the Apocalypse on the last page of the Bible. And you seek to find Noah's ark, to save your species to give meaning to yourself and time. Sometimes the sun smiles at the morning of the seasons rays without permission to warm the weary soul from imaginary journeys to return to the missing Ithaca. The sun hides in the broken twilight in the Pleiades galaxy, which you have never known. Sometimes it happens..., that the tear has dried up to create some green oases in the desert, to give way to a smile roses planted once in the spring...!

Here in the place of churches (Italian impressions)

The bells here at the Vatican site they fall early in the morning and strangely not even the rooster crows hypnotic rhythm, penetrating sound composition that allows you to sit in the recesses of the soul and clears your mind. In the baroque church nearby dome angels painted by the hands of the artist they get my attention more than the white-robed priest probably with pigeons huddled under winter shelter. In the evenings, people here, why not, pray in the alcoves where the resin of the candles lit by the grandparents faith has climbed the walls, maybe for Jesus, maybe God, maybe the cosmos the invisible inspired with the names of saints because man is born and dies in search of the identity of light. Here in the land of churches, the bells speak from morning to evening with the earth and the sky.

London dream

Where you end, I only saw the beginning over the turbulent waters of the Thames history erects gigantic monuments of bridges conceived in the crystal sweat of people iron, stone, beauty wrapped under the cold skin of centuries Tower Bridge. Where you begin, I also saw an end to understand that civilisations are born and die founders, conquerors, and defeated fugitives, under this charming sky; gray and blue looking for a dream, London like you. I saw the hands of the clock to Big Ben move with the rhythm of the present, where day and night speak Shakespeare's language and become imaginary journeys between reality and mystery the golden bell to wake people up...

Poems by Roksana Lais

The study of the heart

The body can be learned about through the anatomical dissection that occurs in the dissecting room. Through detailed dissection, detailed details can be known about the different organs, bone marrow, capillaries and all the other intricate human parts. Through school and higher education, the mind's intellect is developed. No matter how much you study and know about the human body, the human mind, humankind, and love cannot be given any definite definition Yousuf-Zulekha, Radha-Krishna, Romeo-Juliet, Shiri-Farhad, Laila-Majnu, all icons of love and its potential, tragic consequences But despite knowing about their stories, despite studying the science of love, all over the world, countless lovers jump into the fire of love, like a moth to a flame. One feels love in their heart, but where is the heart, where does love live? Where exactly is love's Taj Mahal located? The entire body can be searched but no exact location can be found for where exactly the metaphorical heart really is.

Masked face

How many faces live behind one face, pretending, the burning of unexpressed feelings? How much do people hide? The sun, the heat, and the sky all impact the brain cells creating different symphonies of feelings. Fate plays the cymbal freely to its heart's desire but you cannot disobey fate. There is a barrier to being myself. Why do people only show a masked face? Shown only for their gains. Life is complicated by the game of faces. Strangers and loved ones play many mysterious games. The crying willow, ursa major. The sky is filled with cloud tears. The bottom of a frozen heart awaits mysterious events. Inner faces show a stranger game. With a nauseating feeling, dreams are broken. Reality is broken, madness ensues pure feelings are replaced by pride. The good is lost in all the destruction.

Lonely Depression

Sunflower yellow and sunny hot afternoon but it seems as if a dark blackness causes deafness. The strong wind's blows sound like a witch whispering like hot lead pouring into the ears. An allusion of colourful craftsmanship and strong brush strokes but it tastes like black coffee being drunk in a pale cafe. The meditating mind, the submerged blossoming, glowing laughter. A hot wind blows in the ears. The curve of the hip and the intimate moments of love plays in the mind. The heart beats fast but the nights are cold and lonely. The insulted intellectual, the returned gift are an awful scream of pain in solitude. The heart seeking safeguards from another soft, loving heart but there is only silence all around. There are no magical bonds to be found rejection seems like the sad tune of a violin. Cold, like Christmas Eve in an empty town but a whirlwind of burning fire in the mind's courtyard. The yellow of the sunflower, the brightness of the wheat field, the bright colour of the sun. Silent heartbreak becomes a gift, a painfully cut ear, a present of love to the most beloved. Sitting in depression, you see an indestructible light wanting to dissolve yourself in your love but how sad, no love understood you, Vincent Van Gogh!

Part Seven

Book Reviews

When Poetry meets Philosophy:

Book review of Gauranga Mohanta's "Padmarhizome o Antheiar Pushpadhar" (Lotus-rhizome and Antheia's Flower-tray) (2023)

Reviewed by Dr. Nitai Saha

Gauranga Mohanta's collection of prose poems, "Padmarhizome o Antheiar Pushpadhar" (Lotus-rhizome and Antheia's Flower-tray), published by Golpokar, Dhaka, Bangladesh, immerses a reader in the fragrance of the lotus blossoming in the imperishable pool, evoking a sense of reverence for Antheia. In his poem "Sephalisrot', the poet reflects on the power of pride as death approaches, writing, "Mrityur kachhakachhi ele abhiman bere jay" ("Pride has its sway when death nears."). Through his words, the poet confronts the human tendency to cling to pride even as the inevitability of mortality looms. Mohanta's prose poems transport us to a world of sensory experience, where the scent of the lotus and the power of pride can be felt in equal measure. Through his vivid imagery and introspective musings, the poet invites us to contemplate the complexities of the human experience and the fragility of our existence. Indeed, the utterance takes the poem in particular and the collection in general to a dizzy height of philosophical depth. Mohanta places his own self in the processional stream of Time, and thus achieves a fusion of the particular and the general. He yearns for that mystical truth which will unveil illusion of the world so as to penetrate into the mystery of life and death. It is to this philosopher-poet that we turn, in the hope that under the genial spell of poetry we may be brought with understanding to the more forbidding land of philosophy.

Mohanta's prose poems capture the essence of the night and the sun, expressing them in arresting imagery that seems to defy comprehension. Mohanta's poetry exerts an indomitable effort to match the beauty of nature. While some may find poetry to be cryptic or incomprehensible, his prose poems inspire endless curiosity and imagination in poetry-loving readers. In one such poem, the poet writes, "Jekhana bose thakbar katha noy sekhane bose achhi" ("I am sitting where I should not be sitting"). This line recalls Browning's notion of hand/brain binary in "The Last Ride Together": What hand and brain went ever paired?/What heart alike conceived and dared?/What act proved all its thought had been?/What will but felt the fleshly screen?" Mohanta's rich imagery and evocative language lead us on a journey that blurs the lines between the surreal and the real. In one such poem, the saffron woman transports us to a faraway world where the Greek goddess Antheia weaves a fringe of flowers. Through Mohanta's poetry, we are invited to explore the depths of our imagination and to see the world in new and unexpected ways. Here Poetry and philosophy are happily married and Mohanta, the poet shakes hands with Mohanta, the philosopher. Meditative all along, he spins out philosophy effortlessly and connects man and nature in a way that is an edifying experience for the readers: "Briksher sathe manusher snayabiya kono baibhinya nei".("There is no neurological disparity between man and tree")

The question of neutrality of judgment does not apply to the poet. In this volume of prose poems, the poet is immersed in another world beyond this visible world; but in poetry, the silver lining of beauty shines through the philosophy. "No man", said Coleridge, "was ever yet a great poet without being at the same time a great philosopher." At the same time, the effort to create beauty makes Mohanta socially conscious. No wonder art and society are very often at loggerheads with each other. A poet like Mohanta is neither an analyst nor a statistician, and is even an observer only for the sake of a higher design. He is one who appreciates, and expresses his appreciation so fittingly that it becomes a kind of truth, and a permanently communicable object. That "unbodied joy", the skylark's song and flight, is through the genius of Shelley so faithfully embodied, that it may enter as a definite joy into the lives of countless human beings. The sensuous or suggestive values of nature are caught by Mohanta's quick feeling for beauty, and fixed by his creative activity in the same vein.

The lines from the poem "Briksha" ("Trees") "Janma-kshudha-bedona-byadhi-mrityu niye briksha mulota nirbeg manab"("Trees remain stoic like man in birth-hunger-pain-disease-death.") and "Āghātēr prabolata muchhe phelte pārē śhāsatribhūjēr saralarēkhā ("The straight line of the respiratory triangle can soothe the severity of the wound") deeply resonate with the human experience of birth, hunger, pain, disease, and death. The poet compares the stoic nature of trees to that of humans who endure these struggles. In another line from the same poem, the poet suggests that the straight line of the respiratory triangle can ease the severity of a wound. Such poignant verses deeply affect the poet, leaving him wounded and seeking solace in the murky colours or familiar soil.

Though the poet cannot dissect his own poems, he recognizes the unique circumstances that led him to express his emotions through words. His poetry serves as a testament to the power of language to capture and convey the complexities of the human experience. Poetry involves, then, the discovery and presentation of human experiences that are satisfying and appealing. It is a language for human pleasures and ideals. The use of Imagery is more appealing than the mathematical subtlety, because it transports us to a heterocosm.

The poet has traversed many a mile through the void of silence and released twenty pairs of Eurasian collared doves in honor of Aphrodite, the Greek goddess of love. In the poem "Chaitra Sankranti," the poet reminisces about the green fennel scent of youth at the Sindurmati Mela, which surprisingly captivates us. The visible world around us doesn't fully capture the essence of poetry. Rather, poetry emerges from the beautiful tapestry of the world, which gives rise to the vibrations of our imagination. The prose poems contained in this book unveil an indirect, transformed, and stirring world of life--a heterocosm of poetic fancy.

In "Shephalisrot', the poet underscores an unyielding truth: "Pṛthibir samājē sajjita thākē ēk mithyā ramdhanu, bibarṇo holēi mānuṣh roṅger pralēp chapāẏ" ("An illusory rainbow adorns society, and when it fades, people paint over it with colour"). Meanwhile, in "Benche Thakar Andhokār" ("The Darkness of Living"), the poet conjures a forest lake in the midst of darkness with a melancholic heart. Lastly, in "Tomar Kache Jetey" ("To Reach You"), the yearning of a tired lover's heart is expressed through exquisite verbal felicity: "Tomar kachhe Jetey urte hay anek dur" ("I must traverse a great distance to reach you").

This collection of prose poems by Mohanta presents colour politics with moral and political dimensions, going beyond mere aesthetic appeal. The reader is compelled to exercise moral discrimination while engaging with the texts. Mohanta is not "colour blind" but rather acknowledges the presence of goodness in all colours. The poet justifies the use of "brown" as a positive signifier, suggesting that the culture within the superficial world gains enlightenment through a "brown halo.":

"Kṛittim buddhimattā grohēr sanskṛitir bhetor chhariye dichchhe brown alo"(The culture inside superficial planet's intellect gets illumined by brown halo")

Throughout some of his prose poems, Mohanta explores a rhetoric of 'brown', but always with an uncanny attachment. He uses 'brown' to allude to Acharya Pingala, a renowned ancient Indian poet and mathematician, who first used binary system of numbers as discovered and popularised by an Italian mathematician:

"Itālir goṇitajna ēkdin Alps porbatmālāẏ himālaẏēr rūpāntorito sila ābishkar karēn; Ei barṇomay sila binary saṅkhyā paddhatir sraṣṭā hisebe Pingaler nām prachār kore".

("An Italian mathematician one day discovered the metamorphic rocks of the Himalayas in the Alps; This variegated rock promotes Pingala as the creator of the binary number system")

Mohanta uses colour 'brown('Pingal')' here not in the literal but in the figurative sense, as a reference to neither white nor black but coloured people of the third world. These people occupy an intermediate position along the black-white spectrum of colour classification. It also refers to the prevalence of prejudice among the fair complexioned coloured groups and societies toward blacks/browns, especially those groups or individuals of African/Indian ancestry. His oblique reference to 'brown racism', and resultant intent to present 'brown' as a colour of illuminated wisdom deserves accolades.

Mohanta's art in "Padmarhizome o Antheiar Pushpadhar" involves his ability to express genuinely and sincerely what he himself experiences in the presence of nature, or what he can catch of the inner lives of others, by virtue of his intelligent sympathy. No amount of emotion or even of imagination will profit a poet, unless he can render a true account of them. Both poets and philosophers often adopt a shared perspective, viewing the horizon-line as the ultimate boundary encompassing the entirety of their world. Poetry is not always or essentially philosophical, but may be so; and when the poetic imagination restores philosophy to immediacy, human experience reaches its most exalted state. That is what defines Mohanta's artistic finesse in this volume of prose poems.

Of Concentric Storytelling, Footballs and the Shifting World

Review of Mojaffor's Meet Human Meat and Other Stories

Reviewed by Pina Piccolo

Mojaffor Hossain's latest short-story collection, translated into English from Bangla by a team of 8 stellar translators and published by The Antonym (Kolkata, 2023), cunningly combines in its title "Meet Human Meat and Other Stories" the early 21st century formulaic exhortation "Meet" with the darkly grotesque suggestion of 'civilized' cannibalism consumed in trendy restaurants. Taken from one of the 17 stories that make up the book and is strategically placed at its center, this assonant title with its disquieting echoes introduces the reader to a whole universe of contemporary contradictions, some belonging to mundane, everyday experiences located between Bangladesh and India or the troublesome border between the two and some set in a surrealistic territory of the imagination, uncomfortably close to reality. As a matter of fact the book's opening story revolves around a procession of spirits of differently mutilated people trying to return to a village from which they had fled ahead of an invasion and ends with a story centering on a macabre football that is the object of desire of a group of destitute teen-age boys, kicking their frustration and lack of future around.

One of the salient features of Mojaffor Hossain dense yet airy writing is the variety of storytelling devices the writer effectively wields to keep the reader engaged as they are shifted between locations and characters, points of views and paradoxical situations. The writer relies chiefly on the dynamism of the narrating voice to creatively unfold layers of history, prejudice, deceit, domination, scapegoating as well as the demand for justice and a saner way of life; claims that strike the reader either implicitly (as for example in "All the Sadeqs Are Getting Killed") or explicitly (as occurs in "The Story I Could Never Write").

The storytelling is entrusted sometimes to an individual narrator– whether omniscient, slightly naïve or unreliable ("My Mother Was a Prostitute", "Post Breaking News"), sometimes to two dialoguing/contrasting voices ("Down Memory Lane", "An Ad Seeking the Identity of a Hand", "A River Story"), sometimes a polyphonic chorus or cacophony ("Subservient Country, Independent People", "The Spy", "Land of the Headless") sometimes to a mix of the above ("A Farewell Verse", "The Story I Could Never Write"). Thus a multitude of narrators accompany the reader through the circles of a contemporary hell with its catalogue of raped and burnt women appearing on the edge of the bed to sleepless writers demanding that their story be told; village life with its traditionally appointed bullies and scapegoats coming apart at the seams as technology, bureaucracy and vagaries of modern life seep in; the ongoing religious acrimony between Muslims and Indus and the paradoxical situations and intrigues it gives rise to, and their long standing consequences; the power of the media and hearsay to set up Pirandellian situations in which a living body itself does not suffice to prove one's alive status.

In spite of the jarring, speculative and oftentimes ominous fabric of the stories, Mojaffor Hossein manages to elicit in the reader an underlying sympathy for the characters who are situated on lower rungs of the ladder of abuse (I am thinking of the son in "My Mother Was a Prostitute," or the inept village poet with a grifter's angle in "A Farewell Verse". Though they partake in abuse and scapegoating, by their actions they demonstrate a kind of loyalty to the victim (again the son of the prostitute by choosing to live next to the mother buried in the courtyard of her own home as she is refused proper burial by the village norms against prostitutes).

The character of the inept poet failing in the task the village expects him to perform – i.e. to versify and the scorn that failure brought on him,, reminded me of the notion of concentric circles of stories that I see played out in this book. Salman Rushdie mentioned the importance of this kind of storytelling in his remarks about how Covid had affected this activity, in a 2021 interview reprinted in Lit Hub:

Stories are the things that tell us who we are. And for me, that's the great value of doing this kind of work. We are a narrative animal. We're an animal that understands itself by telling stories. Children want stories very early as a way of understanding the world. And all of us, we live in stories. Families have family stories. Cities have stories of the city. Communities, secular or religious, have stories which define them. Countries have national stories. And we live in these concentric circles of stories, and we understand ourselves through them. Stories contain, in the most beautiful way, what we have been, the potential of what we could be, speculations about how we might be. They are the memory of the human race. And it's one of the beautiful things about being in that world, trying to make stories which become—if I'm lucky—part of that collective memory.

In the concentric stories that Mojaffor Hossain offers in this collection, I detect something Italo Calvino had been advocating in his book *Six Memos for the Millennium* under the rubric 'Lightness'. Here, the lightness is not due to lack of substance, readers are invited to follow an intriguing red balloon buoyed in the air by the contradictions of society, in a polyphonic display of clashing and colluding modernity and tradition, relations between classes, sexes, generations, religions, city and countryside, professions new and old while managing, in a way, to defeat the heaviness and darkness he could have gathered from the dire predicaments the characters are facing. But talking of red balloons and their buoyancy should not deter readers from considering Mojaffor Hossain's ability in bringing the reader closer to earth, to the actual mud and dust of life. In describing the macabre game of soccer played by the destitute boys, in all its elements and surrounding contexts of family, neighborhood, national and international life, the author deploys all his skill in saying and not saying, barely hinting at the nature of what's inside the rags that constitute the football, thus fitting to a T renowned scholar Wolfgang Kayser's remarks about the grotesque as a genre in its modern-day form:

In literature the grotesque appears in a scene or animated tableau. Its representations in the plastic arts, too, do not refer to a state of repose but to an action, a "pregnant moment", or at least — in the case of Kafka — a situation that is filled with ominous tension. In this way the grotesque the kind of strangeness we have in mind is somewhat more closely defined. We are strongly affected and terrified because it is our world which ceases to be reliable, and we feel that we would be unable to live in this changed world. The grotesque instills fear of life rather than death. Structurally, it presupposes that the categories which apply to our world view become inapplicable." The various forms of the grotesque are the most obvious and pronounced contradictions of any kind of rationalism and any systematic use of thought. (Wolfgang Kayser, *The Grotesque in Art and Literature*, page 185).

Pina Piccolo: Italian-American Writer & Translator

A melancholic love letter to Norway || A hybrid memoir

Reviewed by Piyali Basu

Pacemaker

David Toms

Banshee Press

ISBN: 9781838312657

€15

It's a hard life, or to be precise, a strange life. We all are living with the knowledge of this crippling idea, that we probably wouldn't have lived if we were born a few years earlier.

Our author, David Toms, was born in 1988, with this congenital heart defect, and that is how 'Pacemaker' was created. Tom writes at the start of this book, "I am one of a group of people called 'Heart Children' in Ireland. I was born on 19 February 1988 presenting with symptoms in line with transposition of the great arteries, a rare congenital heart defect."

Pacemaker ' is a part memoir and a part prose book, which takes us on a journey from David's childhood through to his teenage years, numerous surgeries, growing up in Waterford, moving to Norway, and, ultimately, surviving a terrifying Covid ordeal. Pacemaker 'settles us into an unsettling idea through David's and we feel the chill in the narrowness of his miss. A thoughtfully written portrayal of each character which the readers might remember for the rest of their lives.

Pacemaker speaks to all of us in its exploration of what it means to live in a fragile yet resilient body, to walk multiple challenging paths, and to overcome them. It is all about David's inner and outer landscape, like walking, which he loves. He invites us to the tramps and tracks of Ireland and then to Norway in a colourful and vibrant way and we must say, he set his mark in every way. His narrative prose beautifully captured the neurological pathways of his brain, his obsession and his drawbacks. Living with a chronic illness is Toms's navigation towards a greater life. Every time he proved that disability is not a winter coat, it's not seasonal, it's permanent, and it's not a traditional level, but an untraditional one.

As a reader, we can feel a sinking in the stomach, a hollowing in our chest, when we read this book, and these are the reasons why I am so glued to David's way of seeing life.

Death is constant, but death is also his favourite teammate too, in his college days and throughout his romances, death was the third wheel in Toms's life.

Can't remember, when was the last time I was so obsessed with a book, but David's writing expertise and his views towards life in a melancholic way remind me of my days in Ireland, my home country, where Nature is alive and the air is cool and crispy, it reminds me of Cork's Barracks and the calm and silent Liffey.

This book is a memoir, a deep, sad love letter to Norway, this book is a letter to his illness and we are bound to follow his journey, a moving, hopeful journey towards eternity.

Journey Across the Veil: An Inspirational Adventure

The Best Seat in the Universe by Grahame Anderson

Reviewed by Louise Whyburd

A beautiful read from start to finish. This book that draws you in from the get go with a heart-warming story of a grandfather who passes away and takes his Grandsons soul across the veil to the other side on adventure onboard his bus. This book is filled with inspirational moments, interesting insights and thought provoking concepts throughout that will help you navigate through life.